NOVA
EXPRESS

NOVA EXPRESS

The Restored Text

William S. Burroughs

EDITED AND WITH AN INTRODUCTION BY
Oliver Harris

Grove Press
New York

First revised edition published by Grove Press in 2014.

Published simultaneously in Canada
Printed in the United States of America

ISBN: 978-0-8021-2208-7
eBook ISBN: 978-0-8021-9722-1

Grove Press
an imprint of Grove/Atlantic, Inc.
154 West 14th Street
New York, NY 10011

Distributed by Publishers Group West

www.groveatlantic.com

14 15 16 17   10 9 8 7 6 5 4 3 2 1

Contents

Acknowledgments vii

Introduction ix

NOVA EXPRESS

 Last Words 1

 So Pack Your Ermines 15

 Chinese Laundry 35

 Crab Nebula 71

 From a Land of Grass Without Mirrors 95

 Gave Proof Through the Night 125

 This Horrible Case 141

 Pay Color 157

Notes 191

Acknowledgments

It is a privilege to edit works by William Burroughs, and a pleasure to thank James Grauerholz for making it possible and for all the support he has given. It's also a pleasure to thank the following for their expert help: Jed Birmingham for assistance with little magazines; Barry Miles for his knowledge of Burroughs' artwork; Jeffrey Miller for insights into the finer points of printing; Keith Seward for razor-sharp feedback; and above all, Véronique Lane, for working with me from start to finish, being by my side in the archival vaults, sharing ideas, reading every word I wrote, and living with the Fish Boys and the Vegetable People for two years.

*   *   *

For the great archival assistance they have provided, I also want to thank: John Bennett of the Rare Books and Manuscript Library at Ohio State University, Columbus; Rob Spindler of the Archives and Special Collections at Arizona State University, Tempe; Isaac Gewirtz, curator of the Berg Collection at the New York Public Library, and his staff; and Michael Ryan and all his staff at the Rare Books and Manuscript Library, Columbia University. I would also like to acknowledge the support of the Research Institute for the Humanities at Keele University. Thanks finally to Jeff Posternak of the Wylie Agency, a great guy to have on your side, and to Peter Blackstock at Grove Press.

Introduction

"THE FUTURE LEAKS OUT"

"THIS IS A BURNING PLANET"

Nova Express begins with a chapter called "Last Words" in a messianic voice warning of End Times. It is a stunning overture to a terminal scenario that after fifty years has lost none of its ferocity. "*Newsweek* says I am basically an old fashioned fire and brimstone preacher," Burroughs noted on the day the book was published; "The Reverend Lee rides again" (*ROW*, 170).[1] *Nova Express*

is actually a mixing deck of many voices—cutting from
a hardboiled detective drawl to the comic rhythms of a
picaresque villain, and from the convulsive beauty of a
Surrealist poet to a tempo as hard and electrical as the
clicking of a Geiger counter—but Burroughs would have
been pleased to sound like a sulphurous Old Testament
authority. For *Nova Express* is nothing if not an analysis
of and tribute to the apocalyptic power of The Word.

Marshall McLuhan, whose own classic *Understanding
Media* appeared the same year, got both the medium—
"an endless succession of impressions and snatches
of narrative"—and the eschatological message: "It is
amusing to read reviews of Burroughs that try to classify
his books as nonbooks or as failed science fiction," he
concluded his own review for *The Nation* in December
1964; "It is a little like trying to criticize the sartorial
and verbal manifestations of a man who is knocking on
the door to explain that flames are leaping from the roof
of our home."[2] *Nova Express* appeared at the height of
the Cold War and the Space Race, when Armageddon
was rarely out of the news or off the screens. 1964 had
opened with the release of Kubrick's *Dr. Strangelove
or: How I Learned to Stop Worrying and Love the Bomb*
and would climax the week *Nova Express* was published
with a U.S. presidential election over which mushroom
clouds had hung, Lyndon Johnson's famous "Daisy Girl"
TV advert linking the prospect of a Barry Goldwater
victory with the countdown to nuclear annihilation. In

short: "This is a burning planet—Any minute now the whole fucking shit house goes up."

Nova Express begins with the blistering Last Words of the mysterious Hassan i Sabbah because time is running out: the book is not just a call-to-arms against those who brought us Hiroshima and Nagasaki, mentioned several times, but a manifesto for global resistance against the 1 percent who run our planet like an alien colony. The book predicts what cataclysms are being "summoned up by an IBM machine and a handful of virus crystals" and describes what dystopian futures are being made on a "soft calculating machine geared to find more and more punch cards." The mainframe in *Dr. Strangelove* was an IBM, but the corporation that bore the Burroughs family name, a major rival to IBM in those days, had already featured in such disaster B-movies as *The Night the World Exploded* (1957), in which a Burroughs B205 calculates the exact time of the planet's destruction. In the month *Nova Express* appeared, November 1964, the Burroughs Corporation supplied NASA with a B5500, an upgrade of the model that had inaugurated "third generation" computer systems; the room-sized solid state machines using transistors and mylar tape magnetic drums that were the first truly self-governing "mechanical brains." Updating his 1952 novel *Queer*, which references "thinking machines," as well as "the electronic brain" that goes berserk in *Naked Lunch*, Burroughs uses the "sound of thinking metal" as one of the voices of *Nova Express*. In 1968 Kubrick's *2001: A Space Odyssey* made the HAL 9000 the sinister star of his sequel to *Dr. Strangelove*, and the following year the Burroughs computer helped launch the Saturn rockets that put a man on the moon. Using technology no more advanced than a pair of scissors, *Nova Express* was a launch vehicle in William Burroughs' own Space Program, his rival mission to invent a "Mythology for the Space Age."

Along with the other volumes of his Cut-Up Trilogy— *The Soft Machine* and *The Ticket That Exploded*—*Nova Express* is a Time Machine, and it's about time we caught up. But despite the wide reach of Burroughs' image across popular culture—or maybe *because* of it—very little is known about the trilogy. How much of these "cut-up novels" are "cut-up"? What order should they be read in, and *how* exactly should we read them? Why is there so little sex in *Nova Express* compared to the other books, and what does its title mean? Since most of what *is* known about the trilogy turns out to be wrong, anyone who thinks *Nova Express* was the last one and the simplest of the three will need to think again.

"I BRING NOT PEACE BUT PIECES"

Nova Express fires the reader into a textual outer space that escapes linear time through montage methods applied at both a structural and syntactical level. As an assault on what Burroughs calls the "Reality Film," the method resembles an accelerated form of cinematic editing, as we're invited to recognize: "Time and place shift in speed-up movie." Repeated across the book, the rapid-fire fragments of text induce a recurrent sense of déjà vu that is deeply disorientating, as is the uncanny sense that Burroughs may have borrowed techniques from one medium to update another but that he is also predicting the media of the future. When "The Subliminal Kid" takes over jukeboxes of the world and cuts in the music with the movies, he precisely replicates the sampling of a digital cultural environment. Likewise, the action of *Nova Express* is modeled on old-fashioned penny arcade pinball machines, "jolting clicking tilting," and yet simulates a console for fantasy video games in codex form: "K9 was in combat with the alien mind screen." With a pun on "canine" that evokes the "human dogs" now in a state of global revolt against their alien masters, "Pilot K9" or "Agent K9" is a technical upgrade of the 1930s comic strip hero in *Secret Agent X-9* scripted by Dashiell Hammett, but today the K9 tag is also immediately recognizable as a science fiction gaming identity.

Traveling in time isn't a theme in *Nova Express*; it's the aim of the form. This is why it's hard to say what is or isn't a "reference," since the text's viral signifiers find their signifieds not only in the past but in the future.

Faced with cut-up passages, the reader can only learn to wait for the "original" words, at which point they take on meaning by discovering new referents. However, since the process happens in both directions at once and the permutations are incalculable, and since the reader's point of intersection with the text changes on every reading, new combinations always keep appearing. As well as being wide-open and open-ended, Burroughs' writing is future-oriented, which is why science fiction was the ideal genre for his cut-up methods.

It wasn't mimesis and it wasn't magic: "I am a chemist not a prophet," says a technical sergeant for The Lazarus Pharmaceutical Company, speaking for Burroughs. The chemistry is a mix of the cryptic, the haunting, and the intertextually impossible: "Good night sweet ladies"? Is that Shakespeare, or T.S. Eliot quoting Shakespeare? "Migrants of ape in gasoline crack of history"? What? Does it really say "Lens googles stuttering light flak"? And Uranian Willy "heard the twittering supersonic threats through antennae embedded in his translucent skull"? Google and Twitter? Does "No bueno" come from *Naked Lunch* or *The Soft Machine* or both? Sometimes a word clicks, a bell rings and the future leaks out (and "his face lights up like a pinball machine," to borrow from *Naked Lunch*), but the reader's flippers can't keep up with the pell-mell rush of verbal steel balls.

Narrative episodes drive the text on while cut-up passages "flow out on ticker tape," and yet Burroughs left most of his material on the cutting-room floor. This is the first revelation about *Nova Express*: just how much *more* there was of it—including collages of literary quotations (Shakespeare, Eliot, Rimbaud, and Joyce in particular) and of newspaper reports about Polaris missiles, the Mariner II Venus probe, A-bomb tests, and high-tech terms: "videosonic—Inertial guidance units—Voice integrators—Direct view control systems—inter valometer computers," and on and on.[3] Burroughs kept only fragments, and it's fascinating to discover in the archival sources that the single word "capsule" in one passage belonged to John Glenn, who piloted his Mercury spacecraft into orbit in 1962 and was feted on his return with one of the largest ever ticker tape parades. A "founding text of the information culture" informed by probability theory and first wave cybernetics,[4] *Nova Express* uses "extremely small particles" of data to experiment with noise and redundancy, to see how much can be left out of the message, and also to show how to get from vacuum tubes to nanotech microchips: "It's the microfilm principle—smaller and smaller." Burroughs juxtaposes the subatomic with the astronomical, referencing white dwarf stars and the Crab Nebula while citing the astronomer Robert Kraft. When K9 says "the human nervous system defines the physics I have constructed," we're invited to see that the book combines extremes of scale to construct its own kind of textual physics.

Nominated for a Nebula Award in 1965, *Nova Express* inspired 1980s cyberpunk writing such as William Gibson's, but it has cut up literary history by continuing to remain more radical than the science fiction it made possible.[5] The book's stream of literary fragments, sampled narratives, shifts in point of view, clips from B-movies and subliminal single frames of current events uncannily maps the digital environment of the Internet that has made Google-eyed cultural DJs of us all. The "futuristic" form of *Nova Express*, which builds on the hybrid geographies of "Interzone" in *Naked Lunch*, doesn't appear antiquated because it's not clean and pure like most 1960s visions of the future, but mixed and dirty. In cinematic terms, it's closer to the tech-noir world of Ridley Scott's *Blade Runner* (1982), which it influenced, than to Kubrick's *Space Odyssey*, although it also has something in common with one of Kubrick's sources: Jean-Luc Godard's *Alphaville*, released six months after *Nova Express* and featuring the gravel-voiced Alpha 60 computer. Significantly, *Alphaville*'s secret agent Lemmie Caution drives a Ford Galaxie but wears a private eye's trench and fedora, and while the film may be set in a dystopian "Zone" it is shot entirely in the night-time streets of Paris in a bleak monochrome, to insist that the future is not in the future; it's already here.

Looking back half a century, *Nova Express* appears both of its times and uncannily prophetic, not just aesthetically, but politically. A Book of Revelations, in it Burroughs plays the role of Willy the Rat, a defector from the American ruling class determined to "call the law" on its true criminality. For Burroughs, revealing "how ugly the Ugly American can be" started at home: alternative drafts of "The Last Words of Hassan i Sabbah" openly invoked his "proud American name" ("Proud of what exactly?"), while one of its earliest versions addressed both sides of his family in accusatory block capitals: "MR ADDING MACHINE BURROUGHS MR ZERO BURROUGHS MR VIRUS BURROUGHS LEE THE PRESS AGENT."[6] His paternal and maternal heritage tied Burroughs to pioneering capitalists not only in business and military computing (the Burroughs Adding Machine) but also in public relations (Uncle "Poison" Ivy Lee, son of the "Reverend Lee" and press agent for Rockefeller and Standard Oil). Burroughs put his privileged haute-bourgeois, classical education to good use by turning it back on itself. He was thinking of Shakespeare's *The Tempest* in the title of his book's penultimate section, "Melted Into Air," but *Nova Express* is born of the insight Karl Marx had into the world market ("All that is solid melts into air, all that is holy is profaned"), updated to include the role of the media to aggravate conflicts and sell back what it steals from us. It wasn't prophecy to Burroughs, it was just straight reportage: "Yep its all there in *Nova Express*," he observed of mid-1960s America, "word for stupid ugly word" (*ROW*, 191).

This is the way *Nova Express* begins, by reversing the duplicitous use of word and image that defines the role of the PR agent and the Mad Man: ratting out the Cold War national security state ("Top Secret—Classified—For The Board"), blowing the whistle on toxic consumer capitalism ("For God's sake don't let that Coca-Cola thing out"), and exposing global ecological disaster ("Not The Green Deal—Don't show them that"). Reviewing *Nova Express*, McLuhan had declared, "We live science fiction." Now, we live *Nova Express*: replace Lazarus Pharmaceuticals by Monsanto, with its genetically modified "terminal seeds"; swap the monopolistic magazine empire of *Time*, *Life*, and *Fortune* (referenced several times) by Rupert Murdoch's News Corporation or the Walt Disney Company; and for Death Dwarfs ("manipulated by remote control") read hunter-killer combat drones over Asia. *Nova Express* is not a book from the past: it addresses our present-time disaster, our still burning planet.

However, history is no more simply a "content" of *Nova Express* than it is a "context" for it. In part, this is because Burroughs mixed up levels of reality as deliberately as he mixed his genres, to make ontologically preposterous hybrids: "Not The Cancer Deal with The Venusians." Lines that didn't make the final cut included: "President Kennedy virtually admitted that at least two known Venusian molluscs were sitting on his cabinet," and "Ben Gurion denied yesterday that any connection exists between what he termed 'the Jewish people' and the crab powers of Minraud."[7] This is one reason the book has not dated and become domesticated as either "historical" or "allegorical": the big picture is always bigger and weirder than any particular history. "The death dwarfs are weapons of the nova mob," Burroughs explained in an interview with the *Paris Review*, two months after his book came out, "which in turn is calling the shots in the cold war."[8] Presidents Kennedy and Johnson are accordingly named in *Nova Express*, but they are not even bit-part players in the galactic conflict led by "Mr. Bradly Mr. Martin." As Inspector Lee insists, "history is fiction," a confidence trickster's "Big Store" operation, involving elaborate sets and a cast of millions. Once they are seen for what they are, however, all the false fronts of the received cultural texts, all the media myths, political theater, and advertising spin can be rewritten, chaotically scrambled, and subjected to ridicule until they lose their power to create solid "reality" and dictate the future. *Nova Express* is not "about" history; it treats history as paper and cuts it up.

If Burroughs' "Last Words" are not "too late," there is "One hope left in the universe: Plan D": "Plan D called for Total Exposure." The title of the book's second section, "Prisoners, Come Out," confirms that Burroughs updates the philosophy lesson of the cave in Plato's *Republic*, and at times readers surely feel like reacting in the same way to the man who says we're all chained in darkness and everything we know and love is an illusion. "Don't listen to Hassan i Sabbah"? Enforced liberation from our temporal existence is more than we bargained for, but it's what Burroughs is offering. In a 1961 typescript he identifies his writing as a war machine for time travel out of time itself: "This is war between those of us who want out and those who want to keep us all locked in time. The cut ups are not for artistic purposes. The cut ups are a weapon a sword. I bring not peace but pieces."[9]

"KUNST UND WISSENSCHAFT"

Before it was published in book form, Burroughs recorded a longer, utterly compelling performance of "Last Words," and I still recall the cold chill of discovering one of the original tapes in a room of the Special Collections Department at Kansas University one winter evening in Lawrence, November 1984. I was immediately mesmerized in my headphones, and have remained so ever since. Three decades later, anyone with access to the Internet can listen to "Last Words" anytime, and follow it by not just more audio tracks from the book but by watching Burroughs perform in *Towers Open Fire*, the 1963 short based on passages from *Nova Express* and *The Ticket That Exploded* directed by Antony Balch. Here his voice, intoning a curse over images of film canisters, is perfectly described as "icily malignant and metallic."[10] Burroughs plays a dozen different roles— from secret agent in black gloves and a fedora hat to gun-toting guerrilla fighter in combat fatigues and a gas mask—and the fact that his gun fires Ping-Pong balls and was bought from Hamleys toy shop in London does nothing to undermine the force of the film or the conviction that Burroughs was anything other than deadly serious.

Our easy digital access to Burroughs' 1960s audiotape recordings and film performances has a double significance for how to read *Nova Express* in the twenty-first century. First, it confirms that his book cannot be confined to the category of the "literary" or its scenario contained within the fiction. In *Nova Express*, it is not the writer who acts out multiple roles in an imaginary war to save the planet. On the contrary: "One of our agents is posing as a writer." What Burroughs was doing was much more than self-dramatization and may have been paranoid self-delusion, but it is categorically *not* postmodern literary self-reflexivity: "We all thought we were interplanetary agents involved in a deadly struggle," he mused in his final novel, *The Western Lands* (1988), before insisting; "The danger and the fear were real enough."[11] Burroughs' absolute immersion in the cut-up project, his evangelical promotion and daily living of it, had a dark side— unleashing for a while an ugly megalomania, misogyny, and anti-Semitism—but it is integral to the power of his texts and our experience of them.

The availability of Burroughs' work in multiple media also establishes that *Nova Express* does not belong to the field of "experimental literature," in the usual sense of formally innovative writing. Up until the publication of *Naked Lunch* in summer 1959, it was still possible to think of Burroughs as "a writer"; not so from that point on. Progressively developing his "third mind" with Brion Gysin, the painter who shared the original cut-up method with him in Paris in October 1959, Burroughs no longer "wrote" but carried out a series of ritualistic *activities* and empirical *operations* in one medium or another, from one technology to another. When Gregory Corso asked what "department" he worked for in a 1961 interview, Burroughs replied, "Kunst und Wissenschaft,"[12] and the Foreword Note to *Nova Express* accordingly frames the book in terms of both the arts and sciences. It's revealing that *Nova Express* not only refers to Gysin's paintings and Dreamachine ("flicker cylinders and projectors") but cross-references them with experimental equipment such as Wilhelm Reich's orgone accumulator and the sensory isolation tanks built by John Lilly, correlating aesthetic and scientific means and ends.

Nova Express is not so much "experimental writing" as a device for conducting experiments on the reader: learning to "read" cut-ups means not only experiencing textual time travel but living in a new medium, maybe to mutate and grow "purple fungoid gills" like the amphibious Fish People. Taking quite literally the scientific meaning of "experiment" and the military sense of "avant-garde," and pushing both to the limits, Burroughs' cut-up project was a decade-long commitment to research and development across a broad range of techniques and technologies in which he collaborated directly with Antony Balch (on films), Ian Sommerville (on audiotapes and photomontages) and Brion Gysin (on the "third mind," a concept and practice of collaboration in itself). The results—in writing, film, tape, photography and collage—were weapons in a war and as much by-products of a process as artistic objects in themselves.

The last decade has begun to catch up with Burroughs, and has seen not only a mass of new scholarly and critical work but the opening up of the enormous archive at the Berg Collection of the New York Public Library, the curating of major artwork exhibitions around the world, the publication of catalogs, the release of films, tapes, letters, and the online digitization of some of the hundreds of texts he contributed to the little magazines of the 1960s mimeograph revolution. The result has been a complete transformation in the Burroughs oeuvre, putting center-stage his cut-up work in media beyond the book form. In 2004 it was still possible to argue that the easy commercial availability of *The Soft Machine, The Ticket That Exploded,* and *Nova Express*, as well as the critical attention paid to them, had misrepresented the cut-up project and perpetuated

Burroughs' reductive reception as a *novelist*: as marketed books, the Cut-Up Trilogy might even be seen as an extraordinary *exception* to the cut-up project, I myself argued.[13] With so much more of the larger project available, now is the time to make the counterargument, and for a new generation to discover the trilogy and to see where it always belonged: not separate from but integrally connected to the full range of Burroughs' unique experiments with word and image.

This is the context for revising the three texts by drawing on archival resources of breathtaking richness, to establish for the first time their manuscript and publishing histories. It is also time to rethink such terms as *cut-up novel* and *cut-up trilogy*. New readers need new scholarship, the state of which has barely advanced since the 1980s, when the first serious but materially flawed academic studies appeared. Drawing on several thousand pages of archival materials—from first drafts and variant typescripts to final long galleys—the notes in this edition aim to reveal the unrecognized complexity of *Nova Express*: they are organized section-by-section because every part has its own untold backstory. The notes therefore aim to make possible new lines of research and reading, and in what follows I offer one such reading, focused on the story that lies behind the book's title. But first, in order to piece together the writing of *Nova Express* we have to unpick the received wisdom about it, starting from the apparent truism that it was the third novel of the Cut-Up Trilogy.

"THE SOFT TICKET"

The Soft Machine, The Ticket That Exploded, and *Nova Express* have been grouped together for fifty years. This is partly because they are so unlike anything else and partly because the identity of each book is blurred by Burroughs' recycling of material across and between them. Running the books together, however, and taking as read the term "Cut-Up Trilogy" (or its thematic alternative, "The Nova Trilogy"), has separated them from their larger context—the many related short texts, photo-collages, scrapbooks, films and tapes that Burroughs made in parallel—and downplayed the important differences between the books (including the almost total lack of sexual material in *Nova Express*). To some, confusion about the trilogy seems not so much inevitable as *intentional*, on the basis that the cut-up project attacked stable identities and linear chronology.

A certain confusion was indeed inherent in the method, since cutting up texts on the scale of Burroughs' project—involving literally thousands of pages of source material, many of which were cut, retyped and cut over and over again—was a process incompatible with achieving a satisfactorily finished product, a definitive text. Burroughs didn't think that *Nova Express* was "in any sense a wholly successful book," but he said the same of *The Soft Machine* and *The Ticket That Exploded*, and for the same reasons.[14] The cut-up method worked well with short texts for little mimeo magazines because the texts were immediate, rough and ephemeral, like the publications themselves: was Burroughs "satisfied" with "Where Flesh Circulates" in *Floating Bear* No. 24 (1962)? The question wasn't relevant. In contrast, the commercially published novel had a fixed form that took time to produce and would last forever. To call *Nova Express* a "cut-up novel" is both inaccurate (it wasn't a novel that was then cut up), and imprecise (how much of it is "cut-up" and how much a "novel"?), but Burroughs himself couldn't avoid calling the book a "novel." It was a contradiction in terms, which is one reason he ended up producing revised editions, so that over a seven-year period the "trilogy" materialized itself as no fewer than six different books: three versions of *The Soft Machine* (1961, 1966, 1968); two of *The Ticket That Exploded* (1962, 1967), and one of *Nova Express* (1964). And as we'll see, that "one" edition of *Nova Express* gives an entirely misleading impression of simplicity.

In the 1966 edition of *The Soft Machine*, Burroughs made a joke out of the resulting confusion (and of his books' lack of commercial success), referring to being paid for the film rights of "a novel I hadn't written called *The Soft Ticket*" and to selling "the Danish rights on my novel *Expense Account.*" But it's not so funny for anyone genuinely interested in the trilogy and how its parts relate one to another. What *is* "the trilogy" when the editions published in the 1960s make possible no fewer than six different permutations and when there's a trilogy alone of *Soft Machines*?

Ironically, "the trilogy" has by default always maintained a single order: first *The Soft Machine*, then *The Ticket That Exploded*, finally *Nova Express*. The sequence keeps faith with the chronology of the first publications of each title: *The Soft Machine* in 1961 (by Olympia Press in Paris); *The Ticket That Exploded* in 1962 (again, Olympia in Paris); and *Nova Express* in 1964 (by Grove Press in New York). The Olympia editions were never published in the United States and went out of print, however, and the available versions are not only different books but have an entirely different chronological order: in Grove editions, the last title, *Nova Express*, was the earliest edition (dating from 1964), while the revised middle title, *The Ticket That Exploded*, became the last edition (published in 1967), and the revised first title, *The Soft Machine*, became the middle volume (published in 1966). Confused? Sketching the development of Burroughs' trilogy over time and relating the books to his work in other media, critics have invariably muddled up the editions and got the history back-to-front. Far from being contra-indicated, an historical approach is long overdue.

The books' reception in the United States and Europe were mirror opposites of each other, since American readers only started the trilogy in 1964 with *Nova Express*, by which time *The Soft Machine* and *The Ticket That Exploded* had been out in Europe for two years. But this is to simplify, since British readers also had a cut-up trilogy-in-one, in the shape of *Dead Fingers Talk* (1963), which was made from revised selections of *Naked Lunch, The Soft Machine,* and *The Ticket.* In 1968 John Calder also brought out the much-revised British edition of *The Soft Machine*, so that the trilogy's first title had now become its final text, and then to cap it all, in 1980 Grove unwisely brought out in one volume a "trilogy" comprising *The Soft Machine, Nova Express,* and *The Wild Boys.*

In light of this confusion's masterpiece, it's less surprising that the history of *Nova Express*, the one "unrevised" edition, turns out to be more complicated than assumed. Constructing the history of its composition clarifies its position within Burroughs' oeuvre, but the initial clues to its status as part of a trilogy are given in the opening pages of the text itself.

One way that *Nova Express* distinguishes itself from the rest of the trilogy is by naming other books by Burroughs, and in its second section it refers to *Naked*

Lunch and *The Soft Machine* twice—in surprising terms: "The purpose of my writing is to expose and arrest Nova Criminals. In *Naked Lunch*, *The Soft Machine* and *Nova Express* I show who they are." Burroughs identifies *Nova Express* as the third of three books, but this is a trilogy beginning with *Naked Lunch* and excluding *The Ticket*—an omission that turns out to be crucial for understanding the "trilogy."[15]

Contrary to the history of publication—in which *Nova Express* appeared in November 1964, almost two years after *The Ticket*—Burroughs had in fact written almost all of *Nova Express,* including this passage, months before he even began *The Ticket.* Had it not been for delays at Grove Press and the speed with which Burroughs wrote *The Ticket That Exploded* for Olympia, *Nova Express* would have followed *The Soft Machine*, so that *The Ticket* would have been the third book of the trilogy. As much a composite text as the others, *Nova Express* was written and re-written over a three-year period and, time-traveling back and forth within the trilogy's history, it would be entirely plausible to place it first, second, and third in different trilogies of composition and publication. Perhaps the most meaningful paradox is that Burroughs began *Nova Express* as a sequel to *The Soft Machine* and completed it as a sequel to *The Ticket That Exploded.* Burroughs' own view was certainly paradoxical: hearing in 1963 that Grove Press had been offered contracts for *The Soft Machine* and *The Ticket*, he wrote confirming to Barney

Rosset that Grove was "the only American publisher for this work but I certainly think *Nova Express* should be published first as a measure of logical sequence."[16] The *logic* is hard to see, but Burroughs wrote *Nova Express* hoping that Grove would publish it before *Naked Lunch*, as a way to strengthen their case against censorship, which is why for this book he cut down the sex.

Finally, it's astonishing to realize that throughout the 1960s Burroughs never once refers to "the cut-up trilogy" in any correspondence, manuscripts or interviews. In fact his only use of the term "trilogy" in this period, in a typescript from early 1962, alludes to the trilogy surprisingly given in *Nova Express*: "My present work is *Novia Express* [sic]—reference is to an exploding star or planet it could happen here—This is the last book of a trilogy—*Naked Lunch The Soft Machine*—The work I am writing now should make it clearer to the reader exactly what I was doing in *The Naked Lunch* and *The Soft Machine*."[17] What's clear is that "the trilogy" is not what we thought it was, and that our readings need to be based on a more accurate history of the writing and rewriting of texts that are both multiple and composite.

"A REWRITE JOB"

In August 1961 Burroughs was living in Tangier at the Villa Muniria, where he had written most of *Naked*

Lunch five years before. After completing *The Soft Machine*, that April he had made a false start on a novel called *The Ugly Spirit*, which was intended to be a "joint operation for Painter and Writer," and spent the summer drawing, painting, making photo-collages and listening to static on transistor radios. At the end of July, Timothy Leary came to visit, bearing hallucinogenic drugs. Leary would later write in vivid detail about that psychedelic summer in Tangier with Burroughs, Allen Ginsberg, Gregory Corso, Ian Sommerville, and Alan Ansen. As well as describing "When the Celestial Messenger Comes Wearing a Fedora," Leary reported Burroughs' decision to write a new kind of cut-up novel, one that would be less "difficult" than *The Soft Machine*.[18] It was in this context that in August Burroughs announced to Brion Gysin: "I am writing a straight action novel that can be read by any twelve year old entitled *The Novia Express*" (*ROW*, 83). A week later, still apparently serious that his new work was suitable for teenage boys, he clarified that this was a "science fiction adventure story."[19] Burroughs would drop one word and then change the spelling of another so that the title has its own trilogy of forms—*The Novia Express, Novia Express, Nova Express*—but, for reasons I will return to, it's significant that he began with a definite title in mind. Having decided the title, identified the genre, and made a start with what became the "Uranian Willy" section—which in places does read like a space invader video game—in mid-August Burroughs left Tangier for a three-month trip to the United States. Leary had invited Burroughs to Massachusetts to research psilocybin mushrooms, and although the trip turned out very badly, it was important for *Nova Express* at this early stage in its writing. The impact shows in the text's categorical warning about hallucinogens—revising Burroughs' earlier enthusiasm and running against the grain of 1960s counterculture—in favor of promoting nonchemical means of consciousness expansion, which implicitly included his own writing. As he had told Leary at the start of the year, "I have achieved pure cut-up highs" (*ROW*, 64). Based in Brooklyn and with little to do but write—"No pot no sex no money" (91)—from September to November 1961 Burroughs concentrated on the book, leaving New York for the Beat Hotel in Paris as soon as he received an advance from Grove.

At the start and end of December 1961, Burroughs sent early chapters to Barney Rosset at Grove Press. More surprisingly, he also mailed them to Henry Wenning, a manuscript dealer in Connecticut. The fact that Burroughs was now selling typescripts of a work-in-progress made *Nova Express* a symbolic landmark in his career. This was not a financially lucrative deal, but the sale separated *Nova Express* both from Burroughs' previous novels and from the many short texts he sent to "no-paying far-out experimental magazines" (*ROW*, 59).

The sales helped sustain Burroughs through times when he needed to pawn the tools of his trade: his typewriter, camera, and tape recorder.

From December 1961 to the end of February 1962, writing first in Paris and then London, Burroughs mailed Rosset more material at least four times, and then on March 30, mailed the first complete manuscript—only to admit three days later that it was "not in as good order as I would like," enclosing more corrections, suggestions and material.[20] Since there's no more "plot" progression than there is "character" development, any structure would have been provisional because multiple permutations were possible. Burroughs' constant shifts in location were also connected, practically as well as figuratively, to the material he produced and the difficulties he had finding the right order for it. The international geography of *Nova Express*' writing history is as revealing as its chronology: as Burroughs explained to Wenning, "my methods of work and constant change of residence traveling with one suitcase makes for difficulty assembling complete typescripts."[21] Barney Rosset encouraged Burroughs to send sections as he wrote them, and several times Burroughs had to ask Rosset to send copies back, having either lost or lost track of what he had written. At least by selling his manuscripts Burroughs preserved them, because his working methods and need to keep moving ensured the casual destruction of much of it.

During the next six months Burroughs started and finished *The Ticket That Exploded* for Olympia Press, assembled *Dead Fingers Talk* for John Calder and began revising *The Soft Machine*—but nothing happened on *Nova Express*. The last two projects suggest he had an agenda in mind when asking Rosset at the start of October 1962 whether Grove had "a definite publication date for *Nova Express*" (he had changed the spelling of the title the previous month): "That was a rush job and I am not satisfied with the arrangement of material and some of the sections could do with a rewrite job."[22] Contrary to appearances, *Nova Express* was *not* the one unrevised volume in the Cut-Up Trilogy, and in the third week of October Burroughs mailed Rosset a "revised and rearranged manuscript" (*ROW*, 115). He added a new chapter in March 1963 and submitted a new ending (which was never used) that October, when the typesetting was done, and then over a year later effectively revised *Nova Express* a second time, so extensive was the work Burroughs did on the galleys in July 1964, now back in Tangier where he had started the book three years earlier.

The three major stages of *Nova Express*' compositional history—the March and October 1962 manuscripts and the July 1964 revised galleys—generated a trilogy of alternative forms and resulted in a composite final text. Piecing together the March 1962 manuscript from incomplete archival copies, it was clearly similar in content to the published text, lacking for certain only three sections ("Pry Yourself Loose And Listen," "Chinese Laundry," and "Inflexible Authority") and including three others that Burroughs later cut. However, the order was completely different and another eight sections differed significantly. The first ten chapters (often titled in block capitals in his first draft) began with "THE NOVIA EXPRESS" (later retitled "Uranian Willy") and ended with "A DISTANT THANK YOU." Other chapters followed in late December and mid-February, and a good deal more of the text was written in the six weeks leading up to his submission of the first complete manuscript on March 30, 1962. This was an especially significant period because Burroughs was now no longer cutting up his material, which is one reason he produced so much so quickly. As he announced on February 20, "I do not use scissors any more" (*ROW*, 99).

In his Foreword Note to *Nova Express* Burroughs acknowledged that he had used an "extension of Brion Gysin's cut-up method which I call the fold-in method," a statement that begs many questions: How did the methods differ, in terms of materials used and results obtained? Is it possible to say which parts of *Nova Express* were cut-up and which folded-in? Should the book be called a "fold-in novel"? Telling Gysin in March 1962 that he was "using more and more cut up method of folding," Burroughs seems to make "fold-in" a subcategory of "cut-up," and while this is not the place to develop a taxonomy of forms, it's obvious that *Nova Express* contains not one but various types of "cut-up" and "fold-in" texts and that we lack the terms to describe and differentiate them—or even to distinguish them from Burroughs' "normal" writing: "he writes naturally now like cut up," Allen Ginsberg observed in September 1962.[23]

Burroughs' 170-page October 1962 manuscript, which was used as the typesetting copy, restructured the material to give it the order of the published text. He revised the titles of more than half a dozen sections, cut one, redacted several others and divided the novel into nine chapters, the last of which would be cut only at the galley stage. In his covering letter, Burroughs referred to its internal divisions as both "chapters" and "sections" and as "sections" and "subsections" (*ROW*, 115). The self-contradiction was typical of Burroughs, and although "section" and "subsection" are more surgically precise, he used "chapter" and "section" more frequently, and I have followed his general if inconsistent practice. In terms of content, the broad direction of manuscript revision was clear: Burroughs redacted cut-up sections and expanded narrative ones. In October 1962 he added two long narratives ("Chinese Laundry" and "Inflexible Authority"), which he suggested to Rosset "would make good advance publicity for the book," potentially in *Evergreen Review*. Although the house journal of Grove Press did not take up the suggestion, it had already published two selections from *Nova Express*, in January and July 1962, and would publish one more in March the following year, while, less strategically, Burroughs contributed other parts to several short-lived little magazines.[24] In March 1963, he added another long piece, the 2,000-word "Pry Yourself Loose" section, adding what might be called a nova noir tone of hardboiled vitriol and giving a stronger narrative drive to the book's opening chapter.

Returning his corrected galleys to Richard Seaver at Grove in July 1964 (a second set had gone, as requested, to Ian Sommerville), Burroughs resumed one last time his familiar refrain: "I found myself dissatisfied with a good deal of the cut up material so the corrected proofs contain considerable deletions and quite a few inserts."[25] These changes were, he insisted, essential to "the integrity and impact of the book." The ten separate inserts he made on the galleys, typed up and Scotch-taped in, added up to some 1,800 words, all inserted into the second half of the manuscript, which was also where he made all the deletions, using a thick black marker pen. By far the longest insert went into the "One More Chance?" section and significantly expanded the material in *Nova Express* about Scientology, a key factor that had been there from the start of the cut-up project. Apart from a long, entirely cut-up ninth chapter that Burroughs canceled completely, the cuts and additions he made at the galley stage balanced out in length.

It's revealing that while everything he canceled on the galleys was cut-up material, so was a third of what he added: he hadn't lost faith in his methods, it was just that the older material now seemed too repetitive (which it was, especially in the ninth chapter). Overall, the revisions didn't much change the balance of the book, the second half of which has roughly twice as much cut-up material as the first half, although precise percentages are impossible to calculate and becoming progressively unable to tell the difference between what is cut-up and what is not is one of the book's strangest effects.[26]

The cut-up text that Burroughs added in 1964 stands out formally through its heavy use of ellipses (. . .), in contrast to his earlier use of the em dash (—). There are 150 ellipses in *Nova Express*, but just one comes from a pre-1964 typescript. Useful for dating Burroughs' material, the ellipses of *Nova Express* also emphasize the larger significance of punctuation. Burroughs not only had an extraordinary ear for speech and idiom and a genius for enigmatic turns-of-phrase but a great sense of rhythm and pace, and he used punctuation to vary the tempo of the reading experience: like a cinematic *dissolve*, ellipses are usually slow, enigmatic; like a cinematic *cut*, the em dash is sharp, rapid and urgent. The visual impact of punctuation on the page also makes a clear gesture against the formal limits imposed by mainstream publication. Commenting on the "multiplicity of punctuation" in the new ending he submitted in October 1963, Burroughs had told Seaver: "This is an experiment with format and the use of punctuation which I have carried further in the work I am doing now."[27] On the other hand, the general practice of Grove's copyeditors was to normalize such distinctive practices as his use of lower case "i" for the first person pronoun and to regularize Burroughs' inconsistency in using punctuation.

Most important, Burroughs makes punctuation itself operate as a sign system, a language, when the dots and dashes are arranged into lines of "supersonic Morse code" at the end of the section "Will Hollywood Never Learn?" The Morse letters were again a gesture, a pragmatic way to assimilate into book form an equivalent to, for example, his "color alphabet," a series of experiments with word and image he developed in spring 1961, inspired by a combination of Rimbaud's poetry and the use of hallucinogens—visually rich experiments which had no commercial possibilities. Visible, rather than audible like phonetic language, the lines of Morse code thus also anticipated the "silent writing of Brion Gysin," embodied in the calligraphic design that closed *The Ticket That Exploded*. Although Grove did not use the "sketch by Brion Gysin for a suggested cover" that Burroughs sent Seaver in July 1964, when *Nova Express* appeared three months later he congratulated his editor on the results: "An excellent job I think as regards cover and typesetting."[28] The question of cover design brings us finally to the book's title, and the bigger picture that lies behind it.

"CURSE GO BACK"

In spring 1965 Burroughs made an untitled collage for his and Gysin's "Book of Methods" (later published as *The Third Mind*) that includes his earlier title for *Nova Express* constructed as a cut-up of words in two different typefaces: a Gothic "The" followed by "NOVA EXPRESS" in white Sans serif capitals against a black background. The title acts as a caption to the picture above it of a train wreck, while the words "By train" appear prominently nearby. The composition also includes typewritten text by Burroughs in two columns (beginning, "you are reading the future"), a photograph of him making tea, and the Spanish word "Sucesos," identifying the train crash as an item in the *sección de sucesos*, the newspaper section dealing with crimes and disasters. In 1966, Jonathan Cape used parts of this collage for the cover of the British edition of *Nova Express*, omitting the Gothic article "The" and adding pictures of locomotive wheels to emphasize the obvious: *Nova Express* names the onrushing apocalyptic train crash of history, the railroad of time, "the total disaster *now* on tracks."

However, to read the title in this way is to risk missing the point Burroughs was making in both book and collage, and indeed in the cut-up project as a whole: what mattered most was not the apparent referential content but the form, the message in the medium itself. The importance of form is precisely established in the *Nova Express* collage by the way it is reproduced in *The Third Mind*, where in miniature it is juxtaposed alongside another *Nova Express* collage. This collage makes two changes to the book's title, omitting the article "The" and, after the same white-on-black capitalized "NOVA," has the word "EXPRESS" in a different typeface. To British readers, the font and spacing of the letters in "EXPRESS" are unmistakable: it is from the masthead of the *Daily Express*. The other semantic content of the word "express"—referring to not trains but newspapers—is activated formally by the typography of the word and by the broadsheet page layout of the collage.[29] The term *nova* may refer to a nuclear explosion in white dwarf stars, but Burroughs was well enough versed in astronomy as well as in Latin to know this was an abbreviation of *stella nova* ("new star"), and that *nova* also designates what is *new* or *news*: it was in this double sense that he originally titled his novel *The Novia Express*.

A year before making these two collages, in spring 1964 as he waited to receive the *Nova Express* galleys,

Burroughs had been building filing systems modeled on
newspaper archives: "Your reporter selects a clipping
from the file labelled *Daily Express*, Saturday, April 25,
1964 (London)."[30] In July, as he corrected the galleys,
he physically framed his book in terms of newspapers
by inserting the same phrase to give a new final line to
both the first and last sections of the text: "September
17, 1899 over New York."[31] Burroughs became obsessed
with this date, using it in many texts, but its significance
lies in its provenance in a newspaper. In February 1964
he wrote Gysin of his discovery: "The *New York Times*
for September 17, 1899 came through a few days ago.
I saw at once that the message was not of content but
format. Newspapers are cut up by format [...] This is
the secret of their power to mould thought feeling and
subsequent events" (*ROW*, 139). Restating what he had
already made explicit in *Nova Express* in terms of "Juxtaposition Formulae" ("Our technicians learn to read
newspapers and magazines for juxtaposition statements
rather than alleged content"), Burroughs was inspired
to produce his own newspaper format pieces using three
columns, and during 1964 and 1965 he made many such
texts. Although these have always been seen as entirely
separate from his book-length cut-up work, the ending
of *Nova Express* insists otherwise: "Well that's about the
closest way I know to tell you and papers rustling across
city desks . . . fresh southerly winds a long time ago."
Those "city desks" of newspaper offices parallel the

sección de sucesos in his *Nova Express* collage and were
a clear reflection of Burroughs' vision in February 1964:
"Why not write a novel as if you were sitting at the city
desk?" (*ROW*, 143). And those "fresh southerly winds"
would be associated with newspapers in the archives
Burroughs later assembled for sale; Folio 108, which he
titled "Fresh Southerly Winds Stir Papers On The City
Desk," gathers together a dozen mid-1960s newspaper-
format publications, from "The Daily Tape Worm" to one
called "The Nova Express."[32]

Burroughs may not have had in mind his late-1950s
character "Fats" Terminal, who "edits a newspaper
known as the *Underground Express*,"[33] but *Nova Express*
was definitely "underground." Not quite, perhaps, like
the underground press of little magazines to which Burroughs contributed—since a publishing house like Grove
was "alternative" but still commercial, not aligned with
the self-publishing networks that sprang up in the 1960s.
Rather, it was underground in its aim to serve a resistance
movement against an occupying power, its cut-up methods intended to sabotage an essentially fascist above-
ground world. *Nova Express* is "about" the Nova Mob,
but from the start Burroughs saw it as opposed to and
directed against what in 1960 he called "the Beaverbrook
Mob," referring to the Anglo-Canadian owner of the *Daily
Express*, and fascist sympathizer, Lord Beaverbrook.[34] In
fact, Beaverbrook was one of a trio of press barons in Burroughs' sights, alongside Henry Luce (*Time, Life, Fortune*)

and William Randolph Hearst (from the *San Francisco Examiner* to New York's *Daily Mirror*). Many early drafts of what became "Last Words," were addressed directly to all three: "PAY IT ALL PAY IT ALL PAY IT ALL BACK. PLAY IT ALL PLAY IT ALL PLAY IT ALL BACK. RIGHT HERE RIGHT NOW FOR ALL TO SEE. MR LUCE BEAVERBROOK HURST TIME SMASH YOUR MACHINE."[35] Dating from as early as May 1960, this and other "Last Words" drafts were written over a year before Burroughs began work on *Nova Express*, but he never used any such material for *The Soft Machine* and would make relatively few references to the press in *The Ticket That Exploded*. However, he saw *Nova Express* in terms of newspapers from first to last.

The most striking instance of how early and how emphatically Burroughs associated the book's original title with newspapers appears in a long canceled passage from the section "Too Far Down The Road." Probably composed in late 1961, the typescript repeats the phrase "To readers of The Daily Express" twice in order to frame a reference to "The Novia Express," and also cites the title of one of Luce's magazines ("Looking through Time"). Readers of "The Novia Express" would have got the point, and this material stayed in until the galley stage in July 1964. Burroughs didn't simply cut it, however: he transferred it from one medium to another, in April 1965 recording "Are You Tracking Me," a sonic experiment that includes the key phrase "To readers of The Daily Express."

In August 1961 the first chapter heading of the manuscript in its earliest draft had carried the original title of
the book as a whole, "THE NOVIA EXPRESS." Here,
the "one hope left in the universe" is to "wise up the
marks": "Show them the rigged wheel of Life-Time-
Fortune. Storm The Reality Studio." The book therefore
opened with not only the clearest possible assault on the
fraudulent "reality" projected by Luce's newsmagazine
empire; in the context of references to *Life, Time,* and
Fortune, the section and book title "The Novia Express"
also identified Burroughs' text as alternative reportage, "news" of a different reality. But it's significant
that the book uses words cut from newspapers quite
recognizably in just three specific sections ("Extremely
Small Particles," "There's A Lot Ended," "Are These
Experiments Necessary?"), and that these are all introduced by dates: from "Dec. 17, 1961—Past Time" to
"March 17, 1962, Present Time Of Knowledge." Attacking the temporality and referentiality standardized by
Time magazine, *Nova Express* mainly uses cut-up news
items that were of passing, topical interest in December
1961 and March 1962 (crime reports, celebrity events),
and renders them deliberately obscure. For Burroughs,
"Present Time" was not determined by public events or
the official historical record but was a point of personal
intersection, and from many pages of cut-up newspaper
source material he chose to keep few fragments of "historical" significance for use in *Nova Express.*

Burroughs' attitudes toward history, news, and time are suggested by the revisions he *didn't* make for the revised manuscript he submitted in October 1962, even though the historical context could scarcely have been more urgent or more resonant. Two days before he mailed his manuscript, Kennedy was addressing Khrushchev on television at the height of the Cuban Missile Crisis, and the Joint Chiefs of Staff were upgrading the alert status for nuclear war to DEFCON 2, its highest-ever condition of readiness. Cut up with tittle-tattle about film stars and murder stories, Burroughs' typescript for "There's A Lot Ended," written in March 1962, had included prophetic "rumors about Castro," but that October he neither restored the line nor updated his manuscript, even though the eyes of the world were on Cuba and the world seemed on the brink of nova.

Burroughs' attack on *Time* was also a personal counter-attack, most directly in response to its review of the Grove Press *Naked Lunch*, which was so offensive he sued the magazine, winning token damages of £5 in November 1963. The *Time* review had also attacked the then-unpublished *Nova Express*, which it described as coming "daringly close to utter babble, according to reports."[36] Burroughs cut up the text from *Time* (and the libel case documents) and recycled the phrase "utter babble" in two magazine-format publications printed in 1965, his own version of *Time* and *APO-33*, in the spirit of what goes around comes around. Or as he put it in

Towers Open Fire, intoning the words over canisters of reality film: "Curse go back."

Of the trinity of media magnates attacked in early drafts of "Last Words," by far the most significant was Henry Luce. *Nova Express* was Burroughs' central weapon against the monopolistic power of Luce's own "trilogy" of *Time*, *Life*, and *Fortune*, titles that not only named but in effect copyrighted Time, Life, and Fortune. Luce's name appears in dozens of typescripts dating from 1960, several addressed directly to him, demanding he dismantle his "Time Machine."[37] Burroughs' public counterattack had started in 1960 with *Minutes to Go*, a manifesto that both addressed potential allies in the cut-up project and identified its primary enemy through an "OPEN LETTER TO LIFE MAGAZINE." This cut-up of *Life*'s mocking feature article on the Beats from November 1959 returned the mockery with interest, in the vein of the comic cuts in *The Drunken Newscaster* tapes Burroughs loved. But the text also announced the future direction of a project that had begun just the month before, when Gysin sliced through newspapers and *Life* magazine advertisements while cutting a mount for a drawing in the Beat Hotel. It identified cut-up methods as a strategy of media *détournement*, as the Paris-based Situationsists called it. From here, it was a short step to *The Third Mind* and *Electronic Revolution* and *The Revised Boy Scout Manual*, handbooks to inspire future

generations of media guerrillas, culture jammers, computer hackers, and pop-up subversives.

In the society of the spectacle, Burroughs understood
that "the real battle" is over the production of reality
itself: of what counts as real in the first place.[38] Given
the balance of power in his rivalry with *Time*, *Life*, and
Fortune, cut-up methods were necessarily terroristic,
waging asymmetrical warfare against a global media
empire seeking to maintain what Luce had envisioned
as a permanent American Century. In that context, *Nova
Express* brilliantly dramatizes how cybernetic feedback
could coincide with imperial blowback by reversing
the function of *Time* magazine. For once the news is
understood as not reporting the past but projecting the
future, Burroughs reasoned that to physically reorder
the news is to scramble the reality it produces, until
"Insane orders and counter orders issue from berserk
Time Machine": "I said The Chief of Police skinned
alive in Baghdad not Washington D.C." The funniest
as well as the most politically ferocious of Burroughs'
Cut-Up Trilogy, *Nova Express* includes within itself a
sense of how ridiculous it was to oppose a media trilogy
that in 1965 had a weekly circulation of more than ten
million with a book whose print run was ten thousand:
"Sure, sure, but you see now why we had to laugh till
we pissed watching those dumb rubes playing around
with photomontage—Like charging a regiment of tanks
with a defective slingshot." Or like fighting the Nova

Mob with a pair of scissors and a Ping-Pong machine gun. Was it just self-delusion to declare that "a box camera and a tape recorder can cut lines laid down by Hollywood and life time fortune"?[39]

Burroughs started *Nova Express* as an "action novel that can be read by any twelve year old," and constructed it both with deadly seriousness and in the adventurous spirit of "Johnny The Space Boy who built a space ship in his barn" (*ROW*, 112)—in other words, against a backdrop of apocalyptic darkness and overwhelming odds, in the doomed but undefeated spirit of eternal hope.

"COMPLETE INTENTIONS FALLING"

The relation between *Nova Express* and newspapers draws attention to a basic distinction for Burroughs between the book form and his newspaper experiments: his little magazine and small pamphlet texts in newspaper format were typically quick, rough, and unrevised productions where he deliberately let stand numerous typos and cancellations as signs of his process of composition. In absolute contrast, Burroughs fully expected his book manuscripts to be professionally typeset and copyedited. He addressed Grove Press in pragmatic terms of publishing norms and editorial corrections: "As regards your enquiries," he wrote Richard Seaver in early October 1963, just as *Nova Express* was about to be typeset, "most of the irregularities you speak of are typing errors to be corrected in the manner you suggest," adding, a couple of weeks later: "As a matter of general orientation, both spelling and punctuation should be normalized and consistent."[40] The agreement between author and publisher was clear and establishes an equally clear context for this new edition of *Nova Express*.

Contrary to media myths, Burroughs did not put his material together haphazardly any more than he wrote it crazed on drugs. Chance operations served particular creative functions that varied over time, but even the early "raw" cut-ups in *Minutes to Go* were carefully edited, representing ways to *escape* the control of language, not abdicate it. "If my writing seems at times ungrammatical," Burroughs explained to his bemused parents in November 1959, as he started to work with cut-up methods, "it is not due to carelessness or accident" (*ROW*, 7). He was equally insistent about the methods themselves, often repeating that the results "must be edited and rearranged as in any other method of composition" (105). The archival evidence confirms the radical creative role he allowed chance in the process of cutting or folding texts and transcribing the results, and he always retained mistakes and typos across his many rough drafts; but the evidence also confirms the rigorous approach he took to the correction of *final* drafts.[41]

Equally, there is no evidence at all that Burroughs accepted as felicitous the kind of contingencies that would usually be called a "corruption," and, far from embracing the unwanted interventions of copyeditors and typesetters, Burroughs did what he could to restore his original intentions. Burroughs *chose* his collaborators, just as he chose the material he cut up and the results he retained. That's why he called on Ian Sommerville, to add a more rigorous hand in proofing the galleys. My own approach to editing *Nova Express* has kept faith with this logic. Apart from giving the opening sections of each chapter their own titles, the roughly one hundred changes for this edition mainly correct typos or restore Burroughs' punctuation (including his occasional use of double colons) and are conventionally based (i.e., supported by multiple manuscript witnesses). The notes detail key changes, comment on apparent errors and twilight zone cases and introduce the richest possible selection of archival material to reveal revisions over time and the intricacy of Burroughs' working methods. While relatively minor, the textual alterations categorically reject the alternative: to fix and fetishize the 1964 Grove edition. *Nova Express* has no final form any more than it allows a definitive reading, since the paradoxical result of its mechanical creative procedures is an organic textuality, a living text that changes on every reading. The poetic complexity of *Nova Express* will always exceed our grasp and yet invite us back, because simply to read and re-read it is the only way to do justice to Burroughs' book, to this textual war machine and homemade spaceship built for time travel, to the radioactive fervor of Reverend Lee's last words.

Oliver Harris
May 2, 2013

1. *Rub Out the Words: The Letters of William S. Burroughs, 1959–1974*, edited by Bill Morgan (New York: Ecco, 2012), 170. After, abbreviated to *ROW*.

2. Marshall McLuhan, "Notes on Burroughs," *The Nation* (December 28, 1964), 517–19.

3. Undated typescript, probably 1963 (William S. Burroughs Papers, 1951–1972, The Henry W. and Albert A. Berg Collection of English and American Literature, New York Public Library, 37.2). After, abbreviated to Berg. Mariner II is cited in Berg 11.28; Polaris in Berg 36.11; Atom bomb fallout in Berg 12.17.

4. See Dennis Redmond's essay <http://members.efn.org/~dredmond/PP2.html>

5. The "condensed" novels of J.G. Ballard would be an obvious exception, but the British writer always insisted Burroughs was an inspiration, not an influence.

6. Typescript, dated May 20, 1960 (Berg 49.1).

7. Undated typescript (Berg 10.11).

8. *Burroughs Live: The Collected Interviews of William S. Burroughs, 1960–1996*, edited by Sylvère Lotringer (New York: Semiotext(e): 2000), 80.

9. Typescript, dated 1961 (Berg 62.9).

10. Peter Wollen, *Paris Hollywood: Writings on Film* (London: Verso, 2002), 31.

11. Burroughs, *The Western Lands* (New York: Viking, 1987), 252.

12. *Burroughs Live*, 42.

13. See "Cutting Up Politics," in *Retaking the Universe: William S. Burroughs in the Age of Globalization* (London: Pluto, 2004), edited by Davis Schneiderman and Philip Walsh, 175–200.

14. Burroughs, *The Job* (New York: Penguin, 1989), 27.

15. One explanation for the presence of *Naked Lunch* might be that Burroughs made his Cut-Up Trilogy from the leftovers of his thousand-page "Word Hoard"; but so far as *Nova Express* is concerned, there's little truth in this often-repeated claim.

16. Burroughs to Rosset, May 24, 1963 (Grove Press Records, Special Collections, Syracuse University.) After, abbreviated to Syracuse.

17. Undated 2-page typescript (Berg 9.16).

18. Timothy Leary, *High Priest* (New York: Ronin, 1995), 225.

19. Burroughs to Gysin, August 18, 1961 (Berg 85.5).

20. Burroughs to Rosset, April 2, 1962 (Syracuse).

21. Burroughs to Wenning, September 23, 1961 (William S. Burroughs Papers, Ohio State University, SPEC.CMS.85, 1.1).

22. Burroughs to Rosset, October 2, 1962 (Syracuse).

23. Ginsberg to Kerouac, September 9, 1962, in *The Letters of Allen Ginsberg*, edited by Bill Morgan (New York: Da Capo, 2008), 270.

24. Burroughs also made three contributions to the German magazine *Rhinozeros* and contributed parts of *Nova Express* to *The Second Coming* in 1962 and Ira Cohen's *Gnaoua* in 1964.

25. Burroughs to Seaver, July 21, 1964 (Berg 75.1).

26. In rough terms, a quarter of the material in chapters 1 to 4 is cut-up, compared with half of the material in chapters 5 to 7. Almost half the book's sections combine cut-up and non-cut-up writing, and of the rest half have just one or the other.

27. Burroughs to Seaver, October 24, 1963 (Syracuse).

28. Burroughs to Seaver, July 21, 1964 and October 25, 1964 (Berg 75.1).

29. At this time, Burroughs made another collage that placed an adapted copy of the front cover of a November 30, 1962 copy of *Time* magazine in between his two *Nova Express* collages. A photograph of this collage is reproduced in *The Art of William S. Burroughs: Cut-Ups, Cut-Ins, Cut-Outs*, edited by Collin Fallows (Nürnberg: moderne Kunst, 2013), 61. According to Barry Miles, it was created at the Hotel Chelsea, New York, in April 1965, and Burroughs used a Spanish language newspaper brought with him from Tangier (e-mail correspondence April 30, 2013). As well as influencing numerous musicians, including an album of the same title by John Zorn (2011), and inspiring Andre Perkowski's cinematic homage (2010), *Nova Express* gave its title to a newspaper in Alan Moore's 1986 comic-book series, *Watchman*.

30. Burroughs, "Tangier," *Esquire* 62.3 (September 1964).

31. In October 1963 Burroughs asked Seaver for two copies of the *New York Times* front page. The *exact* repetition of the line is crucial, although this feature has often been lost in translation, as in the French edition translated by Mary Beach and Claude Pélieu (Paris: Christian Bourgois, 1970). This has "au-dessus de New York, le 17 septembre 1899" the first time but "17 septembre 1899, au-dessus de New York" the second time (9, 189). Unaccountably, the edition also translates the final date "21 July, 1964" as "21 janvier 1964."

32. Folio 108 in the original catalog became Box 38 in the Berg Collection archive.

33. Burroughs, "Word," in *Interzone* (New York: Viking, 1989), 184. Fats Terminal does appear in the "Gave Proof Through the Night" section, on a jukebox playing *The Star-Spangled Banner*.

34. Burroughs to Gysin, August 30, 1960 (Berg 86.8).

35. Undated typescript, probably late 1960 (Berg 48.22).

36. "King of the YADS," *Time* (November 30, 1962), 96-97.

37. "Mr Henry Luce, Do you know what the machine is up to?" begins one typescript (Berg 7.38). A diatribe addressed to Mr Bradly Mr Martin in *The Ticket That Exploded* is clearly a reworking of similar material, but the only time Luce is actually named in the trilogy occurs in the 1968 edition of *The Soft Machine* when a character "goes into his Luce act" (106).

38. *Burroughs Live*, 150.

39. Draft typescript for *The Ticket That Exploded* (Berg 20.39). See also "The Inferential Kid," *The Burroughs File* (San Francisco: City Lights, 1984), 128.

40. Burroughs to Seaver, October 10, 1963 and October 24, 1963 (Syracuse).

41. Burroughs' clearest statement on the subject is quoted in Miles' Introduction to *Le métro blanc* (Paris: Seuil, 1976), a collection of cut-up texts translated into French: "As you know my methods of writing do not allow me to correct rough copies and first drafts [. . .] It is only when I obtain the final form that I correct errors" (12; my translation).

NOVA
EXPRESS

Foreword Note

The section called "This Horrible Case" was written in collaboration with Mr. Ian Sommerville, a mathematician—Mr. Sommerville also contributed the technical notes in the section called "Chinese Laundry"—An extension of Brion Gysin's cut-up method which I call the fold-in method has been used in this book which is consequently a composite of many writers living and dead.

Last Words

LAST WORDS

Listen to my last words anywhere. Listen to my last words any world. Listen all you boards syndicates and governments of the earth. And you powers behind what filth deals consummated in what lavatory to take what is not yours. To sell the ground from unborn feet forever—

"Don't let them see us. Don't tell them what we are doing—"

Are these the words of the all-powerful boards and syndicates of the earth?

"For God's sake don't let that Coca-Cola thing out—"

"Not The Cancer Deal with The Venusians—"

"Not The Green Deal—Don't show them that—"

"Not The Orgasm Death—"

"*Not the ovens—*"

Listen: I call you all. Show your cards all players. Pay it all pay it all pay it *all* back. Play it all play it all play it *all* back. For all to see. In Times Square. In Piccadilly.

"Premature. Premature. Give us a little more time."

Time for what? More lies? Premature? Premature for who? I say to all these words are not premature. These words may be too late. Minutes to go. Minutes to foe goal—

"Top Secret—Classified—For The Board—The Elite—The Initiates—"

Are these the words of the all-powerful boards and syndicates of the earth? These are the words of liars cowards collaborators traitors. Liars who want time for more lies. Cowards who can not face your "dogs" your "gooks" your "errand boys" your "human animals" with the truth. Collaborators with Insect People with Vegetable People. With any people anywhere who offer you a body forever. To shit forever. For this you have sold out your sons. Sold the ground from unborn feet forever. Traitors to all souls everywhere. You want the name of Hassan i Sabbah on your filth deeds to sell out the unborn?

What scared you all into time? Into body? Into shit? I will tell you: "*the word.*" Alien Word "*the.*" "*The*" word of Alien Enemy imprisons "*thee*" in Time. In Body. In Shit. Prisoner, come out. The great skies are open. I

Hassan i Sabbah *rub out the word forever.* If you I cancel all your words forever. And the words of Hassan i Sabbah as also cancel. Cross all your skies see the silent writing of Brion Gysin Hassan i Sabbah: drew September 17, 1899 over New York.

PRISONERS, COME OUT

"Don't listen to Hassan i Sabbah," they will tell you. "He wants to take your body and all pleasures of the body away from you. Listen to us. We are serving The Garden of Delights Immortality Cosmic Consciousness The Best Ever In Drug Kicks. And *love love love* in slop buckets. How does that sound to you boys? Better than Hassan i Sabbah and his cold windy bodiless rock? Right?"

At the immediate risk of finding myself the most unpopular character of all fiction—and history is fiction—I must say this:

"Bring together state of news—Inquire onward from state to doer—Who monopolized Immortality? Who monopolized Cosmic Consciousness? Who monopolized Love Sex and Dream? Who monopolized Life Time and Fortune? Who took from you what is yours? Now they will give it all back? Did they ever give anything away for nothing? Did they ever give any more than they had to give? Did they not always take back what they gave when possible and it always was? *Listen:* Their Garden Of Delights is a terminal sewer—I have been at some pains to map this area of terminal sewage in the so called pornographic sections of *Naked Lunch* and *The Soft Machine*—Their Immortality Cosmic Consciousness and Love is second-run grade-B shit—Their drugs are poison designed to beam in Orgasm Death and Nova Ovens—Stay out of the Garden Of Delights—It is a man-eating trap that ends in green goo—Throw back their ersatz Immortality—It will fall apart before you can get out of The Big Store—Flush their drug kicks down the drain—*They are poisoning and monopolizing the hallucinogen drugs—learn to make it without any chemical corn*—All that they offer is a screen to cover retreat from the colony they have so disgracefully mismanaged. To cover travel arrangements so they will never have to pay the constituents they have betrayed and sold out. Once these arrangements are complete they will blow the place up behind them."

And what does my program of total austerity and total resistance offer *you?* I offer you nothing. I am not a politician. These are conditions of total emergency. And these are my instructions for total emergency if carried out *now* could avert the total disaster *now* on tracks:

"*Peoples of the earth, you have all been poisoned.* Convert all available stocks of morphine to apomorphine.

Chemists, work round the clock on variation and synthesis of the apomorphine formulae. Apomorphine is the only agent that can disintoxicate you and cut the enemy beam off your line. Apomorphine and silence. I order total resistance directed against this conspiracy to pay off peoples of the earth in ersatz bullshit. I order total resistance directed against The Nova Conspiracy and all those engaged in it."

The purpose of my writing is to expose and arrest Nova Criminals. In *Naked Lunch The Soft Machine* and *Nova Express* I show who they are and what they are doing and what they will do if they are not arrested. Minutes to go. Souls rotten from their orgasm drugs, flesh shuddering from their nova ovens, prisoners of the earth to *come out*. With your help we can occupy The Reality Studio and retake their universe of Fear Death and Monopoly—

(Signed) INSPECTOR J. LEE, NOVA POLICE

Post Script Of The Regulator: I would like to sound a word of warning—To speak is to lie—To live is to collaborate—Anybody is a coward when faced by the nova ovens—There are degrees of lying collaboration and cowardice—That is to say degrees of intoxication— It is precisely a question of *regulation*—The enemy is not man is not woman—The enemy exists only where no life is and moves always to push life into extreme untenable positions—You can cut the enemy off your line by the judicious use of apomorphine and silence— *Use the sanity drug apomorphine.*

"Apomorphine is made from morphine but its physiological action is quite different. Morphine depresses the front brain. Apomorphine stimulates the back brain, acts on the hypothalamus to regulate the percentage of various constituents in the blood serum and so normalize the constitution of the blood." I quote from *Anxiety and Its Treatment* by Doctor John Yerbury Dent.

PRY YOURSELF LOOSE AND LISTEN

I was traveling with The Intolerable Kid on The Nova Lark—We were on the nod after a rumble in The Crab Galaxy involving this two-way time stock; when you come to the end of a biologic film just run it back and start over—Nobody knows the difference—Like nobody there before the film.* So they start to run it back and

---

* Postulate a biologic film running from the beginning to the end, from zero to zero as all biologic film run in any time universe—Call this film X1 and postulate further that there can only be one film with the quality X1 in any given time universe. X1 is the film and performers—X2 is the audience who are all trying to get into the film—Nobody is permitted to leave the biologic theatre which in this case is the human body—Because if anybody did leave the theatre he would be looking at a different film Y

the projector blew up and we lammed out of there on the blast—Holed up in those cool blue mountains the liquid air in our spines listening to a little high-fi junk note fixes you right to metal and you nod out a thousand years.* Just sitting there in a slate house wrapped in orange flesh robes, the blue mist drifting around us when we get the call—And as soon as I set foot on Podunk earth I can smell it that burnt metal reek of nova.

---

and Film X1 and audience X2 would then cease to exist by mathematical definition—In 1960 with the publication of *Minutes to Go*, Martin's stale movie was greeted by an unprecedented chorus of boos and a concerted walkout—"We seen this five times already and not standing still for another twilight of your tired Gods."

* Since junk *is* image the effects of junk can easily be produced and concentrated in a sound and image track—Like this: Take a sick junky—Throw blue light on his so-called face or dye it blue or dye the junk blue it don't make no difference and now give him a shot and photograph the blue miracle as life pours back into that walking corpse—That will give you the image track of junk—Now project the blue change onto your own face if you want The Big Fix. The sound track is even easier—I quote from *Newsweek*, March 4, 1963 Science section: "Every substance has a characteristic set of resonant frequencies at which it vibrates or oscillates."—So you record the frequency of junk as it hits the junk-sick brain cells—

"What's that?—Brain waves are 32 or under and can't be heard? Well speed them up, God damn it—And instead of one junky concentrate me a thousand—Let there be Lexington and call a nice Jew in to run it—"

Doctor Wilhelm Reich has isolated and concentrated a unit that he calls "the orgone"—Orgones, according to W. Reich, are the units of life—They have been photographed and the color is blue—So junk sops up the orgones and that's why they need all these young junkies—They have more orgones and give higher yield of the blue concentrate on which Martin and his boys can nod out a thousand years—Martin is stealing *your orgones*—You going to stand still for this shit?

"Already set off the charge," I said to I&I (Immovable and Irresistible)—"This is a burning planet—Any minute now the whole fucking shit house goes up."

So Intolerable I&I sniffs and says: "Yeah, when it happens it happens fast—This is a rush job."

And you could feel it there under your feet the whole structure buckling like a bulkhead about to blow—So the paper has a car there for us and we are driving in from the airport The Kid at the wheel and his foot on the floor—Nearly ran down a covey of pedestrians and they yell after us: "What you want to do, kill somebody?"

And The Kid sticks his head out and says: "It would be a pleasure! Niggers! Gooks! Terrestrial dogs!"—His eyes lit up like a blow torch and I can see he is really in form—So we start right to work making our headquarters in The Land Of The Free where the call came from and which is really free and wide open for any life form the uglier the better—Well they don't come any uglier than The Intolerable Kid and your reporter—When a planet is all primed to go up they call in I&I to jump around from one faction to the other agitating and insulting all the parties before and after the fact until they all say: "By God before I give an inch the whole fucking shit house goes up in chunks."

Where we came in—You have to move fast on this job—And I&I is fast—Pops in and out of a hundred faces in a split second spitting his intolerable insults— We had the plan, what they call The Board Books to

show us what is what on this dead whistle stop: Three
life forms uneasily parasitic on a fourth form that is
beginning to wise up. And the whole planet absolutely
flapping hysterical with panic. The way we like to see
them.

"This is a dead easy pitch," The Kid says.

"Yeah," I say. "A little bit too easy. Something here,
Kid. Something wrong. I can feel it."

But The Kid can't hear me. Now all these life forms
came from the most intolerable conditions: hot places,
cold places, terminal stasis and the last thing any of
them want to do is go back where they came from. And
The Intolerable Kid is giving out with such pleasantries
like this:

"All right take your ovens out with you and pay Hitler
on the way out. Nearly got the place hot enough for you
Jews didn't he?"

"Know about Niggers? Why darkies were born?
Antennae coolers what else? Always a spot for *good*
Darkies."

"You cunts constitute a disposal problem in the worst
form there is and raise the nastiest whine ever heard
anywhere: 'Do you love me? Do you love me? Do you
love me???' Why don't you go back to Venus and fertil-
ize a forest?"

"And as for you White Man Boss, you dead prop in
Martin's stale movie, you terminal time junky, haul your
heavy metal ass back to Uranus. Last shot at the door.

You need one for the road." By this time everybody was
even madder than they were shit scared. But I&I figured
things were moving too slow. ·

"We need a peg to hang it on," he said. "Something
really ugly like virus. Not for nothing do they come
from a land without mirrors." So he takes over this
newsmagazine.

"Now," he said, "I'll by God show them how ugly the
Ugly American can be."

And he breaks out all the ugliest pictures in the
image bank and puts it out on the subliminal so one
crisis piles up after the other right on schedule. And
I&I is whizzing around like a buzz saw and that black
nova laugh of his you can hear it now down all the
streets shaking the buildings and skyline like a stage
prop. But me I am looking around and the more I look
the less I like what I see. For one thing the nova heat
is moving in fast and heavy like I never see it anywhere
else. But I&I just says I have the copper jitters and
turns back to his view screen: "They are skinning the
chief of police alive in some jerkwater place. Want to
sit in?"

"Naw," I said. "Only interested in my own skin."

And I walk out thinking who I *would* like to see
skinned alive. So I cut into the Automat and put coins
into the fish cake slot and then I really see it: Chinese partisans and well armed with vibrating static
and image guns. So I throw down the fish cakes with

tomato sauce and make it back to the office where The
Kid is still glued to that screen. He looks up smiling
dirty and says:
"Wanta molest a child and disembowel it right after?"
"Pry yourself loose and listen." And I tell him. "Those
Tiddly Winks don't fuck around you know."
"So what?" he says. "I've still got The Board Books.
I can split this whistle stop wide open tomorrow."
No use talking to him. I look around some more and
find out the blockade on planet earth is broken. Explor-
ers moving in whole armies. And everybody concerned
is fed up with Intolerable I&I. And all he can say is:
"So what? I've still got . . ./" Cut.
"Board Books taken. The film reeks of burning switch
like a blow torch. Prerecorded heat glare massing Hiroshima. This whistle stop wide open to hot crab people.
Mediation? Listen: Your army is getting double zero in
floor by floor game of 'symbiosis.' Mobilized reasons to
love Hiroshima and Nagasaki? Virus to maintain terminal sewers of Venus?"
"All nations sold out by liars and cowards. Liars who
want time for the future negatives to develop stall you
with more lying offers while hot crab people mass war
to extermination with the film in Rome. These reports
reek of nova, sold out job, shit birth and death. Your
planet has been invaded. You are dogs on all tape. The
entire planet is being developed into terminal identity
and complete surrender."

"But suppose film death in Rome doesn't work and we can get every male body even madder than they are shit scared? We need a peg to evil full length. By God show them how ugly the ugliest pictures in the dark room can be. Pitch in the oven ambush. Spill all the board gimmicks. This symbiosis con? Can tell you for sure 'symbiosis' is ambush straight to the ovens. 'Human dogs' to be eaten alive under white hot skies of Minraud."

And Intolerable I&I's "errand boys" and "strikebreakers" are copping out right left and center:

"Mr. Martin, and you board members, vulgar stupid Americans, you will regret calling in the Mayan Aztec Gods with your synthetic mushrooms. Remember we keep exact junk measure of the pain inflicted and that pain must be paid in full. Is that clear enough Mr. Intolerable Martin, or shall I make it even clearer? Allow me to introduce myself: The Mayan God Of Pain And Fear from the white hot plains of Venus which does not mean a God of vulgarity, cowardice, ugliness and stupidity. There is a cool spot on the surface of Venus three hundred degrees cooler than the surrounding area. I have held that spot against all contestants for five hundred thousand years. Now you expect to use me as your 'errand boy' and 'strikebreaker' summoned up by an IBM machine and a handful of virus crystals? How long could you hold that spot, you 'board members'? About thirty seconds I think with all your guard dogs. And you thought to channel my energies for 'operation total disposal'? Your 'operations' there or here this or that come and go and are no more. *Give my name back.* That name must be paid for. You have not paid. My name is not yours to use. Henceforth I think about thirty seconds is written."

And you can see the marks are wising up, standing around in sullen groups and that mutter gets louder and louder. Any minute now fifty million adolescent gooks will hit the street with switch blades, bicycle chains and cobblestones.

"Street gangs, Uranian born of nova conditions, get out and fight for your streets. Call in the Chinese and any random factors. Cut all tape. Shift cut tangle magpie voice lines of the earth. Know about The Board's 'Green Deal'? They plan to board the first life boat in drag and leave 'their human dogs' under the white hot skies of Venus. 'Operation Sky Switch' also known as 'Operation Total Disposal.' All right you board bastards, we'll by God show you 'Operation Total Exposure.' For all to see. In Times Square. In Piccadilly."

So Pack Your Ermines

SO PACK YOUR ERMINES

"So pack your ermines, Mary—*We* are getting out
of here right now—I've seen this happen before—The
marks are coming up on us—And the heat is moving
in—Recollect when I was traveling with Limestone John
on The Carbonic Caper—It worked like this:: He rents
an amphitheatre with marble walls he is a stone painter
you dig can create a frieze while you wait—So he puts
on a diving suit like the old Surrealist Lark and I am
up on a high pedestal pumping the air to him—Well,
he starts painting on the limestone walls with hydro-
chloric acid and jetting himself around with air blasts
he can cover the wall in ten seconds, carbon dioxide

settling down on the marks begin to cough and loosen their collars."

"But what is he painting?"

"Why it's arrg a theatre full of people suffocating—"

So we turn the flops over and move on—If you keep it practical they can't hang a nova rap on you—Well, we hit this town and right away I don't like it.

"Something here, John—Something wrong—I can feel it—"

But he says I just have the copper jitters since the nova heat moved in—Besides we are cool, just rolling flops is all three thousand years in show business—So he sets up his amphitheatre in a quarry and begins lining up the women clubs and poets and window dressers and organizes this "Culture Fest" he calls it and I am up in the cabin of a crane pumping the air to him—Well the marks are packing in, the old dolls covered with ice and sapphires and emeralds all really magnificent—So I think maybe I was wrong and everything is cool when I see like fifty young punks have showed in aqualungs carrying fish spears and without thinking I yell out from the crane:

"Izzy The Push—Sammy The Butcher—*Hey Rube!*"

Meanwhile I have forgotten the air pump and The Carbonic Kid is turning blue and trying to say something—I rush and pump some air to him and he yells:

"No! No! No!"

I see other marks are coming on with static and camera guns, Sammy and the boys are not making it—These kids have pulled the reverse switch—At this point The Blue Dinosaur himself charged out to discover what the beef is and starts throwing his magnetic spirals at the rubes—They just moved back ahead of him until he runs out of charge and stops. Next thing the nova heat slipped antibiotic handcuffs on all of us.

NABORHOOD IN AQUALUNGS

I was traveling with Merit John on The Carbonic Caper—Larceny with a crew of shoppers—And this number comes over the air to him—So he starts painting The D Fence last Spring—And shitting himself around with air blasts in Hicksville—Stopped ten seconds and our carbon dioxide gave out and we began to cough for such a purpose suffocating under a potted palm in the lobby—

"Move on, you dig, copping out 'The Fish Poison Con—'"

"I got you—Keep it practical and they can't—"

Transported back to South America we hit this town and right away being stung by the dreaded John—He never missed—Burned three thousand years in me playing cop and quarry—So the marks are packing in virus and subject to dissolve and everything is cool—Assimilate ice sapphires and emeralds all regular—So

I walk in about fifty young punks—Sammy and the boys are all he had—One fix—Pulled the reverse switch—Traveling store closing so I don't work like this—John set my medications—Nagasaki in acid on the walls faded out under the rubber trees—He can cover feet back to 1910—We could buy it settling down—Lay up in the Chink laundry on the collars—

"But what stale rooming house flesh—"

Cradles old troupers—Like Cleopatra applying the asp hang a Nova Rap on you—

"Lush?—I don't like it—Empty pockets in the worn metal—Feel it?"

But John says: "Copper jitters since the space sell— The old doll is covered—"

Heavy and calm holding cool leather armchair— Organizes this wispy mustache—I stopped in front of a mirror—Really magnificent in a starched collar—It is a naborhood in aqualungs with free lunch everywhere yell out "Sweet Sixteen"—I walked without Izzy The Push—

"Hey Rube!!"

Came to the Chinese laundry meanwhile—I have forgotten the Chink in front—Fix words hatch The Blue Dinosaur—I was reading them back magnetic—Only way to orient yourself—Traveling with the Chink kid John set throat like already written—"Stone Reading" we call it in the trade—While you wait he packs in Rome—I've checked the diving suit like every night— Up on a high pedestal perform this unnatural act—In acid on the walls—Set your watch by it—So that gives us twenty marks out through the side window and collars—

"But what in St. Louis?"

Memory picture coming in—So we turn over silver sets and banks and clubs as old troupers—Nova Rap on you that night as we walked out—I don't like it— Something picking up laundry and my flesh feel it—

But John says: "Afternoon copper jitters since the caper—Housebreaking can cause this—"

We are cool just rolling—when things go wrong once—show business—We can't find poets and organize this cut and the flesh won't work—And there we are with the air off like beached idiots—Well I think maybe kicks from our condition—They took us—The old dolls on a train burning junk—Thawing flesh showed in aqualungs—Steam a yell out from the crane—

"*Hey Rube!!*"

Three silver digits explode—Meanwhile I have forgotten streets of Madrid—And clear as sunlight pump some air to him and he said: "Que tal Henrique?"

I am standing through an invisible door click the air to him—Well we hit this town and right away aphrodisiac ointment—

"Doc goofed here, John—Something wrong—Too much Spanish—"

"What? It's green see? A green theatre—"

So we turn the marks over and rent a house as old troupers—And we flush out this cool pure Chinese H

from show business—And he starts the whole Green
Rite and organizes this fibrous grey amphitheatre in
old turnip—Meanwhile I have forgotten a heavy blue
silence—Carbonic Kid is turning to cold liquid metal
and run pump some air to him in a blue mist of vaporized flicker helmets—The metal junkies were not making it—These kids intersected The Nova Police—We
are just dust falls from demagnetized patterns—Show
business—Calendar in Weimar youths—Faded poets in
the silent amphitheatre—His block house went away
through this air—Click St. Louis under drifting soot—
And I think maybe I was in old clinic—Outside East
St. Louis—Really magnificent for two notes a week—
Meanwhile I had forgotten "Mother"—Wouldn't you?—
Doc Benway and The Carbonic Kid turning a rumble in
Dallas involving this pump goofed on ether and mixed
in flicker helmets—

"He is gone through this town and right away tape recorders of his voice behind, John—Something wrong—I
can pose a colorless question??"

"Is all right—I just have the silence—Word dust falls
three thousand years through an old blue calendar—"

"William, no me hagas caso—People who told me
I could move on you copping out—said 'Good-Bye' to
William and 'Keep it practical' and I could hear him
hit this town and right away I closed the door when I
saw John—Something wrong—Invisible hotel room is
all—I just have the knife and he said:

"'Nova Heat moved in at the seams—Like three thousand years in hot claws at the window'—

"And Meester William in Tétuan and said: 'I have gimmick is cool and all very technical—These colorless sheets are the air pump and I can see the flesh when it has color—Writing say some message that is coming on all flesh—'

"And I said: 'William tu es loco—Pulled the reverse switch—No me hagas while you wait'—Kitchen knife in the heart—Feel it—Gone away—Pulled the reverse switch—Place no good—No bueno—He pack caso—William tu hagas yesterday call—These colorless sheets are empty—You can look any place—No good—No bueno—Adios Meester William—"

THE FISH POISON CON

I was traveling with Merit Inc. checking store attendants for larceny with a crew of "shoppers"—There was two middle-aged cunts one owning this Chihuahua which whimpered and yapped in a cocoon of black sweaters and Bob Schafer Crew Leader who was an American Fascist with Roosevelt jokes—It happens in Iowa this number comes over the car radio:: "Old Sow Got Caught In The Fence Last Spring"—And Schafer said "Oh my God, are we ever in Hicksville"—Stopped that night in Pleasantville Iowa and our tires gave out we had no tire rations during the war for such a purpose— And Bob got drunk and showed his badge to the locals in a road house by the river—And I ran into The Sailor under a potted palm in the lobby—We hit the local croakers with "the fish poison con"—"I got these poison fish, Doc, in the tank transported back from South America I'm a Ichthyologist and after being stung by the dreaded Candirú—Like fire through the blood is it not? Doctor, and coming on now"—And The Sailor goes into his White Hot Agony Act chasing the doctor around his office like a blowtorch—He never missed—But he burned down the croakers—So like Bob and me when we "had a catch" as the old cunts call it and arrested some sulky clerk with his hand deep in the company pocket, we take turns playing the tough cop and the con cop—So I walk in on this Pleasantville croaker and tell him I have contracted this Venusian virus and subject to dissolve myself in poison juices and assimilate the passers-by unless I get my medicine and get it regular—So I walk in on this old party smelling like a compost heap and steaming demurely and he snaps at me, "What's *your* trouble?"

"The Venusian Gook Rot, doctor."

"Now see here young man my time is valuable."

"Doctor, this is a medical emergency."

Old shit but good—I walked out on the nod—

"All he had was one fix, Sailor."

"You're loaded—You assimilated the croaker—Left me sick—"

"Yes. He was old and tough but not too tough for The Caustic Enzymes Of Woo."

The Sailor was thin and the drugstores was closing so I didn't want him to get physical and disturb my medications—The next croaker wrote with erogenous acid vats on one side and Nagasaki Ovens on the other— And we nodded out under the rubber trees with the long red carpet under our feet back to 1910—We could buy it in the drugstore tomorrow—Or lay up in the Chink laundry on the black smoke—drifting through stale rooming houses, pool halls and chili—Fell back on sad flesh small and pretentious in a theatrical boarding house the aging ham cradles his tie up and stabs a vein like Cleopatra applying the asp—Click back through the cool grey short-change artists—lush rolling ghosts of drunken sleep—Empty pockets in the worn metal subway dawn—

I woke up in the hotel lobby the smell heavy and calm holding a different body molded to the leather chair—I was sick but not needle sick—This was a black smoke yen—The Sailor still sleeping and he looked very young under a wispy mustache—I woke him up and he looked around with slow hydraulic control his eyes unbluffed unreadable—

"Let's make the street—I'm thin—"

I was in fact very thin I saw when I stopped in front of a mirror panel and adjusted my tie knot in a starched

collar—It was a naborhood of chili houses and cheap
saloons with free lunch everywhere and heavy calm bar-
tenders humming "Sweet Sixteen"—I walked without
thinking like a horse will and came to The Chinese Laundry by Clara's Massage Parlor—We siphoned in and The
Chink in front jerked one eye back and went on ironing
a shirt front—We walked through a door and a curtain
and the black smoke set our lungs dancing The Junky
Jig and we lay up on our junk hip while a Chinese kid
cooked our pills and handed us the pipe—After six pipes
we smoke slow and order a pot of tea the Chink kid goes
out to fix it and the words hatch in my throat like already
written there I was reading them back—"Lip Reading"
we call it in the trade only way to orient yourself when
in Rome—"I've checked the harness bull—He comes in
McSorley's every night at 2:20 AM and forces the local
pederast to perform this unnatural act on his person—So
regular you can set your watch by it:: 'I won't—I won't—
Not again—Glub—Glub—Glub.'"—"So that gives us
twenty minutes at least to get in and out through the
side window and eight hours start we should be in St.
Louis before they miss the time—Stop off and see The
Family"—Memory pictures coming in—Little Boy Blue
and all the heavy silver sets and banks and clubs—Cool
heavy eyes moving steel and oil shares—I had a rich St.
Louis family—It was set for that night—As we walked
out I caught the Japanese girl picking up laundry and
my flesh crawled under the junk and I made a meet for

her with the afternoon—Good plan to make sex before a caper—Housebreaking can cause this wet dream sex tension especially when things go wrong—(Once in Peoria me and The Sailor charged a drugstore and we can't find the jimmy for the narco cabinet and the flash won't work and the harness bull sniffing round the door and there we are with The Sex Current giggling ourselves off like beached idiots—Well the cops got such nasty kicks from our condition they took us to the RR station and we get on a train shivering burning junk sick and the warm vegetable smells of thawing flesh and stale come slowly filled the car—Nobody could look at us steaming away there like manure piles—) I woke out of a light yen sleep when the Japanese girl came in—Three silver digits exploded in my head—I walked out into streets of Madrid and won a football pool—Felt the Latin mind clear and banal as sunlight met Paco by the soccer scores and he said: "Que tal Henrique?"

And I went to see my amigo who was taking medicina again and he had no money to give me and didn't want to do anything but take more medicina and stood there waiting for me to leave so he could take it after saying he was not going to take any more so I said, "William no me hagas caso—" And met a Cuban that night in The Mar Chica who told me I could work in his band—The next day I said good-bye to William and there was nobody there to listen and I could hear him reaching for his medicina and needles as I closed the door—When I saw the knife I knew Meester William was death disguised as any other person—Pues I saw El Hombre Invisible in a hotel room somewhere tried to reach him with the knife and he said: "If you kill me this crate will come apart at the seams like a rotten undervest"—And I saw a monster crab with hot claws at the window and Meester William took some white medicina and vomited into the toilet and we escaped to Greece with a boy about my age who kept calling Meester William "The Stupid American"— And Meester William looked like a hypnotist I saw once in Tétuan and said: "I have gimmick to beat The Crab but it is very technical"—And we couldn't read what he was writing on transparent sheets—In Paris he showed me The Man who paints on these sheets pictures in the air—And The Invisible Man said:

"These colorless sheets are what flesh is made from— Becomes flesh when it has color and writing—That is Word And Image write the message that is you on color-less sheets determine all flesh."

And I said: "William, tu éres loco."

NO GOOD—NO BUENO

So many years—that image—got up and fixed in the sick dawn—*No me hagas caso*—Again he touched like that—smell of dust—The tears gathered—In Mexico again he touched—Codeine pills powdered out into the cold Spring air—Cigarette holes in the vast Thing Police—Could give no information other than wind identity fading out—dwindling—"Mr. Martin" couldn't reach is all—Bread knife in the heart—Shadow turned off the lights and water—We intersect on empty walls— Look anywhere—No good—Falling in the dark mutinous door—Dead Hand stretching zero—Five times of dust we made it all the living and the dead—Young form went to Madrid—Demerol by candlelight—Wind hand—The Last Electrician to tap on pane—Migrants arrival— Poison of dead sun went away and sent papers—Ferry boat cross flutes of Ramadan—Dead muttering in the dog's space—Cigarette hole in the dark—give no information other than the cold Spring cemetery—The Sailor went wrong in corridors of that hospital—Thing Police keep all Board Room Reports is all—Bread knife in the heart proffers the disaster accounts—He just sit down on "Mr. Martin"—Couldn't reach flesh on Nino Perdido—A long time between flutes of Ramadan—No me hagas caso sliding between light and shadow—

"The American trailing cross the wounded galaxies con su medicina, William."

Half your brain slowly fading—Turned off the lights and water—Couldn't reach flesh—empty walls—Look anywhere—Dead on tracks see Mr. Bradly Mr. Zero— And being blind may not refuse the maps to my blood whom I created—"Mr. Bradly Mr. Martin," couldn't you write us any better than that?—Gone away—You can look any place—No good—No bueno—

I spit blood under the sliding vulture shadows—At The Mercado Mayorista saw a tourist—A Meester Merican fruto drinking pisco—and fixed me with the eyes so I sit down and drink and tell him how I live in a shack under the hill with a tin roof held down by rocks and hate my brothers because they eat—He says something about "malo viento" and laughs and I went with him to a hotel I know—In the morning he says I am honest and will I come with him to Pucallpa he is going into the jungle looking for snakes and spiders to take pictures and bring them back to Washington they always carry something away even if it is only a spider monkey spitting blood the way most of us do here in the winter when the mist comes down from the mountains and never leaves your clothes and lungs and everyone coughed and spit blood mist on the mud floor where I sleep—We start out next day in a Mixto Bus by night we are in the mountains with snow and the Meester brings out a bottle of pisco and the driver gets drunk down into the Selva came to Pucallpa three days later—The Meester locates a brujo and pays him to prepare Ayahuasca and I take some too and muy mareado—Then I was back in Lima and other places I didn't know and saw the Meester as child in a room with rose wallpaper looking at something I couldn't see— Tasting roast beef and turkey and ice cream in my throat knowing the thing I couldn't see was always out there in the hall—And the Meester was looking at me and I could see the street boy words there in his throat—Next day the police came looking for us at the hotel and the Meester showed letters to the Commandante so they shook hands and went off to lunch and I took a bus back to Lima with money he gave me to buy equipment—

SHIFT COORDINATE POINTS

K9 was in combat with the alien mind screen—Magnetic claws feeling for virus punch cards—pulling him into vertiginous spins—

"Back—Stay out of those claws—Shift coordinate points—" By Town Hall Square long stop for the red light—A boy stood in front of the hot dog stand and blew water from his face—Pieces of grey vapor drifted back across wine gas and brown hair as hotel faded photo showed a brass bed—Unknown mornings blew rain in cobwebs—Summer evenings feel to a room with rose wallpaper—Sick dawn whisper of clock hands and brown hair—Morning blew rain on copper roofs in a slow haze of apples—Summer light on rose wallpaper—Iron mesas lit by a pink volcano—Snow slopes under the Northern shirt—Unknown street stirring sick dawn whispers of junk—Flutes of Ramadan in the distance—St. Louis lights wet cobblestones of future life—Fell through the urinal and the bicycle races—On the bar wall the clock hands—My death across his face faded through the soccer scores—smell of dust on the surplus army blankets—Stiff jeans against one wall—And KiKi went away like a cat—Some clean shirt and walked out—He is gone through unknown morning blew—"No good—No bueno—Hustling myself—" Such wisdom in gusts—

K9 moved back into the combat area—Standing now in the Chinese youth sent the resistance message jolting clicking tilting through the pinball machine—Enemy plans exploded in a burst of rapid calculations—Clicking in punch cards of redirected orders—Crackling shortwave static—Bleeeeeeeeeeeeeeep—Sound of thinking metal—

"Calling partisans of all nations—Word falling—Photo falling—Break through in Grey Room—Pinball led streets—Free doorways—Shift coordinate points—"

"The ticket that exploded posed little time so I'll say 'good night'—Pieces of grey Spanish Flu wouldn't photo—Light the wind in green neon—You at the dog—The street blew rain—If you wanted a cup of tea with rose wallpaper—The dog turns—So many and sooo—"

"In progress I am mapping a photo—Light verse of wounded galaxies at the dog I did—The street blew rain—The dog turns—Warring head intersected Powers—Word falling—Photo falling—Break through in Grey Room—"

He is gone away through invisible mornings leaving a million tape recorders of his voice behind fading into the cold spring air pose a colorless question?

"The silence fell heavy and blue in mountain villages—Pulsing mineral silence as word dust falls from demagnetized patterns—Walked through an old blue calendar in Weimar youth—Faded photo on rose wallpaper under a copper roof—In the silent dawn little grey men played in his block house and went away through an invisible door—Click St. Louis under drifting soot of old newspapers—'Daddy Longlegs' looked like Uncle Sam on stilts and he ran this osteopath clinic outside East St. Louis and took in a few junky patients for two notes a week they could stay on the nod in green lawn chairs and look at the oaks and grass stretching down to a little lake in the sun and the nurse moved around the lawn with her silver trays feeding the junk in—We called her 'Mother'—Wouldn't you?—Doc Benway and me was holed up there after a rumble in Dallas involving this aphrodisiac ointment and Doc goofed on ether and mixed in too much Spanish Fly and burned the prick off the Police Commissioner straight away— So we come to 'Daddy Longlegs' to cool off and found him cool and casual in a dark room with potted rubber plants and a silver tray on the table where he liked to see a week in advance—The nurse showed us to a room with rose wallpaper and we had this bell any hour of the day or night ring and the nurse charged in

with a loaded hypo—Well one day we were sitting out
in the lawn chairs with lap robes it was a fall day trees
turning and the sun cold on the lake—Doc picks up a
piece of grass—

"Junk turns you on vegetable—It's green, see?—A
green fix should last a long time."

We checked out of the clinic and rented a house and
Doc starts cooking up this green junk and the basement was full of tanks smelled like a compost heap of
junkies—So finally he draws off this heavy green fluid
and loads it into a hypo big as a bicycle pump—

"Now we must find a worthy vessel," he said and
we flush out this old goof ball artist and told him it
was pure Chinese H from The Ling Dynasty and Doc
shoots the whole pint of green right into the main line
and the Yellow Jacket turns fibrous grey green and
withered up like an old turnip and I said: "I'm getting
out of here, me," and Doc said: "An unworthy vessel
obviously—So I have now decided that junk is not
green but blue."

So he buys a lot of tubes and globes and they are
flickering in the basement this battery of tubes metal
vapor and quicksilver and pulsing blue spheres and a
smell of ozone and a little high-fi blue note fixed you
right to metal this junk note tinkling through your crystals and a heavy blue silence fell *klunk*—and all the
words turned to cold liquid metal and ran off you man
just fixed there in a cool blue mist of vaporized bank

notes—We found out later that the metal junkies were all radioactive and subject to explode if two of them came into contact—At this point in our researches we intersected The Nova Police—

Chinese Laundry

CHINESE LAUNDRY

When young Sutherland asked me to procure him a commission with the nova police, I jokingly answered: "Bring in Winkhorst, technician and chemist for The Lazarus Pharmaceutical Company, and we will discuss the matter."

"Is this Winkhorst a nova criminal?"

"No just a technical sergeant wanted for interrogation."

I was thinking of course that he knew nothing of the methods by which such people are brought in for interrogation—It is a precision operation—First we send out a series of agents—(usually in the guise of journalists)—to contact Winkhorst and expose him to a battery of stimulus units—The contact agents talk and record the response on all levels to the word units while a photographer takes pictures—This material is passed along to The Art Department—Writers write "Winkhorst," painters paint "Winkhorst," a method actor *becomes* "Winkhorst," and then "Winkhorst" will answer our questions—The processing of Winkhorst was already under way—

Some days later there was a knock at my door—Young Sutherland was standing there and next to him a man with coat collar turned up so only the eyes were visible spitting indignant protest—I noticed that the overcoat sleeves were empty.

"I have him in a strait jacket," said Sutherland propelling the man into my room—"This is Winkhorst."

I saw that the collar was turned up to conceal a gag— "But—You misunderstood me—Not on this level—I mean really—"

"You said bring in Winkhorst didn't you?"

I was thinking fast: "All right—Take off the gag and the strait jacket."

"But he'll scream the fuzz in—"

"No he won't."

As he removed the strait jacket I was reminded of an old dream picture—This process is known as retroactive dreaming—Performed with precision and authority becomes accomplished fact—If Winkhorst did start screaming no one would hear him—Far side of

the world's mirror moving into my past—Wall of glass
you know—Winkhorst made no attempt to scream—
Iron cool he sat down—I asked Sutherland to leave us
promising to put his application through channels—

"I have come to ask settlement for a laundry bill,"
Winkhorst said.

"What laundry do you represent?"

"The Chinese laundry."

"The bill will be paid through channels—As you
know nothing is more complicated and time consuming
than processing requisition orders for so-called 'personal expenses'—And you know also that it is strictly
forbidden to offer currency in settlement."

"I was empowered to ask a settlement—Beyond that
I know nothing—And now may I ask why I have been
summoned?"

"Let's not say summoned—Let us just say invited—It's
more humane that way you see—Actually we are taking
an opinion poll in regard to someone with whom I believe
you have a long and close association, namely Mr. Winkhorst of The Lazarus Pharmaceutical Company—We are
interviewing friends, relatives, co-workers to predict
his chances for reelection as captain of the chemical
executive softball team—You must of course realize the
importance of this matter in view of the company motto
'Always play *soft* ball' is it not?—Now just to give the
interview life let us pretend that you are yourself Winkhorst and I will put the questions directly ketch?—Very

well Mr. Winkhorst, let's not waste time—We know that you are the chemist responsible for synthesizing the new hallucinogen drugs many of which have not yet been released even for experimental purposes—We know also that you have effected certain molecular alterations in the known hallucinogens that are being freely distributed in many quarters—Precisely how are these alterations effected?—Please do not be deterred from making a complete statement by my obvious lack of technical knowledge—That is not my job—Your answers will be recorded and turned over to the Technical Department for processing."

"The process is known as stress deformation—It is done or was done with a cyclotron—For example the mescaline molecule is exposed to cyclotron stress so that the energy field is deformed and some molecules are activated on fissionable level—Mescaline so processed will be liable to produce, in the human subject—(known as 'canine preparations')—uh unpleasant and dangerous symptoms and in particular 'the heat syndrome' which is a reflection of nuclear fission—Subjects complain they are on fire, confined in a suffocating furnace, white hot bees swarming in the body—The hot bees are of course the deformed mescaline molecules—I am putting it simply of course—"

"There are other procedures?"

"Of course but always it is a question of deformation or association on a molecular level—Another procedure consists in exposing the mescaline molecule to certain virus cultures—The virus as you know is a very small particle and can be precisely associated on molecular chains—This association gives an additional tune-in with anybody who has suffered from a virus infection such as hepatitis for example—Much easier to produce the heat syndrome in such a preparation."

"Can this process be reversed? That is can you decontaminate a compound once the deformation has been effected?"

"Not so easy—It would be simpler to recall our stock from the distributors and replace it."

"And now I would like to ask you if there could be benign associations—Could you for example associate mescaline with apomorphine on a molecular level?"

"First we would have to synthesize the apomorphine formulae—As you know it is forbidden to do this."

"And for very good reason is it not, Winkhorst?"

"Yes—Apomorphine combats parasite invasion by stimulating the regulatory centers to normalize metabolism—A powerful variation of this drug could deactivate all verbal units and blanket the earth in silence, disconnecting the entire heat syndrome."

"You could do this, Mr. Winkhorst?"

"It would not be easy—certain technical details and so little time—" He held up his thumb and forefinger a quarter inch apart.

"Difficult but not impossible, Mr. Winkhorst?"

"Of course not—If I receive the order—This is unlikely in view of certain facts known to both of us."

"You refer to the scheduled nova date?"

"Of course."

"You are convinced that this is inevitable, Mr. Winkhorst?"

"I have seen the formulae—I do not believe in miracles."

"Of what do these formulae consist, Mr. Winkhorst?"

"It is a question of disposal—What is known as Uranium and this applies to all such raw material is actually a form of excrement—The disposal problem of radioactive waste in any time universe is ultimately insoluble."

"But if we disintegrate verbal units, that is vaporize the containers, then the explosion could not take place in effect would never have existed—"

"Perhaps—I am a chemist not a prophet—It is considered axiomatic that the nova formulae can not be broken, that the process is irreversible once set in motion—All energy and appropriations is now being channeled into escape plans—If you are interested I am empowered to make an offer of evacuation—on a time level of course."

"And in return?"

"You will simply send back a report that there is no evidence of nova activity on planet earth."

"What you are offering me is a precarious aqualung existence in somebody else's stale movie—Such people made a wide U turn back to the '20s—Besides the whole thing is ridiculous—Like I send back word from Mercury:: 'The climate is cool and bracing—The natives are soo friendly'—or 'On Uranus one is conscious of a lightness in the limbs and an exhilarating sense of freedom'—So Doctor Benway snapped, 'You will simply send back spitting notice on your dirty nova activity—It is ridiculous like when the egg cracks the climate is cool and bracing'—or 'Uranus is mushrooming freedom'—This is the old splintered pink carnival 1917—Sad little irrigation ditch—Where else if they have date twisting paralyzed in the blue movies?—You are offering me aqualung scraps—precarious flesh—soiled movie, rag on cock—Intestinal street boy smells through the outhouse.'"

"I am empowered to make the offer not assess its validity."

"The offer is declined—The so-called officers on this planet have panicked and are rushing the first life boat in drag—Such behavior is unbecoming an officer and these people have been relieved of a command they evidently experienced as an intolerable burden in any case—In all my experience as a police officer I have never seen such a downright stupid conspiracy—The nova mob operating here are stumble bums who couldn't even crash our police line-up anywhere else—"

This is the old needling technique to lure a criminal out into the open—Three thousand years with the force and it still works—Winkhorst was fading out in hot spirals of the crab nebula—I experienced a moment of panic—walked slowly to the tape recorder—

"Now if you would be so kind, Mr. Winkhorst, I would like you to listen to this music and give me your reaction—We are using it in a commercial on the apomorphine program—Now if you would listen to this music and give me advantage—We are thinking of sullen street boy for this spot—"

I put on some Gnaoua drum music and turned around both guns blazing—Silver needles under tons focus come level on average had opened up still as good as he used to be pounding stabbing to the drum beats—The scorpion controller was on screen blue eyes white hot spitting from the molten core of a planet where lead melts at noon, his body half concealed by the portico of a Mayan temple—A stink of torture chambers and burning flesh filled the room—Prisoners staked out under the white hot skies of Minraud eaten alive by metal ants—I kept distance surrounding him with pounding stabbing light blasts seventy tons to the square inch—The orders loud and clear now: "Blast—Pound—Strafe—Stab—Kill"—The screen opened out—I could see Mayan codices and Egyptian hieroglyphs—Prisoners screaming in the ovens broken down to insect forms—Life-sized portrait of a pantless corpse hanged to a telegraph pole ejaculating under a white hot sky—Stink of torture when the egg cracks—always to insect forms—Staked out spines gathering mushroom ants—Eyes pop out naked hanged to a telegraph pole of adolescent image—

The music shifted to Pan Pipes and I moved away to remote mountain villages where blue mist swirled through the slate houses—Place of the vine people under eternal moonlight—Pressure removed—Seventy tons to the square inch suddenly moved out—From a calm grey distance I saw the scorpion controller explode in the low pressure area—Great winds whipping across a black plain scattered the codices and hieroglyphs to rubbish heaps of the earth—(A Mexican boy whistling Mambo, drops his pants by a mud wall and wipes his ass with a page from the Madrid codex)—Place of the dust people who live in sand storms riding the wind—*Wind wind wind* through dusty offices and archives—Wind through the board rooms and torture banks of time—

("A great calm shrouds the green place of the vine people.")

INFLEXIBLE AUTHORITY

When I handed in my report to The District Supervisor he read it through with a narrow smile—"They have distracted you with a war film and given false information as usual—You are inexperienced of course—Totally green troops in the area—However your unauthorized action will enable us to cut some corners—Now come along and we will get the real facts—"

The police patrol pounded into the home office of Lazarus & Co—

"And now Mr. Winkhorst and you gentlemen of the board, let's have the real story and quickly or would you rather talk to the partisans?"

"You dumb hicks."

"The information and quickly—We have no time to waste with such as you."

The D.S. stood there translucent silver sending a solid blast of inflexible authority.

"All right—We'll talk—The cyclotron processes image—It's the microfilm principle—smaller and smaller, more and more images in less space pounded down under the cyclotron to crystal image meal—We can take the whole fucking planet out that way up our ass in a finger stall—Image of both of us good as he used to be—A *stall* you dig—Just old showmen packing our ermines you might say—"

"Enough of that show—Continue please with your statement."

"Sure, sure, but you see now why we had to laugh till we pissed watching those dumb rubes playing around with photomontage—Like charging a regiment of tanks with a defective slingshot."

"For the last time out of me—Continue with your statement."

"Sure, sure, but you see now why we had such lookout on these dumb rubes playing around with a splintered carnival—Charging a regiment of tanks with a defective sanitarium 1917—Never could keep his gas—Just an old trouper is all"—(He goes into a song and dance routine dancing off stage—An 1890 cop picks him up in the wings and brings back a ventriloquist dummy.)

"This, gentlemen, is a death dwarf—As you can see manipulated by remote control—Compliments of Mr. & Mrs. D."

"Give me a shot," says the dwarf. "And I'll tell you something interesting."

Hydraulic metal hands proffer a tray of phosphorescent meal yellow brown in color like pulverized amber— The dwarf takes out a hypo from a silver case and shoots a pinch of the meal in the main line.

"Images—millions of images—That's what I eat— Cyclotron shit—Ever try kicking *that* habit with apomorphine?—Now I got all the images of sex acts and torture ever took place anywhere and I can just blast it out and control you gooks right down to the molecule— I got orgasms—I got screams—I got all the images any hick poet ever shit out—My Power's coming—My Power's coming—My Power's coming—" He goes into a faith healer routine rolling his eyes and frothing at the mouth— "And I got millions and millions and millions of images of Me, Me, Me, meee." (He nods out—He snaps back into focus screaming and spitting at Uranian Willy.) "You hick—You rat—Called the fuzz on me—All right—(Nods out)—I'm finished but you're still a lousy fink—"

"Address your remarks to me," said the D.S.

"All right you hick sheriffs—I'll cook you all down to decorticated canine preparations—You'll never get the apomorphine formulae in time—Never! Never! Never!"—(Caustic white hot saliva drips from his teeth—A smell of phosphorous fills the room)—"Human dogs"—He collapses sobbing—"Don't mind if I take another shot do you?"

"Of course not—After giving information you will be disintoxicated."

"Disintoxicated he says—My God look at me."

"Good sir to the purpose."

"Shit—Uranian shit—That's what my human dogs eat—And I like to rub their nose in it—Beauty—Poetry—Space—What good is all that to me? If I don't get the image fix I'm in the ovens—You understand?—All the pain and hate images come loose—You understand *that* you dumb hick? I'm finished but your eyes still pop out—Naked candy of adolescent image Panama—*Who* look out different?—Cook you all down to decorticated mandrake—"

"Don't you think, Mr. D, it is in your interest to facilitate our work with the apomorphine formulae?"

"It wouldn't touch me—Not with the habit I got—"

"How do you know?—Have you tried?"

"Of course not—If I allowed anyone to develop the formulae he would be *out* you understand?—And it only takes one out to kick over my hypo tray."

"After all you don't have much choice Mr. D."

Again the image snapped back fading now and flickering like an old film—

"I still have the Board Room Reports—I can split the planet wide open tomorrow—And you, you little rat, you'll end up on ice in the ovens—Baked Alaska we call it—Nothing like a Baked Alaska to hold me vegetable—Always plenty wise guys waiting on the Baked Alaska." The dwarf's eyes sputtered blue sparks—A reek of burning flesh billowed through the room—

"I still mushroom planet wide open for jolly—Any hick poet shit out pleasures—Come closer and see my pictures—Show you something interesting—Come closer and watch them flop around in soiled linen—The Garden Boys both of us good as we used to be—Sweet pictures start coming in the hanged man knees up to the chin—You know—Beauty bare and still as good—Cock stand up spurting whitewash—Ever try his crotch when the egg cracks?—Now I got all the images in backward time—Rusty black pants—Delicate gooks in the locker room rubbing each other—I got screams—I *watched*—Burning heavens, idiot—Don't mind if I take another shot—Jimmy Sheffields is still as good as he used to be—Flesh the room in pink carnival—"

A young agent turned away vomiting; "Police work is not pleasant on any level," said the D.S. He turned to Winkhorst: "This special breed spitting notice on your dirty pharmaceuticals—Level—"

"Well some of my information was advantage—It *is* done with a cyclotron—But like this—Say I want to heat up the mescaline formula what I do is put the blazing photo from Hiroshima and Nagasaki under my cyclotron and shade the heat meal in with mescaline—Indetectible—It's all so simple and magnificent really—Beauty bare and all that—Or say I want 'The Drenched Lands' on the boy what I do is put the image from his cock under the cyclotron spurting whitewash in the white hot skies of Minraud."

The death dwarf opens one eye—"Hey, copper, come here—Got something else to tell you—Might as well rat—Everyone does it here the man says—You know about niggers? Why darkies were born?—Travel flesh we call it—Transports better—Tell you something else—" He nods out.

"And the apomorphine formula, Mr. Winkhorst?"

"Apomorphine is no word and no image—It is of course misleading to speak of a silence virus or an apomorphine virus since apomorphine is antivirus—The uh apomorphine preparations must be raised in a culture containing sublethal quantities of pain and pleasure cyclotron concentrates—Sub-virus stimulates antivirus special group—When immunity has been established in the surviving preparations—and many will not survive—we have the formulae necessary to defeat the virus powers—It is simply a question of putting through an inoculation program in the very limited time that remains—Word begets image and image *is* virus—Our facilities are at your disposal gentlemen and I am at your disposal—Technical sergeant I can work for anybody—These officers don't even know what button to push." He glares at the dwarf who is on the nod, hands turning to vines—

"I'm not taking any rap for a decorticated turnip—And you just let me tell you how much all the kids in the office and the laboratory hate you stinking heavy metal assed cunt sucking board bastards."

Technical Deposition of the Virus Power. "Gentlemen, it was first suggested that we take our own image and examine how it could be made more portable. We found that simple binary coding systems were enough to contain the entire image however they required a large amount of storage space until it was found that the binary information could be written at the molecular level, and our entire image could be contained within a grain of sand. However it was found that these information molecules were not dead matter but exhibited a capacity for life which is found elsewhere in the form of virus. Our virus infects the human and creates our image in him.

"We first took our image and put it into code. A technical code developed by the information theorists. This code was written at the molecular level to save space, when it was found that the image material was not dead matter, but exhibited the same life cycle as the virus. This virus released upon the world would infect the entire population and turn them into our replicas, it was not safe to release the virus until we could be sure that the last groups to go replica would not notice. To this end we invented variety in many forms, variety that is of information content in a molecule, which, *enfin*, is always a permutation of the existing material. Information speeded up, slowed down, permutated, changed at random by radiating the virus material with high energy rays from cyclotrons, in short we have created an infinity of variety at the information level, sufficient to keep so-called scientists busy for ever exploring the 'richness of nature.'

"It was important all this time that the possibility of a human ever conceiving of being without a body should not arise. Remember that the variety we invented was permutation of the electromagnetic structure of matter energy interactions which are not the raw material of nonbody experience."

Note From The Technical Department of Nova Police: Winkhorst's information on the so-called "apomorphine formulae" was incomplete—He did not mention alnorphine—This substance like apomorphine is made from morphine—Its action is to block morphine out of the cells—An injection of alnorphine will bring on immediate withdrawal symptoms in an addict—It is also a specific in acute morphine poisoning—Doctor Isbell of Lexington states in an article recently published in *The British Journal of Addiction* that alnorphine is not habit-forming but acts even more effectively as a pain killer than morphine but can not be used because it produces "mental disturbances"—What is pain?—Obviously damage to the image—Junk is concentrated image and this accounts for its pain killing action—Nor could there be pain if there was no image—This may well account for the pain killing action of alnorphine and also for the unspecified "mental disturbances"—So we began our experiments by administering alnorphine in combination with apomorphine.

COORDINATE POINTS

The case I have just related will show you something
of our methods and the people with whom we are called
upon to deal.

"I doubt if any of you on this copy planet have ever
seen a nova criminal—(they take considerable pains to
mask their operations) and I am sure none of you have
ever seen a nova police officer—When disorder on any
planet reaches a certain point the regulating instance
scans POLICE—Otherwise—SPUT—Another planet
bites the cosmic dust—I will now explain something
of the mechanisms and techniques of nova which are
always deliberately manipulated—I am quite well aware
that no one on any planet likes to see a police officer so
let me emphasize in passing that the nova police have
no intention of remaining after their work is done—
That is, when the danger òf nova is removed from this
planet we will move on to other assignments—We do our
work and go—The difference between this department
and the parasitic excrescence that often travels under
the name 'Police' can be expressed in metabolic terms:
The distinction between morphine and apomorphine.
Apomorphine is made by boiling morphine with hydro-
chloric acid. This alters chemical formulae and physiological effects. Apomorphine has no sedative narcotic
or addicting properties. It is a metabolic regulator that
need not be continued when its work is done. I quote

from *Anxiety and Its Treatment* by Doctor John Dent of London: 'Apomorphine acts on the back brain stimulating the regulating centers in such a way as to normalize the metabolism.' It has been used in the treatment of alcoholics and drug addicts and normalizes metabolism in such a way as to remove the need for any narcotic substance. Apomorphine cuts drug lines from the brain. Poison of dead sun fading in smoke—"

The Nova Police can be compared to apomorphine, a regulating instance that need not continue and has no intention of continuing after its work is done. Any man who is doing a job is working to make himself obsolete and that goes double for police.

Now look at the parasitic police of morphine. First they create a narcotic problem then they say that a permanent narcotics police is now necessary to deal with the problem of addiction. Addiction can be controlled by apomorphine and reduced to a minor health problem. The narcotics police know this and that is why they do not want to see apomorphine used in the treatment of drug addicts:

PLAN DRUG ADDICTION

Now you are asking me whether I want to perpetuate a narcotics problem and I say: "Protect the disease. Must be made criminal protecting society from the disease."

The problem scheduled in the United States the use of jail, former narcotics plan, addiction and crime for many years—Broad front "Care" of welfare agencies—Narcotics which antedate the use of drugs—The fact is noteworthy—48 stages—prisoner was delayed—has been separated—was required—

Addiction in some form is the basis—must be wholly addicts—Any voluntary capacity subversion of The Will Capital And Treasury Bank—Infection dedicated to traffic in exchange narcotics demonstrated a Typhoid Mary who will spread narcotics problem to the United Kingdom—Finally in view of the cure—cure of the social problem and as such dangerous to society—

Maintaining addict cancers to our profit—pernicious personal contact—Market increase—Release The Prosecutor to try any holes—Cut Up Fighting Drug Addiction by Malcolm Monroe Former Prosecutor, in *Western World,* October 1959.

As we have seen image *is* junk—When a patient loses a leg what has been damaged?—Obviously his image of himself—So he needs a shot of cooked down image—The hallucinogen drugs shift the scanning pattern of "reality" so that we see a different "reality"—There is no true or real "reality"—"Reality" is simply a more or less constant scanning pattern—The scanning pattern we accept as "reality" has been imposed by the controlling power on this planet, a power primarily oriented towards total control—In order to retain control they have moved to monopolize and deactivate the hallucinogen drugs by effecting noxious alterations on a molecular level—

The basic nova mechanism is very simple:: Always create as many insoluble conflicts as possible and always aggravate existing conflicts—This is done by dumping life forms with incompatible conditions of existence on the same planet—There is of course nothing "wrong" about any given life form since "wrong" only has reference to conflicts with other life forms—The point is these forms should not be on the same planet—Their conditions of life are basically incompatible in present time form and it is precisely the work of the Nova Mob to see that they remain in present time form, to create and aggravate the conflicts that lead to the explosion of a planet that is to nova—At any given time recording devices fix the nature of absolute need and dictate the use of total weapons—Like this:: Take two opposed pressure groups—Record the most violent and threatening statements of group one with regard to group two and play back to group two—Record the answer and take it back to group one—Back and forth between opposed pressure groups—This process is known as "feed back"—You can see it operating in any bar room quarrel—In any quarrel for that matter—Manipulated on a global scale feeds back nuclear war and nova—These conflicts are deliberately created and aggravated by nova criminals—The Nova Mob:: "Sammy

The Butcher," "Green Tony," "Iron Claws," "The Brown
Artist," "Jacky Blue Note," "Limestone John," "Izzy The
Push," "Hamburger Mary," "Paddy The Sting," "The
Subliminal Kid," "The Blue Dinosaur," and "Mr. & Mrs.
D," also known as "Mr. Bradly Mr. Martin" also known as
"The Ugly Spirit" thought to be the leader of the mob—
The Nova Mob—In all my experience as a police officer
I have never seen such total fear and degradation on any
planet—We intend to arrest these criminals and turn
them over to the Biological Department for the indicated
alterations—

Now you may well ask whether we can straighten out
this mess to the satisfaction of any life forms involved and
my answer is this—Your earth case must be processed
by the Biologic Courts—admittedly in a deplorable condition at this time—No sooner set up than immediately
corrupted so that they convene every day in a different location like floating dice games, constantly swept
away by stampeding forms all idiotically glorifying their
stupid ways of life—(most of them quite unworkable of
course) attempting to seduce the judges into Venusian
sex practices, drug the court officials, and intimidate the
entire audience chamber with the threat of nova—In all
my experience as a police officer I have never seen such
total fear of the indicated alterations on any planet—A
thankless job you see and we only do it so it won't have
to be done some place else under even more difficult
circumstances—

The success of the nova mob depended on a blockade of the planet that allowed them to operate with
impunity—This blockade was broken by partisan activity
directed from the planet Saturn that cut the control lines
of word and image laid down by the nova mob—So we
moved in our agents and started to work keeping always
in close touch with the partisans—The selection of local
personnel posed a most difficult problem—Frankly we
found that most existing police agencies were hopelessly
corrupt—the nova mob had seen to that—Paradoxically
some of our best agents were recruited from the ranks of
those who are called criminals on this planet—In many
instances we had to use agents inexperienced in police
work—There were of course casualties and fuck ups—
You must understand that an undercover agent witnesses
the most execrable cruelties while he waits helpless to
intervene—sometimes for many years—before he can
make a definitive arrest—So it is no wonder that green officers occasionally slip control when they finally do move
in for the arrest—This condition, known as "arrest fever,"
can upset an entire operation—In one recent case, our
man in Tangier suffered an attack of "arrest fever" and
detained everyone on his view screen including some of
our own undercover men—He was transferred to paper
work in another area—

Let me explain *how* we make an arrest—Nova criminals are not three-dimensional organisms—(though
they are quite definite organisms as we shall see)

but they need three-dimensional human agents to operate—The point at which the criminal controller intersects a three-dimensional human agent is known as "a coordinate point"—And if there is one thing that carries over from one human host to another and establishes identity of the controller it is *habit*:: idiosyncrasies, vices, food preferences—(we were able to trace Hamburger Mary through her fondness for peanut butter) a gesture, a certain smile, a special look, that is to say the *style* of the controller—A chain smoker will always operate through chain smokers, an addict through addicts—Now a single controller can operate through thousands of human agents, but he must have a line of coordinate points—Some move on junk lines through addicts of the earth, others move on lines of certain sexual practices and so forth—It is only when we can block the controller out of all coordinate points available to him and flush him out from host cover that we can make a definitive arrest—Otherwise the criminal escapes to other coordinates—

We picked up our first coordinate points in London.

Fade out to a shabby hotel near Earl's Court in London. One of our agents is posing as a writer. He has written a so-called pornographic novel called *Naked Lunch* in which The Orgasm Death Gimmick is described. That was the bait. And they walked write in. A quick knock at the door and there it was. A green boy/girl from the sewage deltas of Venus. The colorless vampire creatures from a land of grass without mirrors. The agent shuddered in a light fever. "Arrest Fever." The Green Boy mistook this emotion as a tribute to his personal attractions preened himself and strutted round the room. This organism is only dangerous when directed by The Insect Brain Of Minraud. That night the agent sent in his report:

"Controller is woman—Probably Italian—Picked up a villa outside Florence—And a Broker operating in the same area—Concentrate patrols—Contact local partisans—Expect to encounter Venusian weapons—"

In the months that followed we turned up more and more coordinate points. We put a round-the-clock shadow on The Green Boy and traced all incoming and outgoing calls. We picked up The Broker's Other Half in Tangier.

A Broker is someone who arranges criminal jobs:

"Get that writer—that scientist—this artist—He is too close—Bribe—Con—Intimidate—Take over his coordinate points—"

And the Broker finds someone to do the job like: "Call 'Izzy The Push,' this is a defenestration bit—Call 'Green Tony,' he will fall for the sweet con—As a last resort call 'Sammy The Butcher' and warm up The Ovens—This is a special case—"

All Brokers have three-dimensional underworld contacts and rely on The Nova Guards to block shadows and screen their operations. But when we located The Other Half in Tangier we were able to monitor the calls that went back and forth between them.

At this point we got a real break in the form of a defector from The Nova Mob: Uranian Willy The Heavy Metal Kid. Now known as "Willy The Fink" to his former associates. Willy had long been put on the "unreliable" list and marked for "Total Disposal In The Ovens." But he provided himself with a stash of apomorphine so escaped and contacted our Tangier agent. Fade out

URANIAN WILLY

Uranian Willy The Heavy Metal Kid. Also known as Willy The Rat. He wised up the marks. His metal face moved in a slow smile as he heard the twittering supersonic threats through antennae embedded in his translucent skull.

"Death in The Ovens."

"Death in Centipede."

Trapped in this dead whistle stop, surrounded by The Nova Guard, he still gave himself better than even chance on a crash out. Electrician in gasoline crack of history. His brain seared by white hot blasts. One hope left in the universe: Plan D.

He was not out of The Security Compound by a long way but he had rubbed off the word shackles and sounded the alarm to shattered male forces of the earth:

THIS IS WAR TO EXTERMINATION. FIGHT CELL BY CELL THROUGH BODIES AND MIND SCREENS OF THE EARTH. SOULS ROTTEN FROM THE OR-GASM DRUG, FLESH SHUDDERING FROM THE OVENS, PRISONERS OF THE EARTH COME OUT. STORM THE STUDIO—

Plan D called for Total Exposure. Wise up all the marks everywhere. Show them the rigged wheel of Life-Time-Fortune. Storm The Reality Studio. And retake the universe. The Plan shifted and reformed as reports came in from his electric patrols sniffing quivering down streets and mind screens of the earth.

"Area mined—Guards everywhere—Can't quite get through—"

"Order total weapons—Release Silence Virus—"

"Board Books taken—Heavy losses—"

"Photo falling—Word falling—Break Through in Grey Room—Use Partisans of all nations—*Towers, open fire*—"

The Reality Film giving and buckling like a bulkhead under pressure and the pressure gauge went up and up. The needle was edging to NOVA. Minutes to go. Burnt metal smell of interplanetary war in the raw noon streets swept by screaming glass blizzards of enemy flak. He dispersed on grey sliding between light and shadow down mirror streets and shadow pools. Yes he was wising up the marks. Willy The Fink they called him among other things, syndicates of the universe feeling for him with distant fingers of murder. He stopped in for a cup of "Real English Tea Made Here" and a thin grey man sat at his table with inflexible authority.

"Nova Police. Yes I think we can quash the old Nova Warrants. Work with us. We want names and coordinate points. Your application for Biologic Transfer will have to go through channels and is no concern of this department. Now we'll have a look at your room if you don't mind." They went through his photos and papers with fingers light and cold as spring wind. Grey Police of The Regulator, calm and grey with inflexible authority. Willy had worked with them before. He knew they were undercover agents working under conditions as dangerous as his own. They were dedicated men and would sacrifice him or any other agent to arrest The Nova Mob:

"Sammy The Butcher," "Green Tony," "Iron Claws," "The Brown Artist," "Jacky Blue Note," "Limestone John," "Izzy The Push," "Hamburger Mary," "The Subliminal Kid," "The Green Octopus," and "Willy The Rat," who wised up the marks on the last pitch. And they took Uranus apart in a fissure flash of metal rage.

As he walked past The Sargasso Cafe black insect flak of Minraud stabbed at his vitality centers. Two Lesbian

Agents with glazed faces of grafted penis flesh sat sipping spinal fluid through alabaster straws. He threw up a Silence Screen and grey fog drifted through the café. The deadly Silence Virus. Coating word patterns. Stopping abdominal breathing holes of The Insect People Of Minraud.

The grey smoke drifted   the grey that stops   shift cut   tangle   they breathe   medium   the word   cut shift   patterns   words cut   the insect   tangle cut   shift   that coats   word   cut   breath silence shift   abdominal   cut   tangle   stop   word   holes.

He did not stop or turn around. Never look back. He had been a professional killer so long he did not remember anything else. Uranian born of Nova Conditions. You have to be free to remember and he was under sentence of death in Maximum Security Birth Death Universe. So he sounded the words that end "Word"—

Eye take back color from "word"— Word dust everywhere now like soiled stucco on the buildings. Word dust without color drifting smoke streets. Explosive bio advance out of space to neon.

At the bottom of the stairs Uranian Willy engaged an Oven Guard. His flesh shrank feeling insect claws under the terrible dry heat. Trapped, cut off in that soulless place. Prisoner eaten alive by white hot ants. With a split second to spare he threw his silver blast and caught the nitrous fumes of burning film as he walked through the door where the guard had stood.

"Shift linguals—Free doorways—Cut word lines—
Photo falling—Word falling—Break Through in Grey
Room—Use partisans of all nations—*Towers, open
fire*—"

WILL HOLLYWOOD NEVER LEARN?

"Word falling—Photo falling—Break through in Grey
Room—"

Insane orders and counter orders issue from berserk
Time Machine—

"Terminal electric voice of C—Shift word lines—
Vibrate 'tourists.'"

"I said The Chief of Police skinned alive in Baghdad
not Washington D.C."

"British Prime Minister assassinated in rightist
coup."

"Switzerland freezes all foreign assets—"

"Mindless idiot you have liquidated the Commissar—"

"Cut word lines—Shift linguals—"

Electric storms of violence sweep the planet—
Desperate position and advantage precariously held—
Governments fall with a whole civilization and ruling
class into streets of total fear—Leaders turn on image rays
to flood the world with replicas—Swept out by counter
image—

"Word falling—Photo falling—Pinball led streets."

Gongs of violence and how—Show you something— Berserk machine—"Mr. Bradly Mr. Martin" charges in with his army of short-time hype artists and takes over The Reality Concession to set up Secretary Of State For Ruined Toilet—Workers paid off in SOS—The Greys came in on a London Particular—SOS Governments fade in worn metal dawn swept out through other flesh— Counter orders issued to the sound of gongs—Machine force of riot police at the outskirts D.C.—Death Dwarfs talking in supersonic blats of Morse Code—Swept into orbit of the Saturn Galaxy high on ammonia—Time and place shift in speed-up movie—

"Attack position over instrument like pinball— Towers, open fire—"

Atmosphere and climate shifted daily from carbon dioxide to ammonia to pure oxygen—from the dry heat of Minraud to the blue cold of Uranus—One day the natives forced into heavy reptile forms of overwhelm- ing gravity—next floated in tenuous air of plaintive lost planets—Subway broke out every language—D took pic- tures of a million battle fields—"Will Hollywood never learn?—Unimaginable and downright stupid disaster—"

Incredible forms of total survival emerged clashed exploded in altered pressure—Desperate flesh from short time artists—Transparent civilizations went out talking—

"Death, Johnny, come and took over."

Bradly and I supported by unusual mucus—Stale streets of yesterday precariously held—Paths of desperate position—Shifting reality—Total survival in altered pressure—Flesh sheets dissolving amid vast ruins of berserk machine—"SOS . . . — — —. . . Coughing enemy faces—"

"Orbit Sammy and the boys in Silent Space—Carbon dioxide work this machine—Terminal electric voice of C—All Ling door out of agitated—"

What precariously held government came over the air—Total fear in Hicksville—Secretary Of State For Far Eastern Hotel Affairs assassinated at outskirts of the hotel—Death Diplomats of Morse code supported in a cocktail lounge—

"Oxygen Law no cure for widespread blue cold." The Soviet Union said: "The very people who condemn altered pressure remain silent—"

Displacement into orbit processes—The Children's Fund has tenuous thin air of lost places—Sweet Home Movement to flood it with replicas—

So sitting with my hat on said: "I'm not going to do anything like that—"

Disgusting death by unusual mucus swept into orbit of cosmic vomit—(Tenuous candlelight—Remember I was carbon dioxide)—Rousing rendition of shifting reality— John lost in about 5000 men and women—Everyone else is on The Grey Veil—Flesh frozen to particles called "Good Consciousness" irrevocably committed to the toilet—Colorless slides in Mexican people—Other feature of the code on Grey Veil—To be read so to speak naked—Have to do it in dirty pictures—Reverse instructions on car seat—

"Mindless idiot you have liquidated The Shadow Cabinet—"

Swept out tiny police in supersonic Morse code—Emergency Meeting at entrance to the avenue—

"Calling partisans of all nation—Cut word lines—Shift linguals—Vibrate tourists—Free doorways—Word falling—Photo falling—Break through in Grey Room

—.— .— — — — — .—. —.. ..—. .— .—...—.. —.
— —. .— —. .... — — — — — — — ..—.. —.—..
.—.. ..—. — —."

TOWERS OPEN FIRE

Concentrate Partisans—Take Towers in Spanish Villa—Hill 32—The Green Airborne poured into the garden—Lens googles stuttering light flak—Antennae guns stabbing strafing The Vampire Guards—They pushed the fading bodies aside and occupied The Towers—The Technician twirled control knobs—He drank a bicarbonate of soda and belched into his hand—*Urp.*

"God damned captain's a brown artist—Uranus is right—What the fuck kind of a set is this—?? Not worth a fart—Where's the reverse switch?—Found it—Come in please—*Urp Urp Urp.*"

"Target Orgasm Ray Installations—Gothenburg Freelandt—Coordinates 8 2 7 6—Take Studio—Take Board Books—Take Death Dwarfs—"

Supersonic sex pictures flickered on the view screen—The pilots poised quivering electric dogs—Antennae light guns twisting searching feeling enemy nerve centers—

"*Focus.*"

"*Did it.*"

"*Towers, open fire—*"

Strafe—Pound—Blast—Tilt—Stab—*Kill*—Air Hammers on their Stone Books—Bleep Bleep Bleep—*Death to The Nova Guard—Death to The Vampire Guards—*

Pilot K9 blasted The Scorpion Guards and led Break Through in Grey Room—Place Of The Board Books And The Death Dwarfs—A vast grey warehouse of wire mesh cubicles—Tier on tier of larval dwarfs tube-fed in bottles—The Death Dwarfs Of Minraud—Operation Total Disposal—Foetal dwarfs stirred slowly in green fluid fed through a tube in the navel—Bodies compacted layer on layer of transparent sheets on which was written The Message Of Total Disposal when the host egg cracks—Death Dwarfs waiting transfer to The Human Host—Written on The Soft Typewriter from The Stone Tablets Of Minraud—

"Break Through in Grey Room—Death Dwarfs taken—Board Books taken—"

"Proceed to Sex Device and Blue Movie Studio— Behind Book Shop—Canal Five at Spiegel Bridge—"

"Advancing on Studio—Electric storms—Can't quite get through—"

"Pilot K9, you are hit—back—down—"

The medics turned drum music full blast through his head phones—"Apomorphine on the double"— Frequency scalpel sewing wounds with wire photo polka dots from The Image Bank—In three minutes K9 was back in combat driving pounding into a wall of black insect flak—The Enemy Installation went up in searing white blast—Area of combat extended through the vast suburban concentration camps of England and America—Screaming Vampire Guards caught in stabbing stuttering light blast—

"Partisans of all nation, open fire—tilt—blast— pound—stab —strafe—kill—"

"Pilot K9, you are cut off—back. Back. Back before the whole fucking shit house goes up—Return to base immediately—Ride music beam back to base—Stay out of that time flak—All pilots ride Pan pipes back to base—"

The Technician mixed a bicarbonate of soda survey-ing the havoc on his view screen—It was impossible to estimate the damage—Anything put out up till now is like pulling a figure out of the air—Installations shattered— Personnel decimated—Board Books destroyed—Electric waves of resistance sweeping through mind screens of the earth—The message of Total Resistance on short wave of the world—*This is war to extermination—Shift linguals— Cut word lines—Vibrate tourists—Free doorways—Photo falling—Word falling—Break through in grey room— Calling partisans of all nations—Towers, open fire—*"

Crab Nebula

CRAB NEBULA

They do not have what they call "emotion's oxygen"
in the atmosphere. The medium in which animal life
breathes is not in that soulless place—Yellow plains
under white hot blue sky—Metal cities controlled by
The Elders who are heads in bottles—Fastest brains
preserved forever—Only form of immortality open to
The Insect People of Minraud—An intricate bureaucracy wired to the control brains directs all movement—
Even so there is a devious underground operating
through telepathic misdirection and camouflage—The
partisans make recordings ahead in time and leave the
recordings to be picked up by control stations while

they are free for a few seconds to organize underground activities—Largely the underground is made up of adventurers who intend to outthink and displace the present heads—There has been one revolution in the history of Minraud—Purges are constant—Fallen heads destroyed in The Ovens and replaced with others faster and sharper to evolve more total weapons—The principal weapon of Minraud is of course heat—In the center of all their cities stand The Ovens where those who disobey the control brains are brought for total disposal—A conical structure of iridescent metal shimmering heat from the molten core of a planet where lead melts at noon—The Brass And Copper Streets surround The Ovens—Here the tinkers and smiths work pounding out metal rhythms as prisoners and criminals are led to Disposal—The Oven Guards are red crustacean men with eyes like the white hot sky—Through contact with oven pain and captured enemies they sometimes mutate to breathe in emotions—They often help prisoners to escape and a few have escaped with the prisoners—

(When K9 entered the apartment he felt the suffocation of Minraud crushing his chest stopping his thoughts—He turned on reserve ate dinner and carried conversation—When he left the host walked out with him down the streets of Minraud past the ovens empty and cold now—calm dry mind of the guide beside him came to the corner of 14th and Third—

"I must go back now," said the guide—"Otherwise it will be too far to go alone."

He smiled and held out his hand fading in the alien air—)

K9 was brought to the ovens by red guards in white and gold robes of office through the Brass And Copper Streets under pounding metal hammers—The oven heat drying up life source as white hot metal lattice closed around him—

"Second exposure—Time three point five," said the guard—

K9 walked out into The Brass And Copper Streets— A slum area of vending booths and smouldering slag heaps crossed by paths worn deep in phosphorescent metal—In a square littered with black bones he encountered a group of five scorpion men—Faces of transparent pink cartilage burning inside—stinger dripping the oven poison—Their eyes flared with electric hate and they slithered forward to surround him but drew back at sight of the guard—

They walked on into an area of tattoo booths and sex parlors—A music like wind through fine metal wires bringing a measure of relief from the terrible dry heat— Black beetle musicians saw this music out of the air swept by continual hot winds from plains that surround the city—The plains are dotted with villages of conical paper-thin metal houses where a patient gentle crab people live unmolested in the hottest region of the planet—

Controller of The Crab Nebula on a slag heap of smouldering metal under the white hot sky channels all his pain into control thinking—He is protected by heat and crab guards and the brains armed now with The Blazing Photo from Hiroshima and Nagasaki—The brains under his control are encased in a vast structure of steel and crystal spinning thought patterns that control whole galaxies thousand years ahead on a chessboard of virus screens and juxtaposition formulae—

So The Insect People Of Minraud formed an alliance with the Virus Power Of The Vegetable People to occupy planet earth—The gimmick is reverse photosynthesis— The Vegetable People suck up oxygen and all equivalent sustenance of animal life—Always the colorless sheets between you and what you see taste touch smell eat—And these green vegetable junkies slowly using up your oxygen to stay on the nod in carbon dioxide—

When K9 entered the cafe he felt the colorless smell of The Vegetable People closing round him taste and sharpness gone from the food people blurring in slow motion fade out—And there was a whole tank full of vegetable junkies breathing it all in—He clicked some reverse combos through the pinball machine and left the café—In the street citizens were yacking like supersonic dummies—The SOS addicts had sucked up all the silence in the area were now sitting around in blue blocks of heavy metal the earth's crust buckling

ominously under their weight—He shrugged: "Who am
I to be critical?"

He knew what it meant to kick an SOS habit: White
hot agony of thawing metal—And the suffocating panic
of carbon dioxide withdrawal—

Virus defined as the three-dimensional coordinate
point of a controller—Transparent sheets with virus
perforations like punch cards passed through the host
on the soft machine feeling for a point of intersection—
The virus attack is primarily directed against affective
animal life—Virus of rage hate fear ugliness swirling
round you waiting for a point of intersection and once in
immediately perpetrates in your name some ugly noxious or disgusting act sharply photographed and recorded becomes now part of the virus sheets constantly
presented and represented before your mind screen to
produce more virus word and image around and around
it's all around you the invisible hail of bring down word
and image—

What does virus do wherever it can dissolve a hole and
find traction?—It starts eating—And what does it do with
what it eats?—It makes exact copies of itself that start
eating to make more copies that start eating to make more
copies that start eating and so forth to the virus power
the fear hate virus slowly replaces the host with virus
copies—Program empty body—A vast tapeworm of bring
down word and image moving through your mind screen

always at the same speed on a slow hydraulic-spine axis like the cylinder gimmick in the adding machine—How do you make someone feel stupid?—You present to him all the times he talked and acted and felt stupid again and again any number of times fed into the combo of the soft calculating machine geared to find more and more punch cards and feed in more and more images of stupidity disgust propitiation grief apathy death—The recordings leave electromagnetic patterns—That is any situation that causes rage will magnetize rage patterns and draw around the rage word and image recordings—Or some disgusting sex practice once the connection is made in childhood whenever the patterns are magnetized by sex desire the same word and image will be presented— And so forth—The counter move is very simple—This is machine strategy and the machine can be redirected— Record for ten minutes on a tape recorder—Now run the tape back without playing and cut in other words at random—Where you have cut in and re-recorded words are wiped off the tape and new words in their place— You have turned time back ten minutes and wiped electromagnetic word patterns off the tape and substituted other patterns—You can do the same with mind tape after working with the tape recorder—(This takes some experimentation)—The old mind tapes can be wiped clean—Magnetic word dust falling from old patterns— Word falling—Photo falling—"Last week Robert Kraft of the Mount Wilson and Palomar Observatories reported some answers to the riddle of exploding stars—Invariably he found the exploding star was locked by gravity to a nearby star—The two stars are in a strange symbiotic relationship—One is a small hot blue star—(Mr. Bradly) Its companion is a larger red star—(Mr. Martin) —Because the stellar twins are so close together the blue star continually pulls fuel in the form of hydrogen gas from the red star—The motion of the system spins the hydrogen into an incandescent figure eight—One circle of the eight encloses one star—The other circle encloses the other—supplied with new fuel the blue star ignites."—Quote, *Newsweek,* Feb. 12, 1962—

The Crab Nebula observed by the Chinese in 1054 AD is the result of a supernova or exploding star—Situated approximately three thousand light years from the earth— (Like three thousand years in hot claws at the window— You got it?—)—Before they blow up a star they have a spot picked out as many light years away as possible— Then they start draining all the fuel and charge to the new pitch and siphon themselves there right after and on their way rejoicing—You notice we don't have as much time as people had say a hundred years ago?—Take your clothes to the laundry write a letter pick up your mail at American Express and the day is gone—They are short-timing us as many light years as they can take for the getaway—It seems that there were survivors on The Crab Pitch who are not in all respects reasonable men—And The Nova Law moving in fast—So they start the same old lark sucking all the charge and air and color to a new location and then?—*Sput*—You notice something is sucking all the flavor out of food the pleasure out of sex the color out of everything in sight?—Precisely creating the low pressure area that leads to nova—So they move cross the wounded galaxies always a few light years ahead of the Nova Heat—That is they did—The earth was our set—And they walked right into the antibiotic handcuffs—It will readily be seen that having created one nova they must make other or answer for the first—I mean three thousand years in hot claws at the window like a giant crab in slag heaps of smouldering metal—Also the more novas the less time between they are running out of pitches—So they bribe the natives with a promise of transportation and immortality—

"Yeah, man, flesh and junk and charge stacked up bank vaults full of it—Three thousand years of flesh—So we leave the bloody apes behind and on our way rejoicing right?—It's the only way to live—"

And the smart operators fall for it every fucking time—Talk about marks—One of our best undercover operators is known as The Rube—He perfected The Reverse Con—Comes on honest and straight and the smart operators all think they are conning him—How could they think otherwise until he slips on the antibiotic handcuffs—

"There's a wise guy born every minute," he says. "Closing time gentlemen—The stenographer will take your depositions—"

"So why did I try to blow up the planet?—Pea under the shell—Now you see it now you don't—Sky shift to cover the last pitch—Take it all out with us and hit the road—I am made of metal and that metal is radioactive—Radioactivity can be absorbed up to a point but radium clock hands tick away—Time to move on—Only one turnstile—Heavy planet—Travel with Minraud technicians to handle the switchboard and Venusians to make flesh and keep the show on the road—Then The Blazing Photo and we travel on— Word *is* flesh and word is two that is the human body is compacted of two organisms and where you have two you have word and word is flesh and when they started tampering with the word that was it and the blockade was broken and The Nova Heat moved in—The Venusians sang first naturally they were in the most immediate danger—They live underwater in the body with an air line—And that air line is the word—Then the technicians spilled and who can blame them after the conditions I assigned to keep them technicians—Like three thousand years in hot claws—So I am alone as always—You understand nova is where I am born in such pain no one else survives in one piece—Born again and again cross the wounded galaxies—I am alone but not what you call 'lonely'—Loneliness is a product of dual mammalian structure—'Loneliness,' 'love,' 'friendship,' all the rest of it—I am not two—I am *one*—But to maintain my state of oneness I need twoness in other life forms—Other must talk so that I can remain silent—If another becomes one then I am two—That makes two ones makes two and I am no longer one—Plenty of room in space you say?—But I am not one in space I am one in time—Metal time—Radioactive time—So of course I tried to keep you all out of space—That is the end of time—And those who were allowed out sometimes for special services like creating a useful religious concept went always with a Venusian guard—All the 'mystics' and 'saints'—All except my old enemy Hassan i Sabbah who wised up the marks to space and said they could be one and need no guard no other half no word—

"And now I have something to say to all you angle boys of the cosmos who thought you had an in with The Big Operator—'*Suckers! Cunts! Marks!—I hate you all—And I never intended to cut you in or pay you off with anything but horse shit—And you can thank The Rube if you don't go up with the apes—Is that clear enough or shall I make it even clearer? You are the suckers cunts marks I invented to explode this dead whistle stop and go up with it—*' "

A BAD MOVE

Could give no other information than wind walking in a rubbish heap to the sky—Solid shadow turned off the white

film of noon heat—Exploded deep in the alley tortured
metal Oz—Look anywhere, Dead hand—Phosphorescent
bones—Cold Spring afterbirth of that hospital—Twinges
of amputation—Bread knife in the heart paid taxi boys—
If I knew I'd be glad to look anyplace—No good myself—
Clom Fliday—Diseased wind identity fading out—Smoke
is all—We intersect in the dark mutinous door—Hairless
skull—Flesh smeared—Five times of dust we made it
all—consumed by slow metal fires—Smell of gasoline
envelops last electrician—I woke up with dark information from the dead—Board Room Reports waiting for
Madrid—Arrested motion con su medicina—Soft mendicant "William" in the dark street—He stood there 1910
straw words falling—Dead lights and water—Either way
is a bad move—Better than that?—Gone away can tell
you—No good No bueno—White flash mangled silver
eyes—Flesh flakes in the sky—Explosive twinges of
amputation—Mendicant the crooked crosses and barren
the dark street—No more—No más—Their last end—
Wounded galaxies tap on the pane—Hustling myself—
Clom Fliday—And one fine tell you—No good—No
bueno—

Be cheerful sir our revels touch the sky—The white
film made of Mr. Martin—Rotting phosphorescent bones
carried a gasoline dream—Hand falling—White flash
mangled "Mr. Bradly Mr. Martin"—Thing Police, Board
Room Death Smell, time has come for the dark street—
No more—No más wounded galaxies—I told him you on

aid—Died out down stale streets through convolutions
of our ever living poet—On this green land the dollar twisted to light a last cigarette—Last words answer
you—

Long time between suns behind—Empty hunger cross
the wounded sky—Cold your brain slowly fading—I said
by our ever living poet dead—Last words answer your
summons—May not refuse vision in setting forth the
diary—Mr. Martin Mr. Corso Mr. Beiles Mr. Burroughs
now ended—These our actors, William—The razor inside, sir—Jerk the handle—That hospital melted into
air—Advance and inherit the insubstantial dead—
Flakes fall that were his shadow—

Metal chess determined gasoline fires and smoke
in motionless air—Smudge two speeds—DSL walks
"here" beside me on extension lead from hairless
skull—Flesh-smeared recorder consumed by slow
metal fires—Dog-proof room important for our "oxygen"
lines—Group respective recorder layout—"Throw the
gasoline on them" determined the life form we invaded:
insect screams—I woke up with "marked for invasion"
recording set to run for as long as phantom "cruelties"
are playing back while waiting to pick up Eduardo's
"corrupt" speed and volume variation Madrid—Tape
recorder banks tumescent flesh—Our mikes planning
speaker stood there in 1910 straw word—Either way
is a bad move to The Biologic Stairway—The whole
thing tells you—No good—No bueno outright or

partially—The next state walking in a rubbish heap
to Form A—Form A directs sound channels heat—
White flash mangled down to a form of music—Life
Form A as follows was alien focus—Broken pipes refuse
"oxygen"—Form A parasitic wind identity fading out—
"Word falling—Photo falling" flesh-smeared counter
orders—determined by last Electrician—Alien mucus
cough language learned to keep all Board Room Reports
waiting sound formations—Alien mucus tumescent code
train on Madrid—Convert in "dirty pictures 8"—simple
repetition—Whole could be used as model for a bad
move—Better than shouts: "No good—No bueno"—
    "Recorders fix nature of absolute need:: *occupy*—
'*Here*'—Any cruelties answer him—Either unchanged
or reverse—Clang—Sorry—Planet trailing somewhere
along here—Sequential choice—Flesh plots con su
medicina—The next state according to—Stop—Look—
Form A directs sound channels—Well what now?—Final
switch if you want to—Dead on Life Form B by cutting
off machine if you want to—Blood form determined by
the switch—Same need—Same step—Not survive in
any 'emotion'—Intervention?—It's no use I tell you—
Familiar will be the end product?—Reciprocate complete wires? You fucking can't—Could we become part
of the array?—In The American Cemetery—Hard to
distinguish maps came in at the verbal level—This he
went to Madrid?—And so si learn? The accused was
beyond altered arrival—So?—So mucus machine runs

by feeding in over The American—Hear it?—Paralleled the bell—Hours late—They all went away—You've thought it out?—A whole replaced history of life burial tapes being blank?—Could this 'you' 'them' 'whatever' learn? Accused was beyond altered formations—No good—Machine runs by feeding in 'useless'—Blood spilled over Grey Veil—Parallel spurt—How many looking at dirty pictures—? Before London Space Stage tenuous face maybe—Change—Definite—The disorder gets you model for behavior—Screams?—Laughter?"— Voice fading into advocate:

"Clearly the whole defense must be experiments with two tape recorder mutations."

Again at the window that never was mine—Reflected word scrawled by some boy—Greatest of all waiting lapses—Five years—The ticket exploded in the air—For I dont know—*I do not know* human dreams—Never was mine—Waiting lapse—Caught in the door—Explosive fragrance—Love between light and shadow—The few who lived cross the wounded galaxies—Love?—Five years I grew muttering in the ice—Dead sun reached flesh with its wandering dream—Buried tracks, Mr. Bradly, so complete was the lie—Course—Naturally—Circumstances now Spanish—Hermetic you understand—Locked in her heart of ooze—A great undersea blight—Atlantis along the wind in green neon—The ooze is only colorless question drifted down—Obvious one at that—Its goal?—That's more difficult to tap on the pane—One aspect of virus—An obvious one again—Muttering in the dogs for generalizations—The lice we intersect—Poison of dead sun anywhere else—What was it the old crab man said about the lice?—Parasites on "Mr. Martin"—My ice my perfect ice that never circumstances—Now Spanish cautiously my eyes—And I became the form of a young man standing—My pulse in unison—Never did I know resting place—Wind hand caught in the door—cling—Chocada—to tap on the pane—

Chocada—Again—Muttering in the dogs—Five years—Poison of dead sun with her—With whom?— I dunno—See account on the crooked crosses—And your name?—Berg?—Berg?—Bradly?—"Mr. Martin si" Disaster Snow—Crack—Sahhk—Numb—Just a fluke came in with the tide and The Swedish River of Gothenburg—

THE DEATH DWARF IN THE STREET

Biologic Agent K9 called for his check and picked up supersonic imitation blats of The Death Dwarfs— "L'addition—Ladittion—Laddittion—Garcon— Garcon—Garcon"—American tourist accent to the Nth power—He ordered another coffee and monitored

the café—A whole table of them imitating word forms
and spitting back at supersonic speed—Several pa-
trons rolled on the floor in switch fits—These noxious
dwarfs can spit out a whole newspaper in ten seconds
imitating your words after you and sliding in suggestion insults—That is the entry gimmick of The Death
Dwarfs: supersonic imitation and playback so you think
it is your own voice—(do you own a voice?) they invade
The Right Centers which are The Speech Centers and
they are in the right—in the right—in thee write—
"RIGHT"—"I'm in the right—in the right—You know
I'm in the right so long as you hear me say inside your
right centers 'I am in the right'"—While Sex Dwarfs
tenderize erogenous holes—So The Venusian Gook Rot
flashed round the world—

Agent K9 was with The Biologic Police assigned
to bring the Dwarf Plague under control by disconnecting the dwarfs from Central Control Station:
The Insect Brain Of Minraud enclosed in a crystal
cylinder from which run the cold wires to an array
of calculating machines feeding instructions to The
Death Dwarf In The Street—The brain is surrounded
by Crab Guards charged from The Thermodynamic
Pain And Energy Bank—Crab Guards can not be
attacked directly since they are directly charged by
attack—K9 had been in combat with The Crab Guards
and he knew what can happen if they get their claws
on your nerve centers—

K9 left the café and surveying the street scene he could not but feel that someone had goofed—The Death Dwarfs had in many cases been separated from the human host but they were still charged from Central Control and yacked through the streets imitating words and gestures of everyone in sight—While Sex Dwarfs squirmed out of any cover with a perfunctory, "Hello there," in anyone who stood still for it, dissolved erogenous holes immediately attacked by The Talk Dwarfs so that in a few seconds the unfortunate traveler was torn to pieces which the dwarfs snatch from each other's mouth with shrill silver screams—In fact the noxious behavior of this life form harried the citizens beyond endurance and everyone carried elaborate home-made contrivances for screening out the Talk Dwarfs and a special plastic cover to resist erogenous acids of the Sex Dwarfs—

Without hesitation K9 gave the order: "Release Silence Virus—Blanket area"—So The Silence Sickness flashed round the world at speed of light—As a result many citizens who had been composed entirely of word went ape straight away and screamed through the streets attacking the passers-by who in many cases went ape in turn as The Silence Sickness hit—To combat these conditions, described as "intolerable," political leaders projected stern noble image from control towers and some could occupy and hold up the ape forms for a few days or weeks—Invariably the leader was drained by

the gravity of unregenerate apes, torn in pieces by his
relapsing constituents, or went ape himself on TV—So
the Survivors as they call themselves lived in continual
dread of resistant dwarfs always more frantic from host
hunger—Knowing that at any minute the man next to
you in the street might go Mandril and leap for your
throat with virginal canines—K9 shrugged and put in
a call for Technicians—"The error in enemy strategy is
now obvious—It is machine strategy and the machine
can be redirected—Have written connection in The Soft
Typewriter the machine can only repeat your instructions since it can not create anything—The operation
is very technical—Look at a photomontage—It makes a
statement in flexible picture language—Let us call the
statement made by a given photomontage X—We can
use X words X colors X odors X images and so forth to
define the various aspects of X—Now we feed X into the
calculating machine and X scans out related colors, juxtapositions, affect-charged images and so forth we can
attenuate or concentrate X by taking out or adding elements and feeding back into the machine factors we wish
to concentrate—A Technician learns to think and write
in association blocks which can then be manipulated
according to the laws of association and juxtaposition—
The basic law of association and conditioning is known
to college students even in America: Any object, feeling,
odor, word, image in juxtaposition with any other object
feeling, odor, word or image will be associated with

it—Our technicians learn to read newspapers and magazines for juxtaposition statements rather than alleged content—We express these statements in Juxtaposition Formulae—The Formulae of course control populations of the world—Yes it is fairly easy to predict what people will think see feel and hear a thousand years from now if you write the Juxtaposition Formulae to be used in that period—But the technical details you understand and the machines—all of which contain basic flaws and must be continually overhauled, checked, altered whole blocks of computing machines purged and disconnected from one minute to the next—fast our mind waves and long counts—And let me take this opportunity of replying to the criticisms of my creeping opponents—It is not true that I took part in or instigated experiments defining pain and pleasure thresholds—I used abstract reports of the experiments to evolve the formulae of pain and pleasure association that control this planet—I assume no more responsibility than a physicist working from material presented to an immobilized brain—I have constructed *a* physics of the human nervous system or more accurately the human nervous system defines the physics I have constructed—Of course I can construct another system working on quite different principals— Pain is a quantitative factor—So is pleasure—I had material from purge trials and concentration camps and reports from Nagasaki and Hiroshima defining the limits of courage—Our most precise data came from Lexington

Ky. where the drug addicts of America are processed—
The pain of heroin withdrawal in the addict lends itself
perfectly to testing under control conditions—Pain is
quantitative to degree of addiction and stage of withdrawal and is quantitatively relieved by cell-blanketing
agents—With pain and pleasure limits defined and the
juxtaposition formulae set up it is fairly easy to predict what people will think in a thousand years or as
long as the formulae remain in operation—I can substitute other formulae if I am permitted to do so—No
one has given much thought to building a qualitative
mathematics—My formulae saw to that—Now here is a
calculating machine—Of course it can process qualitative data—Color for example—I feed into the machine
a blue photo passes to the Blue Section and a hundred
or a thousand blue photos rustle out while the machine
plays blues in a blue smell of ozone blue words of all
the poets flow out on ticker tape—Or feed in a thousand
novels and scan out the last pages—That is quality is
it not? Endingness?"

"Green Tony squealed and I'm off for Galaxy X—"

"The whole mob squealed—Now we can move in
for some definitive arrests—Set arrest machinery in
operation—Cover all agents and associations with juxtaposition formulae—Put out scanning patterns through
coordinate points of the earth for Mr. & Mrs. D—Top
Nova Criminals—Through mind screens of the earth
covering coordinate points blocking D out of a hand a

mouth a cold sore—Silver antibiotic handcuffs fitting
D virus filters and—Lock—Click—We have made the
arrest—You will understand why all concepts of revenge
or moral indignation must be excised from a biologic
police agent—We are not here to keep this tired old
injustice show on the road but to stop it short of Nova—"
    "Nova—Nova—Nova—" shriek the Death Dwarfs—
    "Arrest good kind Mr. D?—Why he paid for my her-
nia operation—"
    "That did it—Release Silence Virus—Blanket Area—"
    "Thinking in association blocks instead of words
enables the operator to process data with the speed of
light on the association line—Certain alterations are of
course essential—"

EXTREMELY SMALL PARTICLES

Dec. 17, 1961—Past Time—The error in enemy
strategy is now to be gathered I was not at all close and
the machine can be redirected—These youths of image
and association now at entrance to the avenue carrying
banners of inter language—

Time: The night before adventurers who hope to
form another blazing photo—Injury Headquarters Concentration with reports from Hiroshima—Some of the

new hallucinogens and Nagasaki—Slight overdose of dimethyltryptamine—Your cities are ovens where South American narcotic plants brought total disposal—Brain screams of millions who have controller lives in that place screamed back from white hot blue sky—Can always pull the nova equipped now with tower blasts from Hiroshima and Nagasaki—In such pain he has only one turnstile—

Bureaucracy tuned in on all—Incredibly devious conditions hatch cosmologies of telepathic misdirection—Mind screen movies overlapping make recordings ahead and leave before thinking was recorded—Our most precise data came from U.N. (United Narcotics)—His plan was drug addicts of America slip through the cordon—Pain of heroin failure often the cause of windows to pursue ends not compatible cell-blanketing agent—Our most precise data with The Silent People—Plan was almost superhuman drug burned through his juxtapositions—He was naked now to Nagasaki defining the limits against him—The projector can shift its succinct army before flesh dissolving—

Integrity and bravery are difficulties in the laboratory—Experiments to evolve ill took control this planet—Through the streets Nagasaki defining the limits of bravery—We find nationalisms and clashings to degree of addiction—It is fairly easy to predict inter police taking arms to protect their own forgeries from the taken over—Might reach 500 Ideology Headquarters armed with Board Officers produced synthetically—The hallucinogen drugs bottle three-dimensional coordinate points—New hallucinogens directed against affective animal life—Slight overdose of ugliness fear and hate— The ovens were image dust swirling round you total disposal—Some ugly noxious disgusting act sharply recorded becomes now part of "Photo falling—Word Falling"—Presented and represented before towers open fire—Alien virus can dissolve millions—It starts eating—Screamed back white hot copies of itself— So the Fear Species can replace the host armed now with tapeworm of bring down word and image plus Nagasaki—Injury Headquarters—Dual mammalian structure—Hiroshima People—Or some disgusting officers produced the rest of it—

Attorney General For Fear announced yesterday the discovery that cries of nepotism might "form a new mineral damaging to the President"—Insidious form of high density silica as extremely small particles got into politics with Lyndon B. Johnson, wife of two Negro secret service men—Another Mineral American formed by meteorite impact—"And it would make a splendid good talker," he said—

At these tables there is virtually jostling diplomats— Some displacements of a sedate and celebrated rose garden but ideal for the processes of a quiet river view restaurant—Police juice and the law are no cure for

widespread public petting in chow lines the Soviet
Union said yesterday—Anti-American promptly de-
nounced Kennedy's moribund position of insistence:

"Washington know-how to deal with this sort dem-
onstration in Venezuela of irresponsible propaganda—
Outside Caracas I am deeply distressed at the Soviet
Union's attempt to drag us back just when we was stoned
in violation of the administration's twenty billion dollar
solemn word—"

He begged as a personal thing scattered uprisings—
Error in enemy strategy is switchboard redirected—
Word is TWO that is the noxious human inter language
recorded—And where you have TWO you have odor's
and nationalism's word—They started tampering with
net—Injury Headquarters blockade was broken—
"Calling partisans of all nation—Crab word falling—
Virus photo falling—Break through in Grey Room—"

From a Land of Grass Without Mirrors

FROM A LAND OF GRASS WITHOUT MIRRORS

The cadet stepped out of a jungle of rancid swamp pools covered with spider webs through a slat fence in a place of wooden runways and barriers—walked through a forbidden door and someone said:

"What do you want?"

The cadet looked at the ground and said: "I didn't mean anything."

He walked down a wooden ramp to a school desk of shellacked brown maple where a woman sat.

"Where have you been?"

"I have been to The Far Assembly Meeting—I am on my way back to school—"

"What Assembly Meeting? Where?"

"The Far Assembly Meeting—Over there—"

"That's a lie. The Far Assembly Meeting is in *that* direction."

He composed his face for Basic Pain as he had been taught to compose his face to show nothing.

"I have been to a meeting," he said.

"You have six hours forced work—Guard—"

And the club crushed into his ribs and kidneys and the sides of his neck jabbed his testicles and stomach no matter how he did or did not do the work assigned and loss of composure was punishable by death. Then taken back to World Trade School K9 and whether he walked fast or slow or between slow and fast more bone-crushing shocks fell through him—So the cadets learn The Basic Formulae of Pain and Fear—Rules and staff change at arbitrary intervals—Cadets encouraged or forced into behavior subject to heaviest sanctions of deprivation, prolonged discomfort, noise, boredom all compensation removed from the offending cadets who were always being shifted from one school to another and never knew if they were succeeding brilliantly or washed out report to disposal—

Lee woke with his spine vibrating and the smell of other cigarette smoke in his room—He walked streets swept by color storms slow motion in spinal fluid came to the fish city of marble streets and copper domes—Along canals of terminal sewage—the green boy-girls tend gardens of pink flesh—Amphibious vampire creatures who breathe in other flesh—double sex sad as the drenched lands of swamp delta to a sky that does not change—Where flesh circulates stale and rotten as the green water—by purple fungoid gills—They breathe in flesh—settling slow in caustic green enzymes dissolving body—eating gills adjusted to the host's breathing rhythm—eat and excrete through purple gills and move in a slow settling cloud of sewage—They are in pairs known as The Other Half—the invisible Siamese twin moving in and out of one body—talk in slow flesh grafts and virus patterns exchanging genital sewage breathe in and out of each other on slow purple gills of half sleep with cruel idiot smiles eating Terminal Addicts of The Orgasm Drug under a sign cut in black stone:

> The Nature of Begging
> Need?—Lack.
> Want?—Need.
> Life?—Death.

"It is a warning," said The Prince with a slow bronze smile—"We can do no more—Here where flesh circulates like clothes on stale trade flesh of Spain and Forty-Second Street—scanning pattern of legs—pant smell of The Vagrant Ball Players—"

Lee woke with the green breathing rhythm—Gills slow stirring other cigarette smoke in other gills adjusted to the host by color storms—It is in pairs known as The Other Half sweet and rotten they move in and out and talk in spinal fluid exchanging genital sewage on slow purple gills of half sleep—Addicts of The Orgasm Drug—Flesh juice in festering spines of terminal sewage—Run down of Spain and 42nd St. to the fish city of marble flesh grafts—Diseased beggars with cruel idiot smiles eating erogenous holes inject The Green Drug—Sting insect spasms—It is a warning—We can do not—Doesn't change—Even the sky stale and rotten dissolving—

Lee woke in other flesh the lookout different—His body was covered by transparent sheets dissolving in a green mist—

"Lie still—Wait—Flesh frozen still—Deep freeze—Don't move until you can feel arms and legs—Remember in that hospital after spinal anesthesia and tried to get out of bed to my heroin stash and fell-slid all over the floor with legs like blocks of wood."

He moved his head slightly to one side—Rows and tiers of bunks—A dank packing-house smell—Stinging sex nettles lashed his crotch and hot shit exploded down his thigh to the knee—

"Lie still—Wait—"

The sweet rotten smell of diarrhea swept through the air in waves—The Others were moving now—Larval flesh hanging in rags—Faces purple tumescent bursting insect lust rolled in shit and piss and sperm—

"Watch what everyone else is doing and don't do it
(—General Orders for Emergency Conditions—)"
He could move his arm now—He reached for his stash
of apomorphine and slipped a handful of tablets under
his tongue—His body twisted forward and emptied and
he jetted free and drifted to the ceiling—Looked down
on quivering bodies—crab and centipede forms flashed
here and there—Then red swirls of violence—The caustic green mist settled—In a few minutes there was no
movement—

Lee was not surprised to see other people he knew—
"I brought them with me"—He decided—"We will send
out patrols—There must be other survivors"—

He moved cautiously forward the others fanned out
on both sides—He found that he could move on his
projected image from point to point—He was already
accustomed to life without a body—

"Not much different—We are still quite definite
and vulnerable organisms"—Certainly being without
a body conveyed no release from fear—He looked
down—The green mist had formed a carpet of lichen
over the bunks and floor of what looked like a vast
warehouse—He could see surviving life forms with
body—Green creatures with purple fungoid gills—
"The atmosphere must be largely carbon dioxide," he
decided—He passed a screen through and wiped out
all thought and word from the past—He was conversing with his survivors in color flashes and projected

concepts—He could feel danger—All around him the familiar fear urgent and quivering—

The two agents sat in basement room 1920 Spanish villa—Rotten spermy insect smell of The Green People swirling in bare corners quivering through boneless substance in color blats—He felt out through the open door on thin music down dark streets swept by enemy patrols and the paralyzing white flak—He moved like an electric dog sniffing pointing enemy personnel and installations through bodies and mind screens of the silent fish city his burning metal eyes Uranian born in the face of Nova Conditions—his brain seared by flash blasts of image war—

In this area of Total Conditions on The Nova Express the agents of shadow empires move on hideous electric needs—Faces of scarred metal back from The Ovens of Minraud—Orgasm Drug addicts back from The Venusian Front—And the cool blue heavy metal addicts of Uranus—

In this area the only reason any agent contacts any other agent is for purpose of assassination—So one assumes that any one close to him or her is there precisely to kill—What else? We never knew anything else here— None the less we are reasonably gregarious since nothing is more dangerous than withdrawing from contact into a dead whistle stop—So every encounter quivers with electric suspicion—ozone smell of invisible flash bulbs—

Agents are always exchanging identities as articles of clothing circulate in strata of hustlers—These exchanges marked by last-minute attempts to switch the package and leave you standing with some old goofball bum in 1910 Panama—Lee had such a deal on with the other agent and of course both were falsifying and concealing defects in the merchandise—Of course no agent will allow a trial run since the borrower would be subject to take off with the package and fuck everybody they'll do it every time—So all the deals are sight unseen both parties gathering what information he can delving into the other identity for hidden miles and engineering flaws that could leave him with faulty equipment in a desperate position—His patrols were checking the other agent—Sending in reports—Conveying instructions—intercepting messages—

"Present Controller is The American Woman—Tracer on all connections—Taping all lines in and out—Santa Monica California—She is coming in loud and clear now—"

The young man dropped Time on the bed—His face was forming a smooth brown substance like the side of an electric eel—His left hand dissolved in a crystal bulb where a stinger of yellow light quivered sharp as a hypo needle—Orgasm Sting Ray—Venusian weapon— A full dose can tear the body to insect pieces in electric orgasms—Smaller doses bring paralysis and withered limbs of blighted fiber flesh—Lee hummed a little tune and cut the image lines with his grey screen—The Orgasm Sting dissolved in smoke—Lee picked the boy up by one elbow rigid as a clothing dummy and weightless now Lee guided him down the street steering the body with slight movements of the arm—The screen was empty—The boy sat on Lee's bed his face blank as a plate—The Nova Police moved in calm and grey with inflexible authority—

"'Paddy The Sting' arrested—Host empty—Heavy scar tissue—Surgery indicated—Transfer impractical—"

TOO FAR DOWN THE ROAD

—The Boy, driven too far down the road by some hideous electric hand—I don't know—Perhaps the boy never existed—All thought and word from the past—It was in the war—I am not sure—You can not know the appalling Venusian Front—Obscure hand taping all messages in and out—Last human contacts—suddenly withdrawn—The Boy had never existed at all—A mouth against the pane—muttering—Dim jerky far away voice: "Know who I am? You come to 'indicated accident' long ago . . . old junky selling Christmas seals on North Clark St. . . . 'The Priest' they called him . . . used to be me, Mister" shabby quarters of a forgotten city . . . tin can flash flare . . . smell of ashes . . . wind stirs a lock of hair . . . "Know who I am? hock shop kid like mother used to make . . . Wind and Dust is my name . . . Never Happened is my name . . . Good Bye Mister is my name . . . quiet now . . . I go . . ." (flickering silver smile).

NO GOOD AT THIS RATE

Smell of other cigarette smoke on child track—Proceed to the outer—All marble streets and copper domes inside air—Signature in scar tissue stale and rotten as the green water—Moldy pawn ticket by purple fungoid gills—The invisible Siamese twin moving in through flesh grafts and virus patterns—Exchanging weight on slow purple gills—Addicts of the purpose—Flesh juice vampires is no good—All sewage—Idiot smiles eating erogenous deal—Sweet rotten smell of ice—Insect smell of the green car wreck—The young agent to borrow your body for a special half made no face to conceal the ice—He dies many years ago—He said: "Yes you want to—Right back to a size like that—Said on child track—Screaming on the deal?"

She didn't get it—All possessed by overwhelming inside air—Shoeshine boy, collapse it—Could make or break any place by his male image back in—The shoeshine boy didn't get jump—Wait till the signs are right—And shit sure know to very—Wait a bit—No good—Fast their mind waves and long counts—No use—Don't know the answer—Arsenic two years—Go on treating it—In the blood arsenic and bleeding gums— Now I had my light weight .38 like for protection—

He dies many years ago—"Sunshine of your smile," he said and stomped your ambassador to the mud flats where all died addicted in convulsions of insect—They were addicted to this round of whatever visits of a special kind—

"Grow to a size like that," said Nimum—"So where is my ten percent on the deal?"

The shoeshine boy collapsed and they revived him with secret techniques—The money pinned to an old man's underwear is like that is the best—

So I said: "We can do it here—They won't see us— When I walk with the Dib they can't see me—"

Careful—Watch the exits—Don't go to Paris—Wait till the signs are right—Write to everyone—Wait a bit—No good at this rate—Watch the waves and long counts—No use moving out—Try one if you want to— Right back to the track, Jack—Vampires is no good all possessed by overwhelming Minraud girl—All dies in convulsions—Don't go to Paris—Venusian front— On child track screaming without a body—Still quite definite and vulnerable organisms—Nova signature in scar tissue—Purpose of "assassination" back to a size like that—Her is there precisely to kill—Fast their

mind waves and attempts to switch the package—Know
the answer?: Arsenic two years: Goofball bum in 1910
Panama—They'll do it every time—The young man
dropped Time on us with all the Gods of Life—Giggles
canal talk from the sewage drifting round the gallows
turning cartwheels—Groveled in visits of a special
kind—Know the answer?: Arsenic two years:: Operation completed—WE are blood arsenic and bleeding
gums—

"Are you sure they are not for protection or perhaps
too quick?"

"Quite sure—Nothing here but to borrow your body
for a special purpose":: ("Excellent—Proceed to the
ice")

He dies many years ago—Screen went dead—The
smell of gasoline filled straw hat and silk scarf—Won't
be much left—Have to move fast—Wouldn't know his
name—No use of them better than they are—You want
to?—Right back to the track, Jack—The Controller at
the exits—

WIND HAND TO THE HILT

White sat quietly beaming "humanity's condition"—
Wise Radio Doctor started putting welfare officers in his
portable—The Effects Boys to see if they can do any

locks over the Chinese—Told me to sit down—Gave me
Panorama Comfortable and then said:

"Well? Anything to go by? What are we going to do?"

What weighted the program down was refusal to
leave—

"Well what are you going to do? Perhaps alone?"

"You'd like to do half of it for me would you?"

He slung me out and Worth and Vicky talked use-
fully about that was that—Maybe I've met Two Of A
Kind—They both started share of these people—Vicky
especially sounded him—It wasn't what he had—You
know is why?—What they are meant to do is all?—
Going to get out of it?—An interview with Modigliani
obvious usually sooner than later—I've seen a lot of
these old men you visit on a P&O—You know sixty
seventy years east voyage—Do you see yourself ending up in Cathay?—Trying to pinch suitcase like that
you'll end up buying the deluxe straight—The job will
be there—No cleaner—

If you or any of your pals foretold you were all spirits curtains for them—And trouble for me—Globe is
self you understand until I die—Why do they make
soldiers out of "Mr. Martin?"—Wind hand to the hilt
as it is—work we have to do and the way the flakes
fall—Be trouble in store for me every time—For him
always been and always will be wounded galaxies—We
intersect in a strange and crazy bio advance—On the
night shift working with blind—End getting to know

whose reports are now ended—These our rotten guts
and aching spine accounts—

One more chance he said touching circumstance—
Have you still—Come back to the Spanish bait its
curtains under his blotter—The square fact is many
spirits it's curtains for them—Fed up you understand
until I die—No wish to see The Home Secretary "Mr.
Martin—"

Wind hand to the hilt—work we have to do and way
got the job—Jobbies would like to strike on night shift
working the end of hanging—All good thing come to
answer Mr. Of The Account screaming for a respectable
price—What might be called in air lying about wholesale—*Belt Her*—Find a time buyer before ports are now
ended—These are rotten if they start job for instance—
Didn't last—Have you still—Come back work was
steady at the gate under his blotter—Cover what's left
of the window—Do they make soldiers out of present
food in The Homicide Act as it is?—Blind bargain in
return for accepting "one more chance"—Generous?—
Nothing—That far to the bait and it's curtains—End
getting to know whose price—Punishment and reward
business the bait—No wish to see The Home Secretary
"humanity's condition"—Wise radio doctor reprieving
officers in his portable got the job—So think before
they can do any locks over the Chinese that abolition is
war of the past—Jobbies would like to strike a bargain
instead of bringing you up fair—The end of hanging

generous?—Just the same position—Changed places of years in the end is just the same—What might be called the program was refusal lying about wholesale—Going to do?—Perhaps alone would you?—All good things come to about that was that—Screaming for respectable share of these people—Vicky especially—*Belt her*—Know what they meant if they start job for instance? An interview with further scream along the line—

White sat quietly beaming "human people" out of hospital and others started putting their time on casual—Effects Boys anyway after that—Chinese accusation of a bargain—What are we going to do level on average?—I was on the roof so I had to do Two Of A Kind—They both started before doing sessions—There's no choice—Sounded him—Have to let it go cheap and start do is all—A *journey*, man—The job will be there—No punishment and reward business—

A DISTANT THANK YOU

"I am having in Bill&Iam," she said—

"But they don't exist—tout ça—my dear have you any idea what—certain basic flaws in the—"

"You can afford it—You told me hole is always there to absorb yesterday—and whatever—"

"The Market you understand—Bill tossed a rock and a very dear friend of mine struck limestone with dried excrement purposes. And what purpose more has arisen—quite unlooked for—"

"All the more reason to redecorate Silent Workers—" They had arrived where speech is impossible.

"Iam is very technical," said Bill as he walked around smoking smoke patterns in the room—"Have flash language of The Silent Ones—Out all this crap—Tonight, Madame—Age to grim Gothic Foreman—"

The Studio had set up a desert reek Mayan back to peasant hut—In a few minutes there mountain slope of The Andes—House had stood in the air—

"Limestone country," said Bill—"We might start with a photo-collage of The House—yes?—of course and the statues in clear air fell away to a Mayan Ball Court with eternal gondolas—a terminal life form of bookies and bettors changing black berries in little jade pipes—slow ebb of limestone luck and gills—Controllers of The Ugly Spirit Spinal Fluid—hydraulic vegetable centuries—"

"But what about The House Itself?"

"Lost their enemy—ah yes Madame, The House— You are Lady—Can't we contact them?—I mean well taken care of I hope—"

"I think, Bill, they exist at different pressure—"

"Ah yes The House—Hummm—Permutate at different pressure and sometimes a room is lost in—"

"Bill, they exist at different pressure—"

"In the shuffle?—The Bensons?—But they don't exist—Tout ça c'est de l'invention—There are of course certain basic flaws in the hydraulic machinery but the marl hole is always there to absorb the uh errors—"

At the bottom of the crater was a hole—Bill tossed a rock and the echo fainter and fainter as the rock struck limestone on down—Silence—

"Bottomless you see for practical purposes—and what purpose more practical than disposal??"

Slow The House merged created in silent concentration of the workers from The Land Of Silence where speech is impossible—

"Lucky bastards," Bill always said as he walked around smoking Havanas and directing the work in color flash language of The Silent Ones—showing his plans in photo-collage to grim Gothic foreman—

And The House moved slowly from Inca to Mayan back to peasant hut in blighted maize fields or windy mountain slopes of The Andes—Gothic cathedrals soared and dissolved in air—The walls were made of blocks that shifted and permutated—cave paintings—Mayan relief—Attic frieze—panels— screens—photo-collage of The House in all periods and stages—Greek temples rose in clear air and fell to limestone huts by a black lagoon dotted with gondolas—a terminal life form of languid beautiful

people smoking black berries in little jade pipes*—
And The Fish People with purple fungoid gills—And
The Controllers drifting in translucent envelopes of
spinal fluid with slow hydraulic gestures of pressure
authority—These people are without weapons—so
old they have lost their enemy—

"But they are exquisite," said The Lady. "Can't we
contact them?—I mean for dinner or cocktails?—"

"It is not possible, Madame—They exist at different
pressure—"

"I am having in Bill&Iam"—she said during
breakfast—

Her husband went pale—"My dear, have you any
idea what their fee is?—"

"You can afford it—You told me only yesterday—"

"That was yesterday and whatever I may have told
you in times long past—The Market you understand—
Something is happening to money itself—A very dear
friend of mine found his *special* deposit box in Switzerland filled with uh dried excrement—In short an
emergency a shocking emergency has arisen—quite
unlooked-for—"

"All the more reason to redecorate—There they are
now—"

*Reference to the Pakistan Berries, a small black fruit of narcotic
properties sometimes brought to southern Morocco by caravan—when
smoked conjures the area of black lagoons sketched in these pages—

They had arrived—Bill in "banker drag he calls it now isn't that cute?"

"Iam is very technical"—said Bill puffing slowly on his Havana and watching smoke patterns—"Have to get some bulldozers in here—clean out all this crap— Tonight, Madame, you sleep in a tent like the Bedouin—"

The Studio had set up a desert on the lawn and The Family was moved out—In a few hours there was only a vast excavation where The House had stood—

"Limestone country," said Bill touching outcrops on walls of the crater—

"We might start with a Mayan temple—or The Greeks—"

"Yes of course and the statuary—City Of Marble Flesh Grafts—I envisage a Mayan Ball Court with eternal youths—and over here the limestone bookmakers and bettors changing position and pedestal—slow ebb of limestone luck—and just here the chess players—one beautiful the other ugly as The Ugly Spirit—playing for beauty—slow game of vegetable centuries—"

"But what about The House itself?"—said The Lady—

"Ah yes, Madame, The House—You are comfortable in your present quarters and well taken care of I hope—I think your son is very talented by the way—Hummm— perhaps—ah yes The House—Gothic Inca Greek Mayan Egyptian—and also something of the archaic limestone hut you understand the rooms and walls permutate on hydraulic hinges and jacks—and sometimes a room is lost in—"

"In the shuffle—The Bensons—during breakfast—" Her husband went pale—"C'est l'invention—Fee is?"

"Fee is hydraulic machinery marl yesterday errors told you in times long past—at the bottom of the crater was happening to money itself—echo fainter and fainter special deposit box in Switzerland—"

"A shocking emergency—"

"Bottomless you see for practical pee—practical disposal—There they are now—"

Slow The House merged—created in drag he calls it. "Isn't that cute?—Workers from The Land Of Silence whiffing slowly on his Havana and watching—"

"'Lucky Bill' always said: 'Get some bulldozers in here.'"

The Family was moved and The House moved slowly—only a vast excavation in blighted maize fields and wind—Gothic cathedrals soared on walls of the crater—Blocks shifted relief and panel screens of marble flesh grafts—

"I envisage stages—Gothic Cathedral soured—And over here the limestone huts by a black lagoon dotted position and pedestal—smoke chess players—and Fish People playing for beauty—slow games in their translucent envelopes—"

"Gestures of Pressure Author—" said The Lady—

"You understand so old they are comfortable in present quarters—"

"But they are exquisite"—said Tower Son—(very talented by the way for dinner or cocktails Gothic Inca Mayan Greek Egyptian—and also—)

"You understand the rooms and walls—and sometimes a room is lost—"

"They exist at different pressure playing their slow games by The Black Lagoon—You understand the mind works with une rapidité incroyable but the movements are very slow—So a player may see on the board great joy or a terrible fate see also the move to take or avoid see also that he can not make the move in time—This gives rise of course to great pain which they must always conceal in a round of exquisite festivals—"

The lagoon now was lighted with flicker lanterns in color—floating temples pagodas pyramids—

"The festivals rotate from human sacrifice to dawn innocence when the envelope dissolves—This happens very rarely—They cultivate The Fish People like orchids or pearls—always more exquisite strains blending beauty and vileness—strains of idiot cruelty are specially prized—" He pointed to a green newt creature with purple fungoid gills that stirred in a clear pool of water under limestone outcroppings and ferns—

"This amphibious-hermaphrodite strain is motivated by torture films—So their attractions are difficult to resist—"

The green boy-girl climbed out on a ledge—A heavy narcotic effluvia drifted from his half open mouth—Her squirmed towards the controller with little chirps and giggles—The controller reached down a translucent hand felt absently into the boneless jelly caressing glands and nerve centers—The green boy-girl twisted in spasms of ingratiation—

"They are very subservient as you can see in the right hands—But we must make an excursion to the place of The Lemur People who die in captivity—They are protected—We are all protected here—Nothing really happens you understand and the human sacrifice takes a bow from the flower floats—It is all exquisite and yet would you believe me we are all intriguing to unload this gold brick on some rube for an exit visa—Oh there's my travel agent the controller engaged—"

Playing their slow games by man in the black suit with long mind—works with une rapidité—

"He has been cheating me for months—slow so that a player may see believe the ridiculous travel arrange great joy and see also the move to fastest brain—"

"Yes we have all—Can not make the move in time— This other here—Roles must conceal in anything to go."

"If we could only just flush our flower floats on child track without a body from human sacrifice—"

"Rather bad taste, Old-Thing-Whose-Envelope-Has-Dissolved—The Flayed Man Stand—"

"They cultivate The Fish People—"

"Oh yes whose doing it?"

"*Not* for more exquisite strains—??"

"I tell you nobody can scream—Over there is The Land of The Lemur People—"

"He dissolved after the performance—Beautiful strain of idiot cruelty—"

"So he got his exit visa?—and green newt creature with purple fungoid now?"

"Pool of water under limestone—He has contacted someone—Know is motivated by torture films—"

"Willy The Rube?—I knew him to resist—The green boy climbed hook and he fades out with Effluvia—drifted from his half open mouth all our exquisite food and smoke bones—He fade out in word giggles—He beat Green Tony into The Green Boy-Girl's Boneless Dream Concession—He defend nerve centers—The Green Boy twisted in Sammy The Butcher—"

"Still he may fall for The Hero—They are very subservient—"

"We are an old people you are sus—Make an excursion to the land of persona and statuary—They are protected of course—Here is he now—Really happens you understand—"

"I understand you people need the flower floats—It is all Mongolian Archers—They are—we are all scheming to unload an exit visa—" (The controller engaged short furtive conversation—man in a black suit with one long fingernail and gold teeth—)

"He has been cheating me for months of course they all do—You wouldn't believe the ridiculous travel arrangements they unload on our fastest brains—Yes we have all been laughing stock at one time or another—Here where roles and flesh circulate—There is no place for anything to go—"

"If we could only just flush ourselves down the drain," she said seeing her life time fortunes fade on The Invisible Board—

"Rather bad taste, old thing—Embalm yourself—Tonight is The Festival Of The Flayed Man—"

"Oh yes and whose doing it?—Juanito again?—"

"He dissolved after the last performance—"

"Oh yes he went away—And what is The Travel Agent selling you now?"

"He has contacted someone known as Willy The Rube—perhaps—"

"Willy The Rube??—I know him from Uranus—Think you have him on the hook and he fades out with a train whistle—He beat Green Tony in a game of limestone stud and walked out with The Dream Concession—He defenestrated Izzy the Push and cowboyed Sammy The Butcher."

"Still he may fall for The Hero:: Protect us—We are an old people—Protect our exquisite poisonous life and our *statuary*—Well?"

"Here is he now."

"I understand you people need protection—I am

moving in a contingent of Mongolian Archers—They are expensive of course but well worth it—"

The Mongolian Archers with black metal flesh moved in grill arrangements of a ritual dance flexing their bows—silver antennae arrows sniffing dowsing quivering for The Enemy—

"My dear, they make me terribly nervous—Suppose there is no enemy??"

"That would be unfortunate, Madame—My archers must get relief—You did ask for protection and now—Where are the Lemur People?"

The Lemur People live on islands of swamp cypress peering from the branches and it took many hours to coax them down—Iridescent brown copper color—liquid black eye screens swept by virginal emotions—

"They are all affect you understand—That is why they die in captivity—" A Lemur touched The Rube's face with delicate tentative gestures and skittered again into the branches—

"No one has ever been able to hold a lemur for more than a few minutes in my memory—And it is a thousand years since anyone had intercourse with a lemur—The issue was lost—They are of such a delicacy you understand the least attempt-thought of holding or possessing and they are back in the branches where they wait the master who knew not hold and possess—They have waited a long time—Five hundred thousand years more or less I think—The scientists can never make up their mind about anything—"

The lemur dropped down on Lee's shoulder and playfully nipped his ear—Other lemurs raised sails on a fragile bamboo craft and sailed away over the lagoon under the red satellite that does not change position—

"There are other islands out there where no one has ever been—The lemurs of such delicacy that they die if one sets foot on the island—They exist at different prenatal flesh in black lagoons—"

"You understand silver arrows sniffing pointing incroyable but the movements on The Board a terrible doom: ('Suppose there is no enemy?') Take or avoid but see also that gives rise to great pain—You did a round of exquisite festivals—"

"Me see your lemur people with flicker lights in swamp cypress?"

"Hours to coax them down—Finally the dawn innocence of control sent liquid flickering screens like pearl—All affect, you understand, that is blending beauty and flesh—"

A Lemur touched Lee's face with delicate people who die in captivity—skittering again into the specially prized—this stressing they are back in who will not hold and possess—out on a ledge—a heavy narcotic indeed—thousand years more or less—

The Mongolian Archers with short black conversation of ritual dancing flexed there—dowsing feeling for The Enemy like of course they all do—

"You wouldn't—"

"My dear, they make me terrible arrangements that have been sold to our—"

"That would be unfortunate, Madame—Been laughing stock at one time or ask for protection—and now—"

"Tonight is the festival of Nice Young Emotions—Why they die in captivity—Juanito again?—Where is he now?—"

"Branches no one has ever been—He far now is—"

"They are of such a hat—Is your travel agent selling you attempt or thought of holding the branches where they wait?"

"Perhaps—They have waited a long time—Five Uranus—"

"The Pakistan Berries lay all our dust of a distant thank you on Lee's shoulder—"

REMEMBER I WAS CARBON DIOXIDE

Nothing here now but the recordings—in another country—

"Going to give some riot noises in the old names?"

"Mr. Martin I have survived" (smiles).

"All right young countryman so we took Time
. . . Human voices take over my job now . . . Show
you around alien darkroom . . . their Gods fading . . .
departed file . . . Mrs. Murphy's rooming house left no
address. . . . You remember the 'third stair' it was called?
You wrote last flight . . . seals on North Beach . . . the
lights flashing . . . Clark St. . . . The Priest against
a black sky . . . rocks gathered just *here* on this
beach . . . Ali *there*, hand lifted . . . dim jerky far away
street . . . ash on the water . . . last hands . . . last human
voices . . . last rites for Sky Pilot Hector Clark . . . He
carries the man who never was back . . . Shall these
ticker bones live?? My host had been a long time in
inquisition. . . ."

Through all the streets no relief—I will show you
fear on walls and windows people and sky—Wo weilest
du?—Hurry up please its accounts—Empty is the third
who walks beside you—Thin mountain air here and
there and out the window—Put on a clean shirt and
dusk through narrow streets—Whiffs of my Spain from
vacant lots—Brandy neat—April wind revolving lips
and pants—After dinner sleep dreaming on rain—The
soldier gives no shelter—War of dead sun is a handful
of dust—Thin and tenuous in grey shivering mist of old
Western movies said: "Fill your hand, Martin."

"I can't, son—Many years ago that image—Remember
I was carbon dioxide—Voices wake us and we drown—
Air holes in the faded film—End of smoky shuttered

rooms—No walls—Look anywhere—No good—Stretching zero the living and the dead—Five for rain—Young
hair too—Hurry up please its William—I will show you
fear in the cold spring cemetery—Kind, wo weilest du?"

"Here," said she, "is your card: Bread knife in the
heart—"

"What thinking, William?—Were his eyes—Hurry
up please its half your brain slowly fading—Make yourself a bit smart—It's them couldn't reach flesh—Empty
walls—Good night, sweet ladies—Hurry up please it's
time—Look any place—Faces in the violet light—
Damp gusts bringing rain—"

Got up and fixed in the sick dusk—Again he touched
like that—Smell of human love—The tears gathered—
In Mexico committed fornication but—Cold spring—
besides you can say—could give no information—vast
Thing Police—

"What have I my friend to give you?—Identity fading
out—dwindling—Female smells—knife in the heart—
boy of dust gives no shelter—left no address"

"I'd ask alterations but really known them all—
Closed if you wanted a Greek—I do not find The
Hanged Man in the newspapers—blind eyes—see—
Who walks beside you?" "Will you let me tell you
lost sight a long time ago . . . Smell taste dust on the
window . . . touch . . . touch?? How should I from remote landing dim jerky far away."

"At dawn—Put on a clean shirt in another country—
Soccer scores and KiKi give you?—Empty to the
barrier—Shuttered dawn is far away—Bicycle races
here in this boy were no relief—Long empty noon—
Dead recordings—Moments I could describe that were
his eyes in countries of the world—Left you these
sick dawn bodies—Fading smiles—in other flesh—
Far now—Such gives no shelter—Shifted the visiting
address—The wind at noon—walks beside you?" Piece
of a toy revolver there in nettles of the alley . . . over the
empty broken streets a red white and blue kite.

Gave Proof Through the Night

GAVE PROOF THROUGH THE NIGHT

(*This section, first written in 1938 in collaboration with Kells Elvins who died in 1961, New York, was later cut back in with the "first cut-ups" of Brion Gysin as published in* Minutes to Go.)

Captain Bairns was arrested today in the murder at sea of Chicago—He was The Last Great American to see things from the front and kept laughing during the dark—Fade out

S.S. America—Sea smooth as green glass—off Jersey Coast—An air-conditioned voice floats from microphones and ventilators—:

"Keep your seats everyone—There is no cause for alarm—There has been a little accident in the boiler room but everything is now/"

BLOOOMMM

Explosion splits the boat—The razor inside, sir—He jerked the handle—

A paretic named Perkins screams from his shattered wheelchair:

"You pithyathed thon of a bidth."

Second Class Passenger Barbara Cannon lay naked in First Class State Room—Stewart Hudson stepped to a porthole:

"Put on your clothes, honey," he said. "There's been an accident."

Doctor Benway, Ship's Doctor, drunkenly added two inches to a four-inch incision with one stroke of his scalpel—

"Perhaps the appendix is already out, doctor," the nurse said peering over his shoulder—"I saw a little scar—"

"The appendix *OUT! I'M* taking the appendix out—What do you think I'm doing here?"

"Perhaps the appendix is on the left side, doctor—That happens sometimes you know—"

"Stop breathing down my neck—I'm coming to that—Don't you think I know where an appendix is?—I studied appendectomy in 1910 at Harvard—" He lifted the abdominal wall and searched along the incision dropping ashes from his cigarette—

"And fetch me a new scalpel—This one has no edge to it"—

BLOOOMM

"Sew her up," he ordered—"I can't be expected to work under such conditions"—He swept instruments cocaine and morphine into his satchel and tilted out of The Operating Room—

Mrs. J. L. Bradshinkel, thrown out of bed by the explosion, sat up screaming: "I'm going right back to The Sheraton Carlton Hotel and call the Milwaukee Braves"—

Two Philippine maids hoisted her up—"Fetch my wig, Zalameda," she ordered. "I'm going straight to the captain—"

Mike B. Dweyer, Politician from Clayton Missouri, charged the First Class Lounge where the orchestra, high on nutmeg, weltered in their instruments—

"Play The Star Spangled Banner," he bellowed.

"You trying to corn somebody, Jack?—We got a union—"

Mike crossed to the jukebox, selected The Star Spangled Banner With Fats Terminal at The Electric Organ, and shoved home a handful of quarters—

Oh say can you seeeeeeeeee

The Captain sitting opposite Lucy Bradshinkel—He is shifty redhead with a face like blotched bone—

"I own this ship," The Lady said—

The deck tilted and her wig slipped over one ear—The Captain stood up with a revolver in his left hand—He snatched the wig and put it on—

"Give me that kimona," he ordered—

She ran to the porthole screaming for help like everyone else on the boat—Her head was outlined in the porthole—He fired—

"And now you God damned old fool, *give me that kimona*—"

I mean by the dawn's early light

Doctor Benway pushed through a crowd at the rail and boarded The First Life Boat—

"Are you all right?" he said seating himself among the women—"I'm the doctor."

The Captain stepped lightly down red carpeted stairs—In The Purser's Office a narrow-shouldered man was energetically shoving currency and jewels into a black suitcase—The Captain's revolver swung free of his brassiere and he fired twice—

By the rocket's red glare

Radio Operator Finch mixed a bicarbonate of soda and belched into his hand—"SOS—URP—SOS—God damned captain's a brown artist—SOS—Off Jersey Coast —SOS—Might smell us—SOS—Son of a bitching crew —SOS—URP—*Comrade* Finch—SOS—Comrade in a pig's ass—SOS—SOS—SOS—URP—URP—URP—"

The Captain stepped lightly into The Radio Room— Witnesses from a distance observed a roaring blast and a brilliant flash as The Operator was arrested—The Captain shoved the body aside and smashed the apparatus with a chair—

Our flag was still there

The Captain stiff-armed an old lady and filled The First Life Boat—The boat was lowered jerkily by male passengers—Doctor Benway cast off—The crew pulled on the oars—The Captain patted his bulging suitcase absently and looked back at the ship—

Oh say do that star spangled banner yet wave

Time hiccoughs—Passengers fighting around Life Boat K9—It is the last boat that can be launched—Joe Sargeant, Third Year Divinity student and MRA, slipped through the crowd and established Perkins in a seat at the bow—Perkins sits there chin drawn back eyes shining clutching a heavy butcher knife in his right hand

By the twilight's last gleamings

Hysterical waves from Second Class flood the deck— "Ladies first," screamed a big faced shoe clerk with long teeth—He grabbed a St. Louis matron and shoved her ahead of him—A wedge of shoe clerks formed behind— A shot rang and the matron fell—The wedge scattered— A man with nautical uniform buttoned in the wrong holes carrying a World War I .45 stepped into the last boat and covered the men at the launching ropes—

"Let this thing down," he ordered—The boat hit the water—A cry went up from the reeling deck—Bodies hurtled around the boat—Heads bobbed in the green water—A hand reached out of the water and closed on the boat side—Spring-like Perkins brought down his knife—The hand slipped away—Finger stubs fell

into the boat—Perkins worked feverishly cutting on
all sides:

"Bathdarths—Thons of bidth—Bathdarth—thon
bidth—Methodith Epithcopal God damn ith—"

O'er the land of the freeee

Barbara Cannon showed your reporter her souvenirs
of the disaster: A life belt autographed by the crew and
a severed human finger—

And the home of the brave

"I don't know," she said. "I feel sorta bad about this
old finger."

*Gave proof through the night that our flag was still
there*

sos

The cold heavy fluid settled in a mountain village of
slate houses where time stops—Blue twilight—Place
Of The Silence Addicts—They move in and corner SOS
and take it away in lead bottles and sit there on the nod
in slate houses—On The Cool Blue or The Cold Grey—
leave a wake of yapping ventriloquist dummies—They
just sit there in cool blocks of blue silence and the
earth's crust undulates under their weight of Heavy Time
and Heavy Money—The Blue Heavy Metal People Of
Uranus—Heavy con men selling issues of fraudulent

universe stock—It all goes back into SOS—[Solid Blue Silence.]

"Nobody can kick an SOS habit, kid—All the screams from The Pain Bank—from The Beginning you understand exploded deep in the tortured metal—"

Junk poured through my screaming flesh—I got up and danced The Junky Jig—I had my spoons—That's all I need—Into his spine falling some really great shit lately ("Shoot your way to peat bog") The cold heavy fluid settled—hydraulic beginning you understand— Exploded time stops in blue metal—Suburban galaxies on the nod—blue silence in the turnstile—village of slate houses—This foreign sun in bottles—

Martin came to Blue Junction in a heavy blue twilight where time stops—Slow hydraulic driver got out and moved away—Place of The Silent People—The Foreman showed him to The Bunk House—The men sat in blocks of cool blue silence at a long table and laid out photos in silent language of juxtaposition projecting the work—playing poker for position and advantage—

The work was hard and silent—There were irrigation canals and fish ponds with elaborate hydraulic locks and motors—The windmills and weather maps—(The Proprietor took photos of sky clouds and mountains every day moving arranging his weather maps in a vast flicker cylinder that turned with the wind on roof of The Main Building—Picture panels on walls of The Bunk House and Day Room changed with weather sky and mountain

shadows in a silent blue twilight—The men took photos
of each other and mixed picture composites shifting
combos to wind and water sounds and frogs from the
fish pools—green pastures crisscrossed with black water
and springs overhung with grass where Martin fished
in the evening with Bradly who slept in the bunk next
to his or in his bunk back and forth changing bodies
in the blue silence—Tasks shifted with poker play and
flesh trade—)

Blue—Flicker along the fish ponds—Blue shadows
twilight—street—frogs and crickets—(crisscrossed my
face)

The knife fell—The Clerk in the bunk next to his
bled blue silence—Put on a clean shirt and Martin's
pants—telling stories and exchanging smiles—dusty
motors—The crop and fish talk muttering American
dawn words—Sad rooming house—Picture wan light
on suburban ponds and brown hair—Grey photo pools
and springs over brass bed—Stale morning streets—
sifting clouds and sky on my face—crisscrossed with
city houses—

"Empty picture of a haunted ruin?" He lifted his
hands sadly turned them out . . . "Some boy just wrote
last good-bye across the sky . . . All the dream people
of past time are saying good-bye forever, Mister"

Late afternoon shadows against his back magic of all
movies in remembered kid standing there face luminous
by the attic window in a lost street of brick chimneys

exploded star between us . . . You can look back along the slate shore to a white shirt flapping gunsmoke.

SHORT COUNT

The Heavy Metal Kid returned from a short blue holiday on Uranus and brought suit against practically everybody in The Biologic Courts—

"They are giving me a short count," he said in an interview with your reporter—"And I won't stand still for it—" Fade out

Corridors and patios and porticos of The Biologic Courts—Swarming with terminal life forms desperately seeking extension of canceled permissos and residence certificates—Brokers, fixers, runners, debarred lawyers, all claiming family connection with court officials—Professional half-brothers and second cousins twice removed—Petitioners and plaintiffs screaming through the halls—Holding up insect claws, animal and bird parts, all manner of diseases and deformities received "In the service" of distant fingers— Shrieking for compensations and attempting to corrupt or influence the judges in a thousand languages living and dead, in color flash and nerve talk, catatonic dances and pantomimes illustrating their horrible conditions which many have tattooed on their flesh to

the bone and silently picket the audience chamber—
Others carry photo-collage banners and TV screens
flickering their claims—Willy's attorneys served the
necessary low pressure processes and The Controllers
were sucked into the audience chamber for The First
Hearing—Green People in limestone calm—Remote
green contempt for all feelings and proclivities of the
animal host they had invaded with inexorable moves
of Time-Virus-Birth-Death—With their diseases and
orgasm drugs and their sexless parasite life forms—
Heavy Metal People of Uranus wrapped in cool blue
mist of vaporized bank notes—And The Insect People
of Minraud with metal music—Cold insect brains and
their agents like white hot buzz saws sharpened in the
Ovens—The judge, many light years away from possibility of corruption, grey and calm with inflexible
authority reads the brief—He appears sometimes as
a slim young man in short sleeves then middle-aged
and red faced sometimes very old like yellow ivory—
"My God what a mess"—he said at last—"Quiet all
of you—You all understand I hope what is meant by
biologic mediation—This means that the mediating
life forms must simultaneously lay aside all defenses
and all weapons—it comes to the same thing—and
all connection with retrospective controllers under
space conditions merge into a single being which
may or may not be successful—" He glanced at the
brief—"It would seem that The Uranians represented

by the plaintiff Uranian Willy and The Green People
represented by Ali Juan Chapultepec are prepared to
mediate—Will these two uh personalities please stand
forward—Bueno—I expect that both of you would hesi-
tate if you could see—Fortunately you have not been
uh overbriefed—You must of course surrender all your
weapons and we will proceed with whatever remains—
Guards—Take them to the disinfection chambers and
then to The Biologic Laboratories"—He turned to The
Controllers—"I hope they have been well prepared—
I don't need to tell you that—Of course this is only
The First Hearing—The results of mediation will be
reviewed by a higher court—"

Their horrible condition from a short blue holiday
on Uranus—Post everybody in The Biologic Courts:
Willy's attorney served "Count."—He said in an interview pushing through and still for it—Fade out—
Chambers—Green People—remote green contempt
forms fixers and runners all claiming the animal hosts
they had—(The Court Of Professional Brothers and
Moves Of Vegetable Centuries)—The petitioners and
plaintiffs their green sexless life screaming through
the halls remote mineral calm received—in slate blue
houses and catatonic dances illustrating The Heavy
Metal Kid returned—Many have tattooed in diseases
and brought suit against The Audience Chambers—

"They are giving me a short necessary process"—
Screaming crowds entered the corridors the audience

and the patios—The feeling and proclivities of connection with officials invaded with inexorable limestone and cousins twice removed—Virus and drugs plaintiff and defendant—Heavy Metal People Of Uranus in a thousand languages live robes that grow on them blue and hideous diseases—The little high-fi junk note shrieking for compensation—Spine frozen on the nod color flashes the heavy blue mist of bank notes—The petitioners and plaintiffs screaming through the halls wrapped in: "My God what a mess"—Holding up insect claws remote with all understand I hope what service—He appeared sometimes as whatever remains—All understand I hope what proclivities of the animal means that the mediating lie inexorable moves of Time—

TWILIGHT'S LAST GLEAMING

The Gods of Time-Money-Junk gather in a heavy blue twilight drifting over bank floors to buy con force an extension of their canceled permits—They stand before The Man at The Typewriter—Calm and grey with inflexible authority he presents The Writ:

"Say only this should have been obvious from Her Fourth Grade Junk Class—Say only The Angel Profound Lord Of Death—Say I have canceled your permissos through Time-Money-Junk of the earth—Not knowing what is and is not knowing I knew *not*. All your junk out in apomorphine—All your time and money out in word dust drifting smoke streets—Dream street of body dissolves in light . . ."

The Sick Junk God snatches The Writ: "Put him in The Ovens—Burn his writing"—He runs down a hospital corridor for The Control Switch—"He won't get far." A million police and partisans stand quivering electric dogs—antennae light guns drawn—

"You called The Fuzz—You lousy fink—"

"They are your police speaking your language—If you must speak you must answer in your language—"

"*Stop—Alto—Halt—*" Flashed through all I said a million silver bullets—The Junk God falls—Grey dust of broom swept out by an old junky in backward countries—

A heavy blue twilight drifting forward snatches The Writ—Time-Money-Junk gather to buy: "Put him in The Ovens—Burn his writing—"

"Say only The Angel Profound Lord of D"—Runs down a hospital corridor—Your bodies I have written— Your death called the police—The Junk God sick from "*Stop—Alto—Halt—*" The Junk God falls in a heavy blue twilight drifting over the ready with drawn guns— Time-Money-Junk on all your languages—Yours—Must answer them—Your bodies—I have written your death hail of silver bullets—So we are now able to say *not*. Premature?? I think the auditor's mouth is stopped with his own—With her grey glance faded silver understanding out of date—Well I'd ask alterations but there really isn't time is there left by the ticket that exploded—Any case I have to move along—Little time so I'll say good night under the uh *circumstances*—Now the Spanish Flu would not be again at the window touching the wind in green neon—You understanding the room and she said: "Dear me what a long way down"—Meet Café is closed—if you wanted a cup of tea—burst of young you understand—so many and soo—The important thing is always courage to let go—in the dark—Once again he touched the window with his cool silver glance out into the cold spring air a colorless question drifted down corridors of that hospital—

"Thing Police keep all Board Room Reports"—And we are not allowed to proffer The Disaster Accounts— Wind hand caught in the door—Explosive Bio-Advance Men out of space to employ Electrician—In gasoline crack of history—Last of the gallant heroes—"I'm you on tracks Mr. Bradly Mr. Martin"—Couldn't reach flesh in his switch—And zero time to the sick tracks—A long time between suns I held the stale overcoat— Sliding between light and shadow—Muttering in the dogs of unfamiliar score—Cross the wounded galaxies we intersect—Poison of dead sun in your brain slowly fading—Migrants of ape in gasoline crack of history—Explosive bio advance out of space to neon— "I'm you, Wind Hand caught in the door—" Couldn't reach flesh—In sun I held the stale overcoat—Dead Hand stretching the throat—Last to proffer the disaster account on tracks—See Mr. Bradly Mr.—

And being blind may not refuse to hear: "Mr. Bradly Mr. Martin, disaster to my blood whom I created"—(The shallow water came in with the tide and the Swedish River of Gothenburg.)

This Horrible Case

THE HORRIBLE CASE

Angle boys of the cosmos solicit from lavatories and broom closets of the Biologic Court Buildings charge out high on ammonia peddling fixes on any case from The Ovens Rap to a summons for biologic negligence—After buying a few short fixes in rigged courts, the pleaders defendants court officials and guilty bystanders learn to use a filter screen that scans out whole wave-lengths of ill-intentioned lunacy—This apparatus, sold in corridors and patios of the court buildings, enables any life form in need of legal advice to contact an accredited biologic counselor trained in the intricacies and apparent contradictions of biologic law—The classic case presented

141

to first year students is The Oxygen Impasse: Life Form
A arrives on alien planet from a crippled space craft—
Life Form A breathes "oxygen"—There is no "oxygen"
in the atmosphere of alien planet but by invading and
occupying Life Form B native to alien planet they can
convert the "oxygen" they need from the blood stream of
Life Form B—The Occupying Life Form A directs all the
behavior and energies of Host Life Form B into channels
calculated to elicit the highest yield of oxygen—Health
and interest of the host is disregarded—Development
of the host to space stage is arrested since such development would deprive the invaders by necessity of
their "oxygen" supply—For many years Life Form A
remains invisible to Life Form B by a simple operation
scanning out areas of perception where another life
form can be seen—However an emergency a shocking emergency quite unlooked-for has arisen—Life
Form B *sees* Life Form A—(Watching you have they
thought debarred) and brings action in The Biologic
Courts alleging unspeakable indignities, mental and
physical cruelty, deterioration of mind body and soul
over thousands of years, demanding summary removal
of the alien parasite—To which Form B replies at The
First Hearing: "It was a question of food supply—of
absolute need—Everything followed from that: Iron
claws of pain and pleasure squeezing a planet to keep
the host in body prison working our 'oxygen' plants—
Knowing that if he ever saw even for an instant who

we are and what we are doing—(Switched our way
is doomed in a few seconds)—And now he sees us
planning to use the host as a diving suit back to our
medium where of course Life Form B would be destroyed by alien conditions—Alternative posed by the
aroused partisans fumbling closer and closer to the
switch that could lock us out of Form B and cut our
'oxygen' lines—So what else could we do under the
circumstances? The life form we invaded was totally
alien and detestable to us—We do not have what they
call 'emotions'—soft spots in the host marked for invasion and manipulation—"

The Oxygen Impasse is a basic statement in the al-
gebra of absolute need—"Oxygen" interchangeable
factor representing primary biologic need of a given
life form—From this statement the students prepare
briefs—sift cut and rearrange so they can view the case
from varied angles and mediums:

The trial of The Nova Mob brought in emergency quite
unlooked-for: Broom arisen—sweeps Life Form B—*Sees*
fixes in The Biologic Courts—Deterioration of mind
body and soul buying a few short fixes in rigged Any
Place—Learns the years—the long—the many—such a
place—scans out whole lengths of alien parasite—and
brings action from unspeakable indignities and negligence demanding summary biologic lawyers who never
hustle a form—The best criminal counselor was Uranian
U—His clients from heavy metal—Impression Thing

followed from that Iron Claws Brief—From one interview he got Sammy squeezing a planet in The Switch—The Green Octopus working Vegetable Sentence—And now they have seen there is no "oxygen" in the diving suit—Local life would be destroyed by the "oxygen" they breathe—

"This pressure—Health cut our 'oxygen' lines—so disregarded—"

"So *that* the circumstances?"

"Life of the host beyond 'THE' detestable to us—Would deprive the invaders by soft spots in the host—"

With the material you have nature of absolute need and The First Hearing in Biologic Court—

"Alleging you understand I must fight indignities and cruelties and the natives are all mind body and soul demanding and I can't account for poison—(to which of course I have never lost a client)—Specific facts and cases a question of food supply not adequate—Owed from that the two claws intimidate and corrupt—"

"Enables an arrested criminal of pleasure and pain to squeeze counselor trained in the body-prison contradictions of biologic law—Diving suit of thousand years back to our medium instead of The Reverse Switch—Alternative Word Island—"

So where to first year students of Biologic Law Circumstances?—Life Form A was totally alien crippled space craft—Do not have what they call "emotion's oxygen" in the atmosphere—

A student who represents Life Form A must anticipate questions of the Biologic Prosecutor:—

"How did the space craft 'happen' to be crippled in such convenient proximity?—Was not the purpose of the expedition to find 'oxygen' and extract it by any means?—During many years of occupancy was any effort towards biologic reconversion made by Life Form A prior to intervention of The Biologic Police?—Was not Life Form A conspiring to cut off the 'oxygen' of Life Form B as soon as their 'travel arrangements' were completed? Did they not in fact plan to liquidate Life Form B by cutting off 'emotion's oxygen' the charge on which human and other mammalian life forms run?—(Doctor W. Reich has suggested that human life is activated by units he calls 'orgones' which form a belt around the planet)—Life Form A obviously conspired to blockade the orgone belt and leave Form B to suffocate in a soulless vacuum at the high surface temperatures that obtain on Life Form A's planet of origin: 600 Degrees Fahrenheit—"

In short the plea of need offered by Life Form A is inadequate—To prepare a case would be necessary to investigate the original conditions and biologic history of Life Form A on location—A Biologic Counselor must know his client and be "trained in the body-prison contradictions of biologic law"—It will not be easy for Life Form A to find a counselor willing to handle "this horrible case—"

BRIEF FOR THE FIRST HEARING

   Biologic Counselors must be writers that is only writers can qualify since the function of a counselor is to *create* facts that will tend to open biologic potentials for his client—One of the great early counselors was Franz Kafka and his briefs are still standard—The student first writes his own brief then folds his pages down the middle and lays it on pages of Kafka relevant to the case in hand—(It is not always easy to say what is and is not relevant)—To indicate the method here is a tentative brief for The First Hearing in Biologic Court:— A preparation derived from one page of Kafka passed through the student's brief and the original statement back and forth until a statement of biologic position emerges—From this original statement the student must now expand his case—

QUOTE FROM *The Trial*—FRANZ KAFKA

"I fancy," said the man who was stylishly dressed, "that the gentleman's faintness is due to the atmosphere here—You see it's only here that this gentleman feels upset, not in other places—" Accustomed as they were to the office air felt ill in the relatively fresh air that came up from the stairway—They could scarcely answer him and the girl might have fallen if K had not shut the door with the utmost haste—He had already, so he would relate, won many similar cases either outright or partially—That was very important for the first impression made by the defense frequently determined the whole course of subsequent proceedings—Especially when a case they had conducted was suddenly taken out of their hands—That was beyond all doubt the worst thing that could happen to an advocate—Not that a client ever dismissed an advocate from the case—For how could he keep going by himself once he had pulled in someone to help him?—But it did sometimes happen that a case took a turn where the advocate could no longer follow it—The case and the accused and everything was simply withdrawn from the advocate—Then even the best connection with officials could no longer achieve any result—For even they knew nothing—The case had simply reached the stage where further assistance was ruled out—It had vanished into remote inaccessible courts where even the accused was beyond the reach of an advocate—The advocate's room was in the very top attic so that if you stumbled through the hole your leg hung down into the lower attic in the very corridor where the clients had to wait—

BRIEF FOR FIRST HEARING / / CASE OF LIFE FORM A

They sometimes mutate to breathe *"here"*—The gentleman *is* Biologic Court Building *"here"*—You see it's only "*here*" fixes any case from The Ovens—Not in other places—after buying the relatively fresh air—Life Form A arrives on worst thing that could happen to a space craft—Life Form A breathes from the atmosphere of alien planet—Form A directs all behavior withdrawn from the advocate into channels calculated to no longer achieve health and interest of the host—The case had simply reached to space stage—Assistance was ruled out—Even the accused was beyond years—Life Form A's room was in the very top—

"I fancy," said the man who was on alien planet, "that crippled faintness is due to the 'oxygen'—There is no 'oxygen' this gentleman feels but by invading and occupying 'the office air' they can convert the 'oxygen' up from the stairway of Life Form B."

The first impression made determines whole course of subsequent "oxygen" supply—A shocking emergency case—For how could he keep Form A??—Sees someone to help him but it debarred action in turn—Could scarcely answer the people of Minraud—Brain directs all movement—Use a filter screen that scans the door with intentioned lunacy—Won many similar cases operating through telepathic misdirection—There has been dismissed an advocate from Minraud—Pulled in and replaced—Worst thing that could happen to present heads—Sometimes happened that a case took total weapons—The principal no longer follow it—The case had simply reached molten core of a planet where assistance was ruled out—

"I fancy," said the man, "that this gentleman feels white hot blue skies—Haste he had already so?"

Even so there is a devious underground either outright or partial misdirection—The office air are heads in bottles—Beyond all doubt intend to outthink and replace the advocate—A client revolution—For how could he keep fallen heads to help him?—Metal shimmering heat from the stage where further assistance melts at noon into remote inaccessible courts—

"Word falling—Photo falling stylishly dressed—The gentleman's insane orders and counter orders 'here'— You see it's only 'here'—Accustomed D.C. felt ill in the relatively fresh air, what?—British could scarcely answer him—Shut the door with the utmost haste—"

"Mindless idiot you have won many similar cases—"

Electric defense frequently determined the whole civilization and proceedings—Especially when a case fear desperate position and advantage suddenly taken out of their hands—The case had simply reached incredible life forms—Even the accused was beyond altered pressure— The very top operation—The client of mucus and urine said the man was an alien—Unusual mucus coughing enemy "oxygen" up from the stairway—Speed up movie made such forms by overwhelming gravity supply—Flesh frozen to supply a shocking emergency case—Amino acid directs all movement—won code on Grey Veil—To be read telepathic misdirection—"Office air" they can convert in dirty pictures of Life Form B—liquidate enemy on London

Space Stage—Tenuous air debarred action of yesterday—
Coughing enemy pulled in and replaced—

"The gentleman in body prison working our *'here'*—
You see it's only *'here'* he ever saw even for an instant—
Not in other places—Switched our way is doomed in the
relatively fresh air—That's us—Planning to use the host
could scarcely answer him—Of course Life Form B with
the utmost haste would shut the door that was very important for our 'oxygen' lines—So what else?—Defense
frequently determined the life form we invaded—"

Especially when a case marked for invasion and
manipulation suddenly taken out of their hands—
Dismissed an advocate from Biologic Need once he
had you pulled in to prepare briefs—The trial of The
Nova Mob withdrawn from the advocate—The case had
simply reached rigged any place—Pain and pleasure to
squeeze the "office air" felt contradictions of biologic
stairway—Crippled in such convenient advocate—For
how could he keep means during many years of someone
to help him?—

"I fancy faintness is due to the atmosphere offered by
Life Form A is inadequate—That this gentleman feels
necessary to investigate the original 'office air' story of
Life Form A on location—A came up from the stairway—
He had already counselor willing to handle 'this horrible
case' either outright or partially—You see it's only *'here'*
fixes nature of absolute need—A question of food supply
not alien planet—Form A direct claws intimidate and

corrupt advocate into channels calculated to squeeze host—Assistance back to our medium—"

Life Form A's room was on Ward Island—Crippled in such convenient Life Form B—Minraud an intricate door to cut off "oxygen" of life—Similar case operating through arrangements that could liquidate Life Form B by cutting off advocate from Minraud—

"Life Form A was totally alien," said the man who was an alien—

"Have what they call 'emotion' due to the 'oxygen.'"

"Was not the purpose supply Life Form A prior to intervention directing all movement?"

"Pleader a diving suit back to our medium—Scarcely answer him—Be destroyed by alien conditions—Ally detestable to us—For how could he keep Form A seen parasite?"

The best criminal counselor was similar case operating through metal—Impression followed to present interview—He got Sammy advocate from Minraud— Pulled in and replaced history of Life Form A on location—

Clearly this is a difficult case to defend particularly considering avowed intention of the accused to use the counselor as a diving suit back to their medium where counselor would be destroyed by alien conditions— There is however one phrase in the brief on which a defense can be constructed—"They sometimes mutate to breathe here"—That is if a successful mutation of Life

Form A can be called in as witness—Clearly the whole defense must be based on possibility of mutation and the less said about "absolute biologic need" to maintain a detrimental parasitic existence at the total expense of Form B the better chance of a compromise verdict suspended pending mutation proceedings—

TWO TAPE RECORDER MUTATIONS

"I fancy," said the man, "this gentleman feels totally stupid and greedy Venus Power—Tentacles write out message from stairway of slime—"

"That's us—Strictly from 'Sogginess Is Good For You'—Planning no bones but an elementary nervous system—Scarcely answer him—"

"The case simply at terminal bring down point— Desperate servants suddenly taken out of their hands— Insane orders and counter orders on the horizon—And I playing psychic chess determined the whole civilization and personal habits—"

"Iron claws of pain and pleasure with two speeds— with each recorder in body prison working our 'here' on extension leads—Even for an instant not in operation the host recorder saw the loudspeakers—Way is doomed in relatively soundproof 'room'—Would shift door led to the array—Many recorders important for our oxygen lines—Each to use host connected to its respective recorder layout—For example with nine recorders determined the life form we invaded by three square—Each recorder marked for invasion recording—You see it's only 'here' fixes nature of need set to run for as long as required—'Indignities' and 'cruelties' are playing back while other record—'Intimidate' and 'corrupt' speed and volume variation—Squeeze host back into system—Any number of tape recorders banked together for ease of operation switch in other places— Our mikes are laid out preferably in 'fresh air'—That's us—Planning speaker and mike connected to host— Scarcely answer him—Of course static and moving are possible—Very simplest array would be three lines— Two speeds can be playing especially when a 'case' has four possible states—Fast manipulation suddenly taken out of slow playback—The actual advocate from biologic need in many ways—

"a-Simple hand switching advocate

"b-Random choice fixed interval biologic stairway— The whole thing is switched on either outright or partially—at any given time recorders fix nature of absolute need—Thus sound played back by any 'cruelties' answer him either unchanged or subject to alien planet—

"c-Sequential choice i.e. flesh frozen to amino acid determines the next state according to"—That is a "book"—

Form A directs sound channels—Continuous operation in such convenient Life Form B—Final switching off of tape cuts "oxygen" Life Form B by cutting
off machine will produce cut-up of human form determined by the switching chosen—Totally alien "music"
need not survive in any "emotion" due to the "oxygen"
rendered down to a form of music—Intervention directing all movement what will be the end product?—
Reciprocation detestable to us for how could we become
part of the array?—Could this metal impression follow
to present language learning?—Talking and listening
machine led in and replaced—

Life Form A as follows was an alien—The operator selects the most "oxygen" appropriate material continuous
diving suit back to our medium—Ally information at the
verbal level—Could he keep Form A seen parasitic?—
Or could end be achieved by present interview?—Array
treated as a whole replaced history of life? Word falling photo falling tapes being blank—Insane orders
and counter orders of machine "music"—The Police
Machine will produce a cut-up of it determined by
the switching chosen—Could this alien mucus cough
language learn? Accused was beyond altered sound
formations—Alien Mucus Machine runs by feeding in
overwhelming gravity—Code on Grey Veil parallel the
spread of "dirty pictures"—Reverse instruction raises
question how many convert in "dirty pictures" before
London Space Stage—Tenuous simple repetition to one

machine only—Coughing enemy pulled in whole could be used as a model for behavior—Screams laughter shouts raw material—Voice fading into advocate:

"Clearly the whole defense must be experiments with two tape recorder mutations."

Pay Color

PAY COLOR

"The Subliminal Kid" moved in and took over bars cafés
and juke boxes of the world cities and installed radio trans-
mitters and microphones in each bar so that the music and
talk of any bar could be heard in all his bars and he had
tape recorders in each bar that played and recorded at arbitrary intervals and his agents moved back and forth with
portable tape recorders and brought back street sound and
talk and music and poured it into his recorder array so he
set waves and eddies and tornadoes of sound down all your
streets and by the river of all language—Word dust drifted
streets of broken music car horns and air hammers—The
Word broken pounded twisted exploded in smoke—

Word Falling ///

He set up screens on the walls of his bars opposite mirrors and took and projected at arbitrary intervals shifted from one bar to the other mixing Westerns Gangsters films of all time and place with word and image of the people in his cafes and on the streets his agents with movie camera and telescope lens poured images of the city back into his projector and camera array and nobody knew whether he was in a Western movie in Hongkong or The Aztec Empire in Ancient Rome or Suburban America whether he was a bandit a commuter or a chariot driver whether he was firing a "real" gun or watching a gangster movie and the city moved in swirls and eddies and tornadoes of image explosive bio-advance out of space to neon—

Photo Falling ///

"The Subliminal Kid" moved in seas of disembodied sound—He then spaced here and there and installf opposite mirrors and took movies each bar so that the music and talk is at arbitrary intervals and shifted bars—And he also had recorder in tracks and moving film mixing arbitrary intervals and agents moving with the word and image of tape recorders—So he set up waves and his agents with movie swirled through all the streets of image and brought back street in music from the city and poured Aztec Empire and Ancient Rome—Commuter or Chariot Driver could not control their word dust drifted from outer space—Air hammers word and image explosive bio-advance—A million drifting screens on the walls of his city projected mixing

sound of any bar could be heard in all Westerns and film of
all times played and recorded at the people back and forth
with portable cameras and telescope lenses poured eddies
and tornadoes of sound and camera array until soon city
where he moved everywhere a Western movie in Hongkong
or the Aztec sound talk suburban America and all accents
and language mixed and fused and people shifted language
and accent in mid-sentence Aztec priest and spilled it
man woman or beast in all language—So that People-City
moved in swirls and no one knew what he was going out
of space to neon streets—

"Nothing Is True—Everything Is Permitted—" Last
Words Hassan i Sabbah

The Kid stirred in sex films and The People-City
pulsed in a vast orgasm and no one knew what was film
and what was not and performed all kinda sex acts on
every street corner—

He took film of sunsets and cloud and sky water and
tree film and projected color in vast reflector screens
concentrating blue sky red sun green grass and the
city dissolved in light and people walked through each
other—There was only color and music and silence
where the words of Hassan i Sabbah had passed—

"Boards Syndicates Governments of the earth *Pay*—
Pay back the *Color* you stole—

"Pay Red—Pay back the red you stole for your lying
flags and your Coca-Cola signs—Pay that red back to
penis and blood and sun—

"*Pay Blue*—Pay back the blue you stole and bottled and doled out in eye droppers of junk—Pay back the blue you stole for your police uniforms—Pay that blue back to sea and sky and eyes of the earth—

"*Pay Green*—Pay back the green you stole for your money—And you, Dead Hand Stretching The Vegetable People, pay back the green you stole for your Green Deal to sell out peoples of the earth and board the first life boat in drag—Pay that green back to flowers and jungle river and sky—

"Boards Syndicates Governments of the earth pay back your stolen colors—*Pay Color* back to Hassan i Sabbah—"

PAY OFF THE MARKS?

Amusement park to the sky—The concessioners gathered in a low pressure camouflage pocket—

"I tell you Doc the marks are out there pawing the ground,

"'What's this Green Deal?'

"'What's this Sky Switch?'

"'What's this Reality Con?'

"'Man, we been short-timed?'

"'Are you a Good Gook?'

"'A good Nigger?'

"'A Good Human Animal?'

"They'll take the place apart—I've seen it before—
like a silver flash—And The Law is moving in—Not
locals—This is Nova Heat—I tell you we got to give
and fast—Flicker, The Movies, Biologic Merging Tanks,
The lot—Well, Doc?"

"It goes against my deepest instincts to pay off the
marks—But under the uh circumstances—caught as we
are between an aroused and not in all respects reasonable citizenry and the antibiotic handcuffs—"

The Amusement Gardens cover a continent—There
are areas of canals and lagoons where giant gold fish
and salamanders with purple fungoid gills stir in clear
black water and gondolas piloted by translucent green
fish boys—Under vast revolving flicker lamps along the
canals spill The Biologic Merging Tanks sense withdrawal capsules light and soundproof water at blood
temperature pulsing in and out where two life forms
slip in and merge to a composite being often with deplorable results slated for Biologic Skid Row on the
outskirts: (Sewage delta and rubbish heaps—terminal
addicts of SOS muttering down to water worms and floating vegetables—Paralyzed Orgasm Addicts eaten alive
by crab men with white hot eyes or languidly tortured in
charades by The Green Boys of young crystal cruelty)

Vast communal immersion tanks melt whole peoples
into one concentrate—It's more democratic that way you
see?—Biologic Representation—Cast your vote into the
tanks—Here where flesh circulates in a neon haze and

identity tags are guarded by electric dogs sniffing quivering excuse for being—The assassins wait broken into scanning patterns of legs smile and drink—Unaware of The Vagrant Ball Player pant smell running in liquid typewriter—

Streets of mirror and glass and metal under flickering cylinders of colored neon—Projector towers sweep the city with color writing of The Painter—Cool blue streets between walls of iron polka-dotted with lenses projecting The Blue Tattoo open into a sea of Blue Concentrate lit by pulsing flickering blue globes—Mountain villages under the blue twilight—Drifting cool blue music of all time and place to the brass drums—

Street of The Light Dancers who dance with color writing projected on their bodies in spotlight layers peel off red yellow blue in dazzling strip acts, translucent tentative beings flashing through neon hula hoops—stand naked and explode in white fade out in grey—vaporize in blue twilight—

Who did not know the name of his vast continent?— There were areas left at his electric dogs—Purple fungoid gills stirred in being—His notebooks running flicker screens along the canals—

"Who him?—Listen don't let him out here."

Two life forms entered the cracked earth to escape terrible dry heat of The Insect People—The assassins wait legs by water cruel idiot smiles play a funeral symphony— For being he was caught in the zoo—Cages snarling and coming on already—The Vagrant passed down dusty Arab

street muttering: "Where is he now?"—Listening sifting towers swept the city—American dawn words falling
on my face—Cool Sick room with rose wallpaper—"Mr.
Bradly Mr. Martin" put on a clean shirt and walked out—
stars and pool halls and stale rooming house—this foreign
sun in your brain—visit of memories and wan light—
silent suburban poker—worn pants—scratching shower
room and brown hair—grey photo—on a brass bed—stale
flesh exploded film in basement toilets—boys jack off
from—this drifting cobweb of memories—in the wind of
morning—furtive and sad felt the lock click—

He walked through—Summer dust—stirring St. Louis
schoolrooms—a brass bed—Cigarette smoke—urine as
in the sun—Soccer scores and KiKi when I woke up—
Such wisdom in gusts—empty spaces—Fjords and
Chimborazi—Brief moments I could describe to the
barrier—Pursuits of future life where boy's dawn question
is far away—What's St. Louis or any conveyor distance?
St. Louis on this brass bed? Comte Wladmir Sollohub
Rashid Ali Khan B Bremond d'Ars Marquis de Migre
Principe di Castelcicale Gentilhomo di Palazzo you're a
long way from St. Louis . . . Let me tell you about a score
of years' dust on the window that afternoon I watched the
torn sky bend with the wind . . . *white white white as far
as the eye can see ahead a blinding flash of white* . . . (The
cabin reeks of exploded star). . . . Broken sky through
my nostrils—Dead bare knee against the greasy dust—
Faded photo drifting down across pubic hair, thighs, rose

wallpaper into the streets of Pasto—The urinals and the bicycle races here in this boy were gone when I woke up—Whiffs of my Spain down the long empty noon— Brief moments I could describe—The great wind revolving lips and pants in countries of the world—Last soldier's fading—Violence is shut off Mr. Bradly Mr.—I am dying in a room far away—last—Sad look—Mr. Of The Account, I am dying—In other flesh now—Such dying— Remember hints as we shifted windows the visiting moon air like death in your throat?—The great wind revolving lip smoke, fading photo and distance—Whispers of junk, flute walks, shirt flapping—Bicycle races here at noon— boy thighs—Sad—Lost dog—He had come a long way for something not exchanged . . . sad shrinking face . . . He died during the night. . . .

SMORBROT

Operation Sense Withdrawal* is carried out in silent lightless immersion tanks filled with a medium of salt bouillon at temperature and density of the human body

---

*The most successful method of sense withdrawal is the immersion tank where the subject floats in water at blood temperature sound and light withdrawn—loss of body outline, awareness and location of the limbs occurs quickly, giving rise to panic in many American subjects—Subjects frequently report feeling that another body is floating half in and half out

—Cadets enter the tank naked and free floating a few inches apart—permutate on slow currents—soon lose the outlines of body in shifting contact with phantom limbs—Loss of outline associated with pleasant sensations—frequently orgasms occur—

K9 took off his clothes in a metal-lined cubicle with a Chinese youth—Naked he felt vertigo and a tightening of stomach muscles as they let themselves down into the tank and floated now a few inches apart warm liquid swirling through legs and genitals touching—His hands and feet lost outline—There was sudden sharp spasm in his throat and a taste of blood—The words dissolved— His body twisted in liquid fish spasms and emptied through his spurting penis—feeling other spasms shiver through the tank—He got out and dresses with a boy from The Alameda—Back in flesh—street boy words in his throat—Kerosene light on a Mexican about twenty felt his pants slide down his stomach his crotch unbuttoned sighed and moved his ass off—He was naked now in lamp—Mexican rolled marijuana cigarette— naked body of the other next to his turning him over on his stomach—his crotch unbuttoned wind and water

of the body in the first part—Experiments in sense withdrawal using the immersion tanks have been performed by Doctor Lilly in Florida—There is another experimental station in Oklahoma—So after fifteen minutes in the tank these marines scream they are losing outlines and have to be removed—I say put two marines in the tank and see who comes out— Science—Pure science—So put a marine and his girl friend in the tank and see who or what emerges—

sounds—sighed and moved his ass in shadow pools on rose wallpaper—brass bed stale against him—Felt naked body of the other explode in his spine—Room changed with flesh—Felt his pants slide—The cadet's ass was naked now—A few inches apart in the tank the Mexican—His lips felt propositions—A few inches apart K9 moved his ass in scratching shower—Wave of pleasure through his stomach—He was floating moving in food—City of Chili Houses exploded in muscles and the words went in—There in his throat—Kerosene light on with street boy—Outskirts of The City—First spurts of his crotch—

The naked cadets entered a warehouse of metal-lined cubicles—stood a few inches apart laughing and talking on many levels—Blue light* played over

---

*Reference to the orgone accumulators of Doctor Wilhelm Reich—Doctor Reich claims that the basic charge of life is this blue orgone-like electrical charge—Orgones form a sphere around the earth and charge the human machine—He discovered that orgones pass readily through iron but are stopped and absorbed by organic matter—So he constructed metal-lined cubicles with layers of organic material behind the metal—Subjects sit in the cubicles lined with iron and accumulate orgones according to the law of increased returns on which life functions—The orgones produce a prickling sensation frequently associated with erotic stimulation and spontaneous orgasm—Reich insists that orgasm is an electrical discharge—He has attached electrodes to the appropriate connections and charted the orgasm—In consequence of these experiments he was of course expelled from various countries before he took refuge in America and died in a federal penitentiary for suggesting the orgone accumulator in treating cancer—It has occurred to this investigator that orgone energy can be concentrated to disperse the miasma of idiotic prurience and anxiety that

their bodies—Projectors flashed the color writing of
Hassan i Sabbah on bodies and metal walls—Opened
into amusement gardens—Sex Equilibrists perform on
tightropes and balancing chairs—Trapeze acts ejaculate
in the air—The Sodomite Tumblers doing cartwheels
and whirling dances stuck together like dogs—Boys
masturbate from scenic railways—Flower floats in the
lagoons and canals—Sex cubicles where the acts performed to music project on the tent ceiling a sky of
rhythmic copulation—Vast flicker cylinders and projectors sweep the gardens writing explosive bio-advance
to neon—Areas of sandwich booths blue movie parlors
and transient hotels under ferris wheels and scenic
railways—soft water sounds and frogs from the canals—K9 stood opposite a boy from Norway felt the
prickling blue light on his genitals filling with blood
touched the other tip and a warm shock went down his
spine and he came in spasms of light—Silver writing
burst in his brain and went out with a smell of burning metal in empty intersections where boys on roller
skates turn slow circles and weeds grow through cracked
pavement—
Mexican rolled cigarette the soft blue light deep in
his lungs—Mexican hands touching felt his pants slide

blocks any scientific investigation of sexual phenomenon—Preliminary
experiments indicate that certain painting—like Brion Gysin's—when
projected on a subject produced some of the effects observed in orgone
accumulators—

down in soundless explosion of the throat and a taste of blood—His body twisted—Sleeps naked now—wind and water sounds—Outskirts of the city—shadow areas of sandwich booths and transient hotels under scenic railways—

We drank the beer and ate the smorbrot—I dropped half a sandwich in my lap and she wiped the butter off with a napkin laughing as the cloth bulged under her fingers my back against a tree the sun on my crotch tingling filling with blood she opened my belt and: "Raise up, darling," pulled my pants down to the knee—

We ate the smorbrot with hot chocolate from the thermos bottle and I spilled a cup of chocolate in my lap and jumped up and she wiped the chocolate off with a paper napkin and I dodged away laughing as the cloth bulged under her fingers and she followed me with the napkin and opened my belt—I felt my pants slide down and the sun on my naked crotch tingling and filling with blood—We did it half undressed—When I came there was silver light popped in my eyes like a flash bulb and looking over her shoulder I saw little green men in the trees swinging from branch to branch turning cartwheels in the air—And sex acts by naked acrobats on tightropes and balancing poles—Jissom drifting cobwebs through clear green light—Washed in the stream and pulled up my pants—We rode back to Copenhagen on my motor scooter—I left her in front of her flat block and arranged a meeting for Sunday—As she walked away I could see the grass stains on the back of her dress—That night I was blank and went back to a bar in Neuerhaven where I can usually find a tourist to buy drinks—and sat down at a table with a boy about my age—I noticed he had a very small narrow head tapering from his neck which was thick and smooth and something strange about his eyes—The iris was shiny black like broken coal with pinpoint green pupils—He turned and looks straight at me and I got a feeling like scenic railways in the stomach—Then he ordered two beers—"I see that you are blank," he said—The beers came—"I work with the circus," he said—balancing his chair—"Like this on wires—never with net—In South America I did it over a gorge of a thousand meters in depth."

Balancing he drank the Tuborg—"There are not many who can see us—Come and I will show you our real acts."

We took a cab to the outskirts of the city—There was a warm electric wind blowing through the car that seemed to leave the ground—We came to what looked like a ruined carnival by a lake—In a tent lit by flickering blue globes I met more boys with the same narrow head and reversed eyes—They passed around a little pipe and I smoked and felt green tingling in my crotch and lips—A Negro drummer began pounding his drum with sticks—The boys got up laughing and passing the pipe and talking in a language like bird calls and took off their clothes—They climbed a ladder to the high wire and walked back and forth like cats—A magic lantern projected color writing on their bodies that looked like Japanese tattooing—They all got erections and arching past each other on the wire genitals touched in a shower of blue sparks—One boy balanced a steel chair on the wire and ejaculated in a crescendo of drum beats and flickering rainbow colors—jissom turning slow cartwheels dissolved in yellow light—Another boy with earphones crackling radio static and blue sparks playing around his yellow hair did a Messerschmitt number—the chair rocking in space—tracer bullets of jissom streaking cross interstellar void—(Naked boys on roller skates turn slow circles at the intersection of ruined suburbs—falling through a maze of penny arcades—spattered the cracked concrete weeds and dog excrement—) The boys came down from the wire and one of them flicked my jacket—I took off my clothes and practiced balancing naked in a chair—The balance point was an electrical field holding him out of gravity—The charge built up in his genitals and he came in a wet dream the chair fluid and part of his body—That night made sex with the boy I met in Neuerhaven for the first time with each other in space—Sure calm of wire acts balanced on ozone—blue electric spasms—Smell of burning metal in the penny arcade I got a hard on looking at the peep show and Hans laughed pointing to my fly: "Let's make the roller coaster," he said—The cashier took our money with calm neutral glance—A young

Italian clicked us out—We were the only riders and as
soon as the car started we slipped off our shorts—We
came together in the first dip as the car started up the
other side throwing blood into our genitals tight and
precise as motor parts—open shirts flapping over the
midway—Silver light popped in my head and went out
in blue silence—Smell of ozone—You see sex is an electrical charge that can be turned on and off if you know
the electromagnetic switchboard—Sex is an electrical
flesh trade—It is usually turned on by water sounds—
Now take your sex words on rose wallpaper brass bed—
Explode in red brown green from colors to the act on
the association line—Naked charge can explode sex
words to color's rectal brown green ass language—The
sex charge is usually controlled by sex words forming
an electromagnetic pattern—This pattern can be shifted
by substituting other factors for words—Take a simple
sex word like "masturbate"—"jack off"—Substitute
color for the words like: "jack"—red "off"—white—
red—white—Flash from words to color on the association screen—Associate silently from colors to the
act—Substitute other factors for the words—Arab drum
music—Musty smell of erections in outhouses—Feel
of orgasm—Color-music-smell-feel to the million sex
acts all time place—Boys red-white from ferris wheels,
scenic railways, bridges, whistling bicycles, tree houses
careening freight cars train whistles drifting jissom in
winds of Panhandle—shivering through young bodies

under boarding house covers rubbly outskirts of South American city ragged pants dropped to cracked bleeding feet black dust blowing through legs and genitals— Pensive lemur smell of erection—cool basement toilets in St. Louis—Summer afternoon on car seats to the thin brown knee—Bleak public school flesh naked for the physical the boy with epilepsy felt The Dream in his head struggling for control locker room smells on his stomach—He was in The Room with many suitcases all open and drawers full of things that had to be packed and only a few minutes to catch the boat whistling in the harbor and more and more drawers and the suitcases won't close arithmetical disorder and the wet dream tension in his crotch—The other boys laughing and pointing in the distance now as he got out of control silver light popped in his eyes and he fell with a sharp metal cry—through legs and genitals felt his pants slide—shivering outskirts of the city—wind of morning in a place full of dust—Naked for a physical orgasms occur— tightening stomach muscles—scenic railways exploded in his crotch—Legs and genitals lost outline careening through dream flesh—smell of the mud flats—warm spurts to sluggish stream water from the tree house—a few inches apart laughing in the sunlight jissom cartwheels in the clear air of masturbating afternoons—pulled up my pants— Explosion of the throat from color to the act jumped up laughing in the transient hotels—careening area of sand- wich booths—Silver writing burst in moonlight through a Mexican about twenty shifting his crotch sighed and moved

naked now a few inches in his hand—pleasure tingling
through cracked bleeding feet—With phantom limbs his
cock got hard sensations on roller skates—slow intersection of weeds and concrete—Penny arcades spattered light
on a Mexican about twenty—Wet dreams of flight sighed
in lamp—Flash from word to color sex acts all time place
exploded in muscles drifting sheets of male flesh—Boys on
wind of morning—first spurts unbuttoned my pants—Area
of sandwich booths and intolerable scenic railways he came
wet dream way—(In the tree house black ants got into our
clothes pulling off shirts and pants and brushing the ants
off each other he kept brushing my crotch—"there's an ant
there" and jacked me off into the stream of masturbating
afternoons)—Hans laughed pointing to my shorts—Pants
to the ankle we were the only riders—Wheee came together
in the first dip open shorts flapping genitals—Wind of
morning through flesh—Outskirts of the city—

ITS ACCOUNTS

Now hazard flakes fall—A huge wave rolled treatment
"pay back the red you stole"—Farewell for Alexander—
Fading out in Ewyork, Onolulu, Aris, Ome, Oston—Sub
editor melted into air—I Sekuin hardly breathe—Dreams
are made of might be just what I am look: Prerecorded
warning in a woman's voice—Scio is pulling a figure

out of logos—A huge wave bowled a married couple off what you could have—Would you permit that person in Ewyork, Onolulu, Aris, Ome, Oston?—One assumes a "beingness" where past crimes highlighted the direction of a "havingness"—He boasted of a long string of other identities—She gave no indication of fundamental agreement—We returned to war—Process pre-clear in absurd position for conditions—Scio is like pulling a figure out of The Homicide Act—Logos got Sheraton Call and spent the weekend with a bargain—Venus Vigar choked to passionate weakness—The great wind identity failed—So did art loving Miss West—Every part of your dust yesterday along the High Street Air—The flakes fall that were his cruelest lawyer: show you fear on walls and windows treatment—Farewell trouble for Alexander—Pay back the red you stole living or dead from the sky—Hurry up please its accounts—Empty thing police they fading out—Dusk through narrow streets, toilet paper, and there is no light in the window—April wind revolving illness of dead sun—Woman with red hair is a handful of dust—Departed have left used avenue—Many years ago that youngster—It was agony to breathe in number two intake—Dreams of the dead—Prerecorded warning—Remember I was carbon dioxide—It is impossible to estimate the years in novitiate postulating Sheraton Carlton Call—Loose an arrow—Thud—Thing Police fading out in Ewyork, Onolulu, Aris, Ome, Oston—See where he struck—Oh

no discounts and compensations—Stop tinkering with
what you could have—Must go in time—Stop tinkering
with recompense—You'll know me in dark mutinous
mirrors of the world—Yesterday along high street massive treatment:: "Pay back the red you stole"—A shame
to part with it?? Try various farewell trouble?? Near curtains for them and trouble shuffled out of the die—Along
high street account reaching to my chest—Pay back the
red you stole happened—Effects Boys said farewell to
Alexander Bargain—"What are we going to do? Thing
police they fading out—Sub editor melted into air—So
I had to do Two Of A Kind on toilet paper—Obvious
sooner that air strip."

"It was agony to breathe—What might be called the
worried in number two intake—Barry going to do?—
Partisans of all nation learn all about it—Red Hair we
were getting to use on anyone—Pit too—Going to get
out of it?"

A colorless question drifted down corridors of that
hospital—"I Sekuin—Tell me what you would permit
to remain?"

SIMPLE AS A HICCUP

Mr. Martin, hear us through something as simple as a
hiccup tinkering with the disaster accounts—All Board

Room Reports are classified as narcotic drugs—Morphine is actually "Mr. Martin," his air line the addict—I have said the basic techniques: every reason to believe the officers dictate in detail with a precise repetition of stimuli place of years—Techniques of nova reports are stimuli between enemies—Dimethyltryptamine pain bank from "disagreeable symptoms"—Overdose by precise repetition can be nightmare experience owing to pain headphones send nova spirit from Hiroshima and Nagasaki—"Mr. Martin," hear us through mushroom clouds—Start tinkering with disaster brains and twisting all board room reports—Their pain line is the addict—Pain bank from the torture chambers—Every reason to believe the officers torn into insect fragments by precise repetition of years—Tortured metal pain spirit Uranian born of nova conditions send those blasts—Great wind revolving the nova spirit in image flakes—Every part of your translucent burning fire head shut off, Mr. Bradly, in the blue sky writing of Hassan i Sabbah—That hospital melted in Grey Room—Writing of Hassan i Sabbah postulating you were all smoke drifting from something as simple as a hiccup—I have said the basic techniques of the world and mutilated officers dictate in detail with iron claws of the chessmen place of years—Hassan i Sabbah through all disaster accounts—Last door of nova and all the torture expanding drugs—Pressure groups teach mechanisms involved—Disaster of nova pulsed need dictates use of throat bones—I Sabbah

walk in the recordings write dripping faucet and five
flashes per second—The rhythmic turrets destroy enemy
installations—Cortex winds overflowing into mutinous
areas hearing color seeing "Mr. Bradly Mr. Martin"—
Just time—Just time—I quote from Anxiety And Its
Treatment in Grey Room—Apomorphine as a hiccup—
Hassan i Sabbah through apomorphine acts on the hypothalamus and regulates blood serum of the world and
mutilated officers—Melted a categorical "no mercy for
this enemy" as dust and smoke—

THERE'S A LOT ENDED

New York, Saturday March 17, Present Time—For
many he accidentally blew open present food in The Homicide Act—Anyway after that all the top England spent
the weekend with a bargain—Intend to settle price—I
had work in Melbourne before doing sessions—Austra-
lia in the gates—Dogs must be carried—Reluctant to
put up any more Amplex—Go man go—There's a lot
ended—Flashes The Maharani of Check Moth—The
clean queen walks serenely down dollars—Don't listen
to Hassan i Sabbah—We want Watney's Woodbines and
all pleasures of the body—Stand clear of The Garden
Of Delights—And love slop is a Bristol—Bring together
state of news—Inquire on hospital—At the Ovens Great

Gold Cup—Revived peat victory hopes of Fortria—
Premature Golden sands in Sheila's cottage?—You want
the name of Hassan i Sabbah so own the unborn?—Cool
and casual through the hole in thin air closed at hotel
room in London—Death reduces the college—Seriously
considered so they are likely to face lung cancer dis-
ciplinary action—

Venus Vigar choked to death with part-time
television—Ward boy kept his diary thoughts and
they went back meticulously to the corridor—He
pointed out that the whole world had already watched
Identikit—"Why, we all take satisfaction—Rode
a dancing horse on sugar avenue—Prettiest little
thought you ever saw"—

The capsule was warm in Soho—An operation
has failed to save American type jeans—Further
talks today with practical cooperation—There are
many similarities—Solicitor has ally at Portman
Clinic—The Vital Clue that links the murders is
JRR 284—Finished off in a special way just want to
die—When his body was found three young men are
still dancing the twist in The Swede's Dunedin muck
spreading The New Zealand after 48 hours in his bed
sitter—Stephen film was in the hospital—Definition
of reasonable boy body between his denials—Identity
popped in flash bulb breakfast—Yards and yards of
entrails hung around the husband irrevocably committed to the toilet—The Observer left his friend in

Cocktail Probation—Vanished with confessed folk singer—Studio dresser John Vigar found dead on the old evacuation plan—The body, used in 1939, year of Vigar's birth, was naked—Both men had been neatly folded—As the series is soon ending are these experiments really necessary? Uncontrolled flash bulbs popped in rumors—Said one: "All this is typical Dolce just before Christ Vita—"—Quiet man in 624A said the tiny bedroom as doctor actor would never do—Police examined the body counter outside little groups of denials—Miss Taylor people hung around the husband—He plays Mark even Anthony with Liz—There was great bustle through the red hair—Born in Berlin and made his first threat to peace at the age of 17—Hanratty was then brought up as a Jew—Over 100 police in unfashionably dressed women search for boy who had protested definition of "reasonable friend" and "circumstantial police"— Prime haggling going on—Sir, I am delighted to see that/ writes about/ I am quite prepared to/ Last attention is being paid to routine foundations on the Square Generation/ The light woman is at the clear out/ if they wish to live their moment without answering to me/ this of course they will not do

James swaggering about in arson to be considered— Murder in the operating theatre at Nottingham— Stephen said to be voting through yards and yards of entrails irrevocably committed to the toilet—

ONE MORE CHANCE?

Scientology means the study of "humanity's condition"
—Wise radio doctor—Logos Officers in his portable—
The Effects Boy's "scientology release" is locks over the
Chinese—Told me to sit by Hubbard guide—
   "What are you going to do?—That person going to
get out of 'havingness'??"
   Will cover the obvious usually sooner than later—
Globe is self you understand until assumed unwit-
tingly "reality" is made out of "Mr. Martin"—To agree
to be Real *is* "real" and the way the flakes fall—Game
conditions and no game every time—For him always
been a game consists of "freed galaxies"—End getting
an effect on the other team now ended—Look around
here it's curtains for them—Be able to not know his
past circumstances—Scio is knowing and wind hand
to the hilt—Work we have logos you got it? Dia through
noose—Jobbies would like to strike—Release certificate is issued for a respectable price—Find a process
known as "overwhelming," what?—Come back work
was what you could have—What would you permit that
person—?? Food in The Homicide Act??—Look around
and accept "one more chance"?? "Havingness" bait and
it's curtains—End anatomy of games—The fundamental
reward business the bait—The cycle of "Humanity's
condition"—Apparent because we believe it—One assumes a "beingness" over the Chinese—Like to strike

a bargain: Other identities—Is false identity—In the
end is just the same—Fundamentally agreement—
All games for respectable share of these "barriers"
and "purposes"—Know what they mean if they start
"no-effect"??

Cool and casual the anatomy of games closed at hotel
room in London—

The District Supervisor looked up with a narrow
smile. "Sit down young man and smoke . . . occupational
vice what? . . . only vice left us . . . You have studied
Scientology of course?"

"Oh yes sir . . . It was part of our *basic* training
sir . . . an unforgettable experience if you'll pardon the
expression sir . . ."

"Repeat what you know about Scientology."

"The Scientologists believe sir that words recorded during a period of unconsciousness . . .
(anesthesia, drunkenness, sleep, childhood amnesia
for trauma) . . . *store* pain and that this pain store can
be plugged in with key words represented as alternative
mathematical formulae indicating number of exposures
to the key words and reaction index, the whole battery feeding back from electronic computers . . . They
call these words recorded during unconsciousness *engrams* sir . . . If I may say so sir the childhood amnesia for trauma is of special interest sir . . . The child
forgets sir but since the controllers have the engram
tapes sir any childhood trauma can be plugged in at any

time . . . The pain that *overwhelms* that person is known as *basic basic* sir and when *basic basic* is wiped off the tape . . . Oh sir *then* that person becomes what they call a *clear* sir . . . Since Lord Lister sir . . . since the introduction of *anesthesia* sir . . ." (Amnesia smiled) "Oh let me yes sir tell you about a score of years' dust on the expression sir . . . If you'll pardon the expression sir are known as engrams sir."

"You have occupational experience?"

"Oh yes sir . . . It was part of our Basic Scientology Police Course sir"

"You have studied the risks of 'dancing'?"

"Sir the Scientologists believe this pain can be plugged in from Oaxaca photo copies and middle ages jacking off in deprostrated comrades"

(The living dead give a few cool hints . . . artificial arms and legs . . . soulless winded words)

"With the advent of *General Anesthesia* sir words recorded during *operations* became . . . (The nurse leans over the doctor's shoulder dropping cigarette ashes along the incision—'What are you looking for?' snarls the doctor . . . 'I know what I'm doing right enough . . . appendectomy at least . . . But why stop there?? Enemy anesthetized we advance . . . Fetch me another scalpel . . . This one's filthy . . .' Chorus of street boys outside: 'Fingaro?? one cigarette?? please thanks you very much . . . You like beeg one? . . . son

bitch bastard . . .' 'Go away you villainous young toads'
snarls the doctor pelting them with tonsils . . . Wish I
had an uterine tumor . . . like a bag of cement . . . get
one of them with any luck . . . You nurse . . . Put out that
cigarette . . . You *wanta cook my patient's lungs out*??"
    Shrill screams from maternity blast through the loud-
speaker . . . The Technician mixes a bicarbonate of soda
and belches into his hand . . . 'Urp urp urp . . . Fucking
set picks up every fart and passes it along' A hideous
squawk of death rattles smudges the instrument panel
out of focus . . . White no smell of death from a cell
of sick junkies in the prison ward swirls through the
operating room . . . The doctor sags ominously severing
the patient's femoral artery . . . 'I die . . . I faint . . . I
fail . . . Fucking sick Coolies knock all the junk right
out of a man . . .' He staggers towards the narco cabinet trailing his patient's blood . . . 'GOM for the love
of God') It's a little skit I wrote for the *Post Gazette*
sir . . . Anesthesia on stage sir words recorded during operations became the most reliable engrams . . .
Operation Pain they called it sir . . . I can feel it now
sir . . . in my tonsils sir . . . ether vertigo sir . . . (*The patient is hemorrhaging . . . nurse . . . the clamps . . . quick
before I lose my patient*) . . . Another instrument of these
pain tourists is the *signal switch* sir . . . what they call
the 'yes no' sir . . . 'I love you I hate you' at supersonic
alternating speed . . . Take orgasm noises sir and cut

them in with torture and accident groans and screams
sir and operating-room jokes sir and flicker sex and
torture film right with it sir" . . .

"And what is your counter?"

"Just do it sir . . . in front of everybody sir . . . It
would have a comic effect sir . . . We flash a sex pic
with torture in the background sir then snap that torture
pic right in your bloody face sir . . . if you'll pardon
the expression sir . . . we do the same with the sound
track sir . . . *varying distances* sir . . . It has a 3D effect
sir . . . right down the old middle line sir . . . if you'll
pardon the expression sir . . . the razor inside sir . . .

"Jerk the handle . . . It sounds like this sir: 'Oh my
God I can't stand it . . . That hurts that hurts that hurts so
gooood . . . Ooooooohhhh fuck me to death . . . Blow his
fucking guts out . . . You're burning up baby . . . whole
sky burning . . . I'll talk . . . Do it again . . . Come in
. . . Get out . . . Slip your pants down . . . What's that??
nurse . . . the clamps . . . Cut it off . . .' with the pics
sir . . . popping like fireworks sir . . . sex and pain
words sir . . . vary the tape sir . . . switch the tape
sir . . .

"Now all together *laugh laugh laugh* . . . Oh sir we
laugh it right off the tape sir . . . We *forget* it right off the
tape sir . . . You see sir we can *not know it* if we have the
engram tapes sir . . . simple as a hiccup sir . . . melted a
categorical no mercy for this enemy as dust and smoke
sir . . . The man who never was reporting for no duty

sir . . . A young cop drew the curtains sir . . . Room for
one more operating-room joke inside sir"
   You can still see the old operating room kinda run
down now . . . Do you begin to see there is no patient
there on the table?

ARE THESE EXPERIMENTS NECESSARY?

Saturday March 17, 1962, Present Time Of Knowledge—Scio is knowing and open food in The Homicide
Act—Logos you got it?—Dia through noose—England
spent the weekend with a bargain before release certificate is issued—Dogs must be carried reluctant to the
center—It's a grand feeling—There's a lot ended—This
condition is best expressed queen walks serenely down
dollar process known as overwhelming—What we want
is Watney's Woodbines and the Garden Of Delights—
And what could you have?—What would you? State of
news?—Inquire on hospital? what?—Would you permit
that person revived peat victory hopes of Fortria? Pre-
clear to look around and discover Sheila's Cottage?—
Death reduces the cycle of action—Venus Vigar choked
to death in the direction of "havingness"—His diary
thoughts they went back other identities—The whole
world had valence is false identity—Further talks
today with "barriers" and "purposes"—Vital clue that

links the murders is: game one special way just want to die—Spreading the New Zealand after film was in the hospital—Yards of entrails hung about the toilet—The observer left his scio and vanished with confessed folk singer logos—Dia through noose found dead on the old evacuation—Release certificate of Vigar's birth is issued naked—This condition is best expressed uncontrolled flash bulbs popped process known as "overwhelming"—

"Sir I am quite prepared—other identities—Woman is at the clear out if is fundamentally agreement"—

"Look around here and tell me are these experiments really necessary?"—All this to "overwhelm"—? Apparency bustle through the red hair—I have said Scio Officers at any given time dictate place of years—Dead absolute need condition expressed process known as "overwhelming"—Silence—Don't answer—What could that person "overwhelm?"—Air?—The great wind revolving what you could have—What would you?—Sound and image flakes fall—It will be seen that "havingness" no more—

Paralyzed on this green land the "cycle of action"— The cycle of last door—Shut off "Mr. Bradly Mr. Apparent Because We Believe It"—Into air—You are yourself "Mr. Bradly Mr. Other Identities"—Action is an apparency creating and aggravating conflict—Total war of the past—I have said the "basic pre-clear identities" are now ended—Wind spirits melted "reality need" dictates use of throat bones—"Real is real" do get your heavy

summons and are melted—Through all the streets time
for him be able to not know his past walls and windows
people and sky—Complete intentions falling—Look
around here—No more flesh scripts dispense Mr.—
Heard your summons—Melted "Mr. Bradly Mr. Martin"

MELTED INTO AIR

Fade out muttering: "There's a lover on every corner
cross the wounded galaxies"—

Distant fingers get hung up on one—"Oh, what'll
we do?"

Slowly fading—I told him you on tracks—All over for
sure—I'm absolutely prophesized in a dream grabbing
Yuri by the shirt and throwing last words answer his Yu-
goslavian knife—I pick up Shannon Yves Martin may not
refuse vision—Everybody's watching—But I continue the
diary—"Mr. Bradly Mr. Martin?"—You are his eyes—I
see suddenly Mr. Beiles Mr. Corso Mr. Burroughs presence on earth is all a joke—And I think: "Funny—melted
into air"—Lost flakes fall that were his shadow: This
book—No good junky identity fading out—

"Smoke is all, boy—Dont intersect—I think now I
go home and it's five times—Had enough slow metal
fires—Form has been inconstant—Last electrician to
tap on the bloody dream"—

"I see dark information from him on the floor—He pull out—Keep all Board Room Reports—Waiting chair to bash everybody—Couldn't reach tumescent daydream in Madrid—Flash a jester angel who stood there in 1910 straw words—Realize that this too is bad move—No good—No bueno—Young angel elevated among the subterraneans—Yas, he heard your summons—Nodded absently—"

"And I go home having lost—Yes, blind may not refuse vision to this book—"

CLOM FLIDAY

I have said the basic techniques of nova are very simple consist in creating and aggravating conflicts— "No riots like injustice directed between enemies"—At any given time recorders fix nature of absolute need and dictate the use of total weapons—Like this:: Collect and record violent Anti-Semitic statements—Now play back to Jews who are after Belsen—Record what they say and play it back to the Anti-Semites—Clip clap— You got it?—Want more?—Record white supremacy statements—Play to Negroes—Play back answer—Now The Women and The Men—No riots like injustice directed between "enemies"—At any given time position of recorders fixes nature of absolute need—And dictates the use of total weapons—So leave the recorders running and get your heavy metal ass in a space ship— Did it—Nothing here now but the recordings—Shut the whole thing right off—*Silence*—When you answer the machine you provide it with more recordings to be played back to your "enemies" keep the whole nova machine running—The Chinese character for "enemy" means to be similar to or to answer—Don't answer the machine—Shut it off—

"The Subliminal Kid" took over streets of the world— Cruise cars with revolving turrets telescope movie lenses and recorders sweeping up sound and image of the city around and around faster and faster cars racing through all the streets of image record, take, play back, project on walls and windows people and sky—And slow moving turrets on slow cars and wagons slower and slower record take, play back, project slow motion street scene—Now fast—Now slow—slower—*Stop*—Shut off—No More— My writing arm is paralyzed—No more junk scripts, no more word scripts, no more flesh scripts—He all went away—No good—No bueno—Couldn't reach flesh—No glot—Clom Fliday—Through invisible door—Adios Meester William, Mr. Bradly, Mr. Martin—

I have said the basic techniques creating and aggravating conflict officers—At any given time dictate total war of the past—Changed place of years in the end is just the same—I have said the basic techniques of Nova reports are now ended—Wind spirits melted

between "enemies"—Dead absolute need dictates use
of throat bones—On this green land recorders get your
heavy summons and are melted—Nothing here now but
the recordings may not refuse vision in setting forth—
Silence—Don't answer—That hospital melted into
air—The great wind revolving turrets towers palaces—
Insubstantial sound and image flakes fall—Through all
the streets time for him to forbear—Blest be he on walls
and windows people and sky—On every part of your dust
falling softly—falling in the dark mutinous "No more"—
My writing arm is paralyzed on this green land—Dead
Hand, no more flesh scripts—Last door—Shut off Mr.
Bradly Mr.—He heard your summons—Melted into
air—You are yourself "Mr. Bradly Mr. Martin—" all
the living and the dead—You are yourself—There be—

Well that's about the closest way I know to tell you
and papers rustling across city desks . . . fresh southerly
winds a long time ago.

September 17, 1899 over New York

July 21, 1964
Tangier, Morocco
William Burroughs

Notes

Abbreviations

NEX   *Nova Express*, Grove Press, 1964.
March 1962 MS   First Draft of *Nova Express*, sent to Barney Rosset,
                March 30, 1962 (typescripts in several archival
                collections, mainly OSU 2.2, 2.3, 2.4, 3.5).
October 1962 MS Second Draft of *Nova Express*, 170-page type-
                script dated October 24, 1962 and sent to Bar-
                ney Rosset that day (a single typescript used
                as the typesetting manuscript, OSU 4.9).
ASU   William Seward Burroughs Papers 1938–1997,
                Special Collections, Arizona State University.
Berg   William S. Burroughs Papers, 1951–1972, The
                Henry W. and Albert A. Berg Collection of Eng-
                lish and American Literature, New York Public
                Library.

CU   Columbia University (William Burroughs or
                  Jack Kerouac Collections).
OSU   William S. Burroughs Papers, Ohio State Uni-
                  versity, SPEC.CMS.85.
SU   Grove Press Records, Special Collections,
                  Syracuse University.

Foreword Note

"The section called 'This Horrible Case'": the October 1962
MS refers to "Section VII" and "Section III." The change from
numbering was made on the long galleys, where "section" is
written in and the word "chapter" canceled, so that the book
opens with a history of revision relating to its structure and the
identification of its separate parts. Unlike the first editions of
The Soft Machine (1961) and *The Ticket That Exploded* (1962),
Nova Express was published with a contents list of chapters.
This was probably based on a two-page typescript entitled
"Section Heading And Layout of *Nova Express*" (Berg 36.7),
which Burroughs mailed Barney Rosset in October 1962.
The list included an anomaly in using "Chinese Laundry"
as both a chapter and a section heading. (The same anomaly
also applied to the single-section Chapter 9, which was cut
in the galley stage.) This duplication has been generalized
for each chapter in this edition.

Last Words

LAST WORDS

The stunning opening of *Nova Express* has the richest manuscript
history of any section and contains some of its earliest material.
However, it was not originally intended for the book and had a
curiously tentative relationship to the first draft manuscript that
Burroughs mailed Barney Rosset on March 30, 1962. Writing from

London on that date, Burroughs suggested that "Last Words" be "used as a foreword or preface" (*ROW*, 102), which was how it had been recently published along with two other prefatory texts in *Evergreen Review* 6.22 (January 1962).

Appearing under the title "LAST WORDS OF HASSAN I SABBAH," the *Evergreen* version is textually almost identical and differs mainly in punctuation (using fewer em dashes, more periods, block capitals instead of italics, and lower-case first-person "i"—all characteristic of early drafts).

"Last Words" was therefore a last-minute addition to Burroughs' first draft manuscript and a paratext rather than part of the text proper—just as it had been in *Evergreen Review*, where it precedes and is distinguished from actual "episodes" of his novel. Burroughs had originally sent "Last Words" to Rosset from New York in September 1961 as he began work on *Nova Express*, and gave a brief account of both the circumstances of its original composition and its current purpose, enclosing "the testament of Hassan i Sabbah which came to me under mescaline over a year ago and which I consider to be a final statement of what I am doing in *Naked Lunch* and *The Soft Machine* and the novel now in progress entitled *The Novia Express*. 'Play it all play it all play it all back. For all to see.' I hope you can include this statement in *The Naked Lunch*" (Burroughs to Rosset, September 27, 1961; SU). Since Burroughs had just arrived in New York following a disastrous visit to Timothy Leary, his identification of "Last Words" as mescaline-inspired is almost as revealing as his intention to publish the text in Grove's forthcoming edition of *Naked Lunch*. As Burroughs indicates, its origins go back another year, to spring 1960.

Writing from London, on June 21, 1960, Burroughs mailed an early version to Allen Ginsberg, then in Pucallpa, Peru, in response to his friend's plea for help after taking the drug *yagé* ("write, fast, please"), and the letter published three years later in *The Yage Letters* includes most of the opening and closing lines of "Last Words" as published in *Nova Express* (Burroughs and Ginsberg, *The Yage Letters Redux* [San Francisco: City Lights, 2006], 65). The letter also demonstrates the essential formal feature of Burroughs' text in the many drafts he would compose during mid to late 1960, beginning: "LISTEN TO MY LAST WORDS ANY WORLD" (70). The setting of the text in block capitals, which declares its urgency in visual terms, goes back to the earliest manuscript, dated by Burroughs "May 20, 1960 *Past Time*" (CU; Ginsberg Collection). On this date he wrote to Dave Haselwood that "these LAST WORDS OF HASSAN SABBAH might be used as a Post Script to *The Exterminator*," the pamphlet he was then co-authoring with Brion Gysin (Burroughs to Haselwood, May 20, 1960; The Outsider Magazine Collection, Northwestern University). Before it appeared in *Nova Express*, therefore, "Last Words" had not only appeared complete in one publication (*Evergreen Review*) and partially in another (*The Yage Letters*) but had also been proposed to appear in two others (the Grove Press *Naked Lunch* and *The Exterminator*).

In May 1960 Burroughs had sent a "final version" to Haselwood: "The first version was flaked out here and there so that Mr K came off better than he deserves. I think it is all said now" (Burroughs to Haselwood, May 22, 1960; Auerhahn Press records, Bancroft Library, University of California, Berkeley). Two variant early drafts from 1960 have survived that identify the mysterious "Mr K," who is the clue to a very different "Last Words" than the version published in *Nova Express*. One typescript begins: "AND YOU MR K MR KRUSHEV WHO THOUGHT TO MONOPOLIZE SPACE UNDER THE NAME OF HASSAN SABBAH" (ASU 7). The other draft names the Soviet leader in a context that mixes political, media and business figures, and is indicative of the range of explicit reference that characterized many of Burroughs' early drafts of "Last Words" material, elaborating on the generic phrasing "boards, syndicates, and governments of the earth": "YOU WANT HASSAN SABBAH TO EXPLAIN THAT? TO TIDY THAT UP . . . YOU HAVE THE WRONG NAME AND THE WRONG NUMBER MR LUCE GETTY ROCKEFELLER ANSLINGER KRUSHEV" (Berg 49.1).

Other drafts of "Last Words" include racist and sexist invective, signs of an ugly anti-Semitism and misogyny that went unchecked during Burroughs' early, messianic period. Sometimes, he would edit this out: "Deleted [Ezra] Poundish Anti-Semitism" he told Gysin, referring to similar materials intended for their proposed sequel to *The Exterminator* (Burroughs to Gysin, August 30, 1960; Berg). Other times, he would address it openly, asking, "WHY DO THE JEWS ALWAYS MANOEVER ONE INTO ANTI-SEMITISM?" or seek to transcend it by identifying everyone as a victim of the same anti-human conspiracy: "I HAVE PULLED THE BIG CON HEY RUBE SWITCH. MARKS OF THE WORLD WOMEN JEWS COMMUNISTS ALL ALL ALL. WE HAVE ALL BEEN TAKEN. [. . .] DON'T KILL THE JEWS AND THE WOMEN. RUB OUT THEIR WORDS" (Berg, 48.22).

Although the fit seems perfect—Hassan i Sabbah is invoked far more in *Nova Express* than in *The Soft Machine* or *The Ticket*—the "Last Words" section was therefore drawn from a very large body of alternative, overlapping and expanded drafts composed from mid-1960 onward. Above all, these earlier forms reveal the specifically political investment of Burroughs with the text. The material was also formally distinctive, the text always typed in block capitals, at least until summer 1961 when Burroughs cut up "Last Words" and experimented with variations similar in layout to the spaced lines that would appear in the "Uranian Willy" section (Berg 26.13).

1   "Listen to my last words anywhere": before this line, a post-September 1962 version has: **"You may call Hassan i Sabbah to write for you. You will stay to write for Hassan i Sabbah: Last words of Hassan i Sabbah"** (ASU 7).

2   "Listen: I call you all": before this phrase, one draft headed "THE TESTAMENT OF HASSAN I SABBAH" has: "**'These things take time and that's my business**—' / As usual?" (Berg 12.4).

2   "Play it all play it all play it *all* back": corrects *NEX* 4 ("Play it all pay it all"), which reproduced an error made in the October 1962 MS; all other manuscript witnesses and recorded versions confirm the typographical error.

2   "In Times Square. In Piccadilly": one 1960 typescript has a

variant that changes the order and adds Paris to New York and London: **"IN PICCADILLY IN TIMES SQUARE IN PLACE DE LA CONCORDE"** (Berg 48.22). The Parisian reference also appears in the 1960/61 spoken-word version of "Last Words" recorded by Ian Sommerville, which features on *Nothing Here Now but the Recordings* (1981).

2   "Alien Word '*the*': one draft continues: *"'The' Golden Word of Alien Enemy that exists only where no life is*. [. . .] **I Hassan i Sabbah rub out The Golden Word forever"** (Berg 11.15).

3   "And the words of Hassan i Sabbah as also cancel": what *appears* to be a typographical error occurs in all witnesses from the earliest drafts to final galleys, and in the first, 1961 edition of *The Soft Machine*, where these lines also appear.

3   "writing of Brion Gysin Hassan i Sabbah": one early draft continues with a fragment from *The Tempest*; **"leave not a wrack behind"** (Berg 12.4); while another, much later draft, continues; **"///////////////////////////////"** (Berg 12.8).

3   "September 17, 1899 over New York": the section's final phrase was only inserted onto the galleys in July 1964, at which time it was also added onto the last page of the book. The date and place recur across a mass of short texts in the mid-1960s, some clarifying that what was being recycled were fragments from the front page of the September 17, 1899 *New York Times*. The page itself, copies of which Burroughs asked Richard Seaver to send him in October 1963, is unremarkable except for a reference to "the Bradley-Martins."

PRISONERS, COME OUT

As for "Last Words," Burroughs asked Barney Rosset to add this section to the March 1962 manuscript of *Nova Express* as part of a "preface." The section was clearly written later than "Last Words," and its central warning against hallucinogens echoes in tone and substance Burroughs' May 6, 1961 letter to Timothy Leary describing recent bad trips on DMT: "I would like to sound a word of urgent warning with regard to the hallucinogen drugs with special reference to Dimethyl-tryptamine" (*ROW*, 73). The section was most likely composed in September 1961, in the wake of Burroughs' acrimonious split with Leary that month, when he also delivered a paper to the American Psychological Symposium promoting nonchemical alternatives to drugs such as DMT. Burroughs told Ginsberg the section "expressed quite clearly" what he thought "about Leary and his project" (*ROW*, 98). Compounding Burroughs' antipathy was Leary's indirect connection to Henry Luce and his wife Clare Boothe Luce, whose enthusiasm for LSD was reflected in the drug's remarkably extensive and positive coverage in *Time* and *Life*.

The section appeared in *Evergreen* in January 1962 with only minor differences under its original title: "OPEN LETTER TO MY CONSTITUENTS AND CO-WORKERS IF ANY REMAIN FOR THE END OF IT."

3   "And *love love love* in slop buckets": one draft, titled like the version in *Evergreen Review*, has an alternative line: **"Sacred mushrooms and mescaline for the asking. And something better than that. Hash and junk in one shot"** (Berg 11.15).

3   "and history is fiction": several typescripts add **"—toute ca c'est invention—"** (Berg 11.15, ASU 7), anticipating the phrase, used correctly, in "A Distant Thank You."

3   "Bring together state of news—Inquire onward from state to doer": the surprising textual origins of this opening line of Inspector Lee's address on behalf of Hassan i Sabbah, which had previously appeared in *The Exterminator* along with other parts of this passage, are revealed in a draft typescript: **"I swear by the night and all that it brings together / that you shall march onwards from state to state / if an evil doer brings you a piece of news inquire first into its truth"** (Berg 58.28). Reference is to Book 49 *Al-Hujurat* ("The Chambers") and Book 84 *Inshiqaq* ("The Rending") of *The Koran*.

4   *"Naked Lunch* and *The Soft Machine"*: corrects *NEX* 6 ("and *Soft Machine"*). Due to a change made by the copyeditor in the final long galleys (OSU 5.12), the 1964 edition introduced a confusion in the titles of Burroughs' books by dropping the definite article in order to impose an incorrect consistency.

4   *"hallucinogen drugs"*: in a sign of how new the term was, the copyeditor notes **"check spelling"** besides **"hallucigen,"** which was how Burroughs spelled the word on his typescript (OSU 4.10) and how it appeared in *Evergreen Review.*

4   "blow the place up behind them": closing speech marks have been added here, and cut before "And what does my program," undoing changes made by the copyeditor in keeping with manuscripts (OSU 4.9, ASU 7) and *Evergreen Review.*

5   "I order total resistance directed against The Nova Conspiracy and all those engaged in it": an early draft (no date, but not later than early 1962) has the most substantive variant on these and following lines: **"I order total resistance to The Novia Conspiracy. Rub out their words and images forever.**

   A narcotics agent infiltrated the beatniks by writing bad poetry. WE are not bad writers but our purpose is ultimately the same: to expose and arrest Novia Criminals. In *The Naked Lunch, The Soft Machine* and *The Novia Express* i have shown who they are and what they are doing and what they will do if they are not arrested. These books were written to expose and arrest criminals. Minutes to go. This is war to extermination" (ASU 7).

5   "engaged in it": closing speech marks have been added here, and cut from before "The purpose" and from around "Signed . . . Police," in keeping with both manuscripts (OSU 4.9, ASU 7) and *Evergreen Review.*

5   "prisoners of the earth to *come out*": the "to" is not in any manuscript witnesses or *Evergreen Review* but the apparent error was allowed to stand in the galleys.

5   "(Signed)": one typescript and *Evergreen Review* have: **"Signed The Regulator Interstellar Board of Health"** (Berg 11.18). The original made more sense of what follows in the text, which is "Post Script Of The Regulator," while the use of the term "Post Script" and the signature confirm the original titling of "Prisoner, Come Out" as an "OPEN LETTER."

6   "Apomorphine is made from morphine": underscoring the centrality of the drug to his book, the note was an addition Burroughs made in October 1963.

PRY YOURSELF LOOSE AND LISTEN

This section appeared in neither the March or October 1962 manuscripts, but was composed in spring 1963 (note its reference to *Newsweek* March 4, 1963). That it was added to the manuscript at this time—as a five-page typescript on legal-sized paper (ASU 4.3 and OSU 4.9)—can be inferred from Burroughs' letter to Rosset of March 15: "Enclose another chapter for *Nova Express*. This chapter to be inserted immediately after 'Prisoners, Come Out'. I think it makes the following section ('Pack Your Ermines, Mary') considerably clearer" (*ROW*, 120). The section was published incomplete (ending "You have to move fast on this job"), with minor differences, in *Gnaoua* 1 (Spring 1964). Brilliantly capturing its terrific vitriol, Burroughs' live recording of the section is one of the standout tracks on *The Best of William Burroughs* (1998).

6   "We were on the nod": the first draft of this line is both more and less precise astronomically: **"We were on the nod in Uranus after a rumble in a remote galaxy"** (Berg 15.46).

6   "theatre [. . .] theatre": corrects *NEX* 8 ("theater"). Although on the galleys (OSU 5.11) Burroughs specifically asked to

respect his choice of British spelling, the copyeditor pre-
ferred the American spelling for "theatre" and "amphitheatre." Burroughs wrote to Seaver: "As I have noted on your
letter 'grey' 'theatre' should remain English" (October 24,
1963; SU). The one instance of "gray" (in *NEX* 115) has
been corrected to "grey" for this edition (p. 121).

8   "The Intolerable Kid and your reporter": the first draft continues: **"He's a great guy is I&I or at least he's big—
But Jesus Christ I hate him—Everyone does that of
course being his profession—"** (Berg 15.46).

8   "And I&I is fast": heavily canceled on the typescripts is
the original name before "I&I" was inserted; **"Percussion
Paul"** (OSU 4.9, ASU 4.3).

11   "split this whistle stop wide open tomorrow": one long early
draft continues: **"And he rips into action—I mean he
jumps right onto board and they are in a car three
hundred miles an hour across solid ice—The Board
Director at the wheel with the Kid clamped on him
shoving his foot right down to the floor—'All right
you board gooks—You called me—You want action—
I'll by God show you action—faster! Faster! Faster!
Faster and uglier'—And The Board is shitting and
pissing themselves as they begin to see just who they
have called and just how much of a shit he cares what
happens to them in the blow up—The whole fucking
machine in a long fast skid for nova—** [. . .]

**"And I had to laugh till I pissed seeing those two-
bit welching board bastards getting the nigger gook
errand boy routine back with compound interest—
Then I dig The Kid is wising up the marks and I say
'What's with you? You wig already?'**

**"He just looks at me and says—'Maybe I got a new
angle—Sheets are empty many years.'**

**"'Well,' I says, 'It's about time—The old angle is
worn down to a white dwarf.'"** (Berg 37.15).

So Pack Your Ermines

SO PACK YOUR ERMINES

Titled "The Carbonic Caper" in all drafts until Burroughs retyped it for the October 1962 MS, this section was written shortly before he mailed Rosset the March 1962 MS. On March 15 he refers to "a section I had just written entitled The Carbonic Caper" in the course of explaining to Jack Kerouac how he had folded in this material together with the closing lines of *The Subterraneans* to form the penultimate section of *Nova Express*, "Melted Into Air" (Burroughs to Kerouac, March 15, 1962; CU, Kerouac Collection). Earlier drafts show a large number of very minor revisions, indicating the care Burroughs took to revise small details: e.g., the Carbonic Kid "is turning purple" and "screams" in first draft (OSU 2.2), but "is turning blue" and "yells" in second draft (OSU.4.9), which is near verbatim the final text.

15   "I was traveling with Limestone John": early drafts (Berg 15.56, OSU 2.2) lack the opening lines and begin here.

15   "It worked like this::": restores the double colon that Burroughs indicated on the October 1962 MS, only one of which was not canceled by the copyeditor (after "special purpose"; *NEX* 100, p. 105 here); thirteen other double colons have been restored throughout the text.

NABORHOOD IN AQUALUNGS

A cut-up of the previous section, "So Pack Your Ermines," and the following section, "The Fish Poison Con," this section was almost certainly written at the same time (March 1962) and as a second part of what was then titled "The Carbonic Caper." The earliest version (OSU 2.2), a rough 4-page typescript, lacks the final 30 words and has about 360 more, almost half of which were canceled on the manuscript. Cut-up variants in this draft include permutations such as "Then he was an American fascist with old Surrealist lark." Although the section is at first frustrating, its beautifully judged recycling and recombination of phrase fragments makes it one of the most evocative on repeat readings.

THE FISH POISON CON

The earliest complete manuscript of this section is a 6-page type-script using this title and identified by Burroughs (possibly for Barney Rosset but much more likely in late 1961 for the benefit of the manuscript dealer Henry Wenning) as "1st draft" of "Chapter 12" (OSU 2.4). The section was therefore moved from the second half of the March 1962 MS toward the beginning of the October 1962 MS. This typescript lacks about 100 words and has just over 100 more, and differs in phrasing and punctuation, including having far fewer capitalizations (e.g., for phrases like "Old Sow Got Caught In The Fence"). There is also a "2nd draft" which shows only minor differences from the published version, principally an even more extensive use of lower case first-person "i" than in the first draft. The section was published in *Evergreen Review* 7.29 (March 1963) almost verbatim except for one significant differ-ence: the text continues with the second half of "No Good—No Bueno" (from "I spit blood" onward). Burroughs recorded most of the section for his 1965 album *Call Me Burroughs*.

21   "checking store attendants for larceny": the first draft con-tinues: **"and a rattier crew never went on tour"** (OSU 2.4).

21   "Bob Schafer": in first draft the name is spelled alternately **"Schrmersrr"** and **"Shremser"** and he is **"a frustrated Fascist and Roosevelt hater"** (OSU 2.4). In late 1942 Burroughs really did travel through Iowa with Merit Inc., or more precisely Merit Protective Services of Chicago, while working as a fraud investigator together with Robert J. "Bob" Schremser.

22   "White Hot Agony Act": in first draft: **"And The Sailor could go into this Agony Act and change form like**

a horse picture and chase the doctor around his office with strange metal snarls and heat himself white hot while he gave off this smell of blowtorches and ozone" (OSU 2.4).

23   "The Caustic Enzymes of Woo": a certain obscurity and incompleteness is one of the essential features of the cut-up mythology, but archival typescripts reveal that Burroughs worked out more than shows, as is the case here: **"The Children Of Wu: The Pain Planet which runs on Theta waves"** (Berg 40.4).

23   "the drugstores was closing": the typesetter of the October 1962 MS corrected the plural to singular ("drugstore" in *NEX* 24), but Burroughs' use of idiomatic expression is confirmed by his spoken-word recording of the section.

23   "pool halls and chili": echoing a line in *Naked Lunch*, the first draft continues: **"Out of junk in East St Louis and i was traveling with Irene Kelly and her was sporting woman and we ~~hit the sex charge and~~ made it five times arc lights flickering ~~over our mineral copulations~~"** (OSU 2.4).

24   "Lip Reading": in first draft this is related to what a canceled line refers to as **"host hopping"** (OSU 2.4).

24   "Cool heavy eyes": the first draft features a pun here: **"The cool ~~financier~~ finance seer eyes"** (OSU 2.4).

26   "Meester William was death": the first draft has: **"Meester William was ~~The Cuban~~ death disguised as any other person—And then I saw Meester William in a hotel room ~~wanted me to go to bed with him and I wouldn't because~~ tried to reach him with the knife and he said: 'If you kill me who will pilot this ship?'"** (OSU 2.4).

26   "transparent sheets": the first draft continues: **"~~like glass but thin and easy to move~~—And in Paris i saw this painter who ~~used to run a night club in Tangier~~ was painting on these sheets pictures in the air"** (OSU 2.4).

NO GOOD—NO BUENO

Manuscript evidence, as well as their appearance together in *Evergreen Review* 7.29 (March 1963), confirms that this section was written as a continuation of "The Fish Poison Con." Burroughs made a small number of minor revisions directly onto his manuscript, such as changing "wheeling vultures" to "sliding vultures" and "a bottle of aguardiente" to "a bottle of pisco," while revising lowercase first-person "i" to upper case (OSU 2.4). Three-quarters of the section comes from *The Soft Machine*, the majority deriving from the "white score" section near the end of the 1961 edition (retitled "Dead on Arrival" and moved to the opening of both later editions).

27   "smell of dust": the October 1962 MS continues: "**—must be love—Must be love.**"

28   "Mr. Bradly Mr. Martin": a recurrent figure across the trilogy, embodying principles of dualism and conflict, he has a particular meaning in the context of *Nova Express*, clarifying why Burroughs so often refers in manuscripts and related texts to C.S. Lewis, author of his own "Space Trilogy." In an early draft of his 1963 text "The Beginning Is Also The End," Burroughs has Bradly Martin declare: "**I've been called everything in the book. Mr C.S. Lewis refers to me as The Bent One**" (Berg, 16.1).

28   "looking at something I couldn't see": the first draft continues with the line: "**but it must have been what makes maricas**" (i.e., homosexuals) (OSU 2.4).

29   "the thing I couldn't see": the first draft continues with a canceled line: "**worse than hunger and mist and The Civil Guard**" (OSU 2.4).

SHIFT COORDINATE POINTS

This section was titled "Pinball Led Street" up to and including the October 1962 MS, where the old title was canceled and the new one written in by Burroughs. Identifying a "1ˢᵗ draft" version as "Chapter 18" (OSU 2.2), he moved it from near the end of the March 1962 MS toward the beginning of the October 1962 MS; the result of this restructuring is that "Shift Coordinate Points" came to precede "Coordinate Points," which appeared near the start of the March 1962 MS. Although Burroughs identified this as "1st draft" (for the benefit of Wenning in late 1961), an earlier version exists (Berg 4.35), which reveals significant variant material.

29   "K9 was in combat": the earliest draft has two substantially different variants of the opening paragraphs, the longer of which begins: **"Pin ball led street with elect of doorway—Shift lingual—Vibrate tourists—free doorways—Word falling—Photo falling—Break through in grey Room—**

As soon as the hash hit K9 was in combat with the Novia Guard—Thinking metal armed with electromagnetic claws feeling for the virus punch cards twisting pulling him into vertiginous spins feeling the full weight of the alien mind screen's crushing mineral hate for mammalian life—'Back—Stay out of those claws—Shift lingual—Shift word patterns—Cut Word lines—Shift coordinate points—'" (Berg 4.35). Also starting "As soon as the hash hit," the other version continues: **"K9 moved in occupying the enemy mind screen taking over view points and right centers and ego positions—Feeling the full weight and evil of the alien screen the crushing mineral hate for mammalian life forms—The novia guards—He was all the way in now the guard weaker his claws fading in smoke—"**

30   "So many and sooo—": the first draft continues with a paragraph canceled on the October 1962 MS: **"Intersected in The Dark Guards—A machine with cool silver blew purple iodine and red nitrous fumes down corridors of that hospital to musical clock hands—Blue fashion plates faded opposite mirrors and hovered out—He**

walked through air hammers of coal gas and dust—"
(OSU 2.2).

31   "Doc Benway and me": the earliest draft has **"Me and The
Sailor,"** and it is the Sailor who sells the aphrodisiac and
has the idea for a green fix (Berg 4.35).

33   "At this point in our researches": on the first draft the last
word is canceled and Burroughs inserted the phrase **"Research Project"** (OSU 2.2). The earliest draft has longer
final lines: **"At this point in our researches we had
a spot of bother with the biologic intersected The
Nova Police—And furthermore the metal junkies
were radioactive and subject to go up any place if two
of them came together—So they lived in continual
fear and hatred of each other and continual gang
warfare—"** (Berg 4.35).

Chinese Laundry

CHINESE LAUNDRY

Despite its length, this has one of the lightest archival histories
of any section: five pages of early drafts in three Berg Collection
folders and the full six-page typescript in the October 1962 MS.
This is because "Chinese Laundry," together with the next section, "Inflexible Authority," almost certainly comprise the "ten
pages of new material" referred to by Burroughs when sending
Rosset his manuscript in October 1962 (*ROW*, 115). (Although
the detail is not given in the published version, the archival
original of Burroughs' letter specifies that these "ten pages" are
to replace existing pages 20–29 in the manuscript—where "Chinese Laundry" and "Inflexible Authority" are paginated 20–29
[Berg 75.1].) There is no evidence to clarify what the original ten
pages were that Burroughs cut, although they probably included
Chapter VII, "Pure Song of New Before the Traveller" (a title
derived from Rimbaud's poem "Genie"), published in *Evergreen*

Review in January 1962. The October 1962 MS is near verbatim and, with its spelling of "nova" rather than "novia," dates from after September that year.

35   "The Lazarus Pharmaceutical Company": Lazarus Pharmaceuticals was just one of many satirical business names Burroughs invented at this time, and in one typescript it is listed among others playing on phrases from *Nova Express*: **"Focus Uranium Limited Shitola, Trak Tell and Tell, Martin Air Lines, Cobra Copper Kansas A.J., National Towers, OPEN FIRE—Keystone Concrete, Martin Chain, Lazarus Pharmaceuticals—Bell and Trak— Strafe pound blast, tilt Lynch Gass&Light—Vampire shares sagged sluggishly [. . .] Transvestite Airlines, Chemical Corn, Kali Polaroid, Bradly Bronze, Death Dwarf Packing, Ward Fruit, Burroughs B&M [. . .] General Fidelity of Minraud"** (Berg 36.11). Other variations include specific military references, such as **"Polaris missile for searing white blast—Hiroshima Optics, Nagasaki Pit & Forge"** (Berg 36.11). One page referring to **"Standard and Poor's Index"** has the phrase **"Crazy new highs for 1962"** (36.11), while another mixes in *Nova Express* phrases to declare a stock market crash: **"Dow Jones Average explodes—paper moon—Gongs of violence and how"** (36.10). In May 1962, Wall Street was indeed hit by a "flash crash," in which companies such as IBM lost over 5% of their share value in less than twenty minutes. Burroughs' cut-up crash—which probably followed rather than preceded the "real thing"—also features in Anthony Balch's 1963 film *Towers Open Fire*, where he intones instructions to sell stock in a list of companies from Mayan Cosmetics to Lazarus Pharmaceuticals over archival newsreel of the 1929 Wall Street Crash (and the front page of the London *Evening Standard*, reporting another crash in late 1962 alongside coverage of the John Vassall spy case).

INFLEXIBLE AUTHORITY

Like "Chinese Laundry," this section was written shortly before completion of the October 1962 MS. There is also a two-page early draft of the opening half, which has a few minor variants (Berg 5.5).

43   "The District Supervisor": on an early draft he is identified as **"the Inspector"** (Berg 5.5).

44   "The police patrol pounded into the": the early draft continues: **"virus machine headquarters in America England Switzerland and France—"** (Berg 5.5).

45   "This, gentlemen, is a death dwarf": a related typescript defines the death dwarf as **"a synthetic organism"** and **"a parasitic creature"** (Berg 6.3), while another expands on its role as an antihuman instrument radio-controlled from enemy installations, including **"Life Time Fortune Headquarters NYC—There is also an encephalographic center in Wisconsin—No doubt others exist—But if these could be taken over and the equipment used to confuse and destroy enemy broadcast the whole conspiracy would collapse—because the Death Dwarf is only a transmitter"** (Berg 49.31).

45   "My Power's coming": on the early draft the death dwarf turns into **"a Negro faith healer"** who spits at **"the young agent"** rather than at Uranian Willy (Berg 5.5).

47   "Jimmy Sheffields is": corrects *NEX* 47 ("Jimmy Sheffield is"), an error introduced by the copyeditor on the galleys (OSU 5.12). "Jim Sheffield" is a character in Henry Kuttner's novel *Fury*, cited in *The Ticket That Exploded*.

COORDINATE POINTS

This long section is one of the most heavily redrafted of all and underwent several revisions of title: "THE NOVIA POLICE" (OSU 2.3); "The Biologic Police and Courts" (OSU 2.4); "THE BIO-LOGIC POLICE" (Berg 36.3), until Burroughs wrote "Coordinate

Points" onto his October 1962 MS. The very first time Burroughs refers to writing *Nova Express*, in an August 7, 1961 letter to Gysin, he would allude to this material, sending a photograph "to illustrate chapter on The Novia Police" (*ROW*, 83).

Early drafts make the material more explicit as a lecture address and include several passages discussing in detail the concept of criminality. Some of these drafts were clearly written early in the history of the *Nova Express* manuscript: one draft includes the early variant spelling "novae criminals" and "novae mob" (Berg 11.28); another uses the term "Novia Guard," rather than "Mob" (OSU 2.4). Burroughs identified the "1st draft" six-page typescript, titled "THE NOVIA POLICE," as "Chapter II" of his March 1962 manuscript (OSU 2.3). Complicating this history is an early, five-page typescript entitled "The Biologic Police and Courts," which Burroughs identified as "Chapter 14" (OSU 2.4). This typescript begins with a version of material that appears almost halfway into the section as published and then continues with most of "This Horrible Case," suggesting that these two sections were originally joined.

Central to most drafts is the subsection "PLAN DRUG ADDIC-TION." An autograph note by Burroughs written onto the OSU 2.3 typescript identifies this page as an "original cut up made in 1959 before Novia Express was started or conceived"; the manuscript page is near verbatim compared to the published text, the main difference being the absence of em dashes and the use instead of three- or four-dot ellipses. This was one of Burroughs' earliest cut-up texts and one he would return to over time in different ways, from making a collage with this title in 1965 that cut up almost the entire page from the Grove edition of *Nova Express*, to reproducing the text in the British edition of *The Soft Machine* (1968) and in several magazines including *Mayfair* (August 1969).

Burroughs' fondness for the whole section is evident in how extensively he reworked drafts of it and from his inclusion of an expanded section in *The Ticket That Exploded* ("the nova police") that includes almost a thousand words of "Coordinate Points" verbatim.

He expressed his feelings in a letter to Alan Ansen in early 1963: "Did you like the nova police in *Ticket*?—I endeavoured to distil an archetype of the perfect police officer in Inspector Lee and find that the part has taken over to an extent where some of my old connections have been alienated—Well it's all show business what?" Burroughs signed his letter "Bill B / Inspector J Lee / Nova Police" (Burroughs to Ansen, January 23, 1963; ASU).

51   "The case I have just related": this opening sentence appears as an overtype onto the October 1962 MS, and was clearly added by Burroughs to integrate the preceding two sections after they were included in this manuscript.

51   "I doubt if any of you": the rest of this line was revised in almost every draft: **"have ever seen a criminal"** (Berg 11.4); **"have ever really seen a criminal"** (Berg 11.40); **"have ever seen a criminal for what they are"** (ASU 7). The most substantial variant of this paragraph, a one-page carbon, is probably the earliest: **"I am sure none of you have ever seen a police man before and many of you retain romantic concepts of 'The Criminal' [. . .] A criminal is quite simply some one who will do anything for money—Throw acid in a baby's face? Straightaway if the price is right? You got it? Servants scheduled for 'Total Disposal' no matter what they were promised—Now you understand something about the structure of the enemy and the servants it employs—The enemy has no feeling and conceives feeling in others as a weakness to be exploited—By any means—"** (Berg 12.10). Another early variant begins: **"Ladies and gentlemen may I have your attention please—I am Inspector J Lee of the Novae Police— boo booo—Exactly—Now I doubt if any of you on this copy planet have ever seen a novae criminal"** (Berg 11.28).

51   "Apomorphine": one typescript develops the role of apomorphine further and continues with a discussion of criminality

that includes an unusual autobiographical reference: **"Of course morphine is only one police problem and a minor one at this intersection point. Morphine alone never exploded a planet. Certain of the hallucinogen drugs Venusian imports can explode the planet. The control of these drugs is now a more pressing problem. Apomorphine is the key to all drug control. Now let us look at ordinary criminals a moment. They are important as tools used by the Novia mob. What is a thief? Someone who confiscates property of doubtful ownership as all property is on this planet. No. A thief is someone who takes from you what is yours. I quote a Texas sheriff Robert Vail Ennis on the subject of theft. 'It's no good taking from a man what he makes honest'"** (Berg 11.24). Sherriff Ennis arrested Burroughs in 1948: see Rob Johnson's *The Lost Years of William S. Burroughs: Beats in South Texas* (Texas A&M, 2006). The similar passage on the March 1962 MS concludes its definition of a thief with an allusion to Henry Luce's magazine empire: **"They monopolize life time and fortune. They take sex and love dream and function from you so that you will buy it back at house odds"** (OSU 2.3).

52   "First they create a narcotic problem": in one typescript: **"First they import morphine from Uranus"** (ASU 7).

52   "PLAN DRUG ADDICTION": Burroughs' manuscript page identified as the **"original cut up made in 1959"** (OSU 2.3) has a few unused words in the opening paragraph (**"Protect the disease from its crime"**) and in the penultimate paragraph (**"only sick people understand that menace [. . .] direct dreaming of Narcotics Commissioner"**).

54   "remain in present time form": one very early draft continues with an illustration of stupid life forms, and concludes: **"The Novia Guard has turned loose on the world the terrible weapon of mass stupidity"** (OSU 2.4).

55   "'Iron Claws'": the clue to the identity of this member of
the Nova Mob is given in "Simple as a Hiccup," where the
phrase occurs followed by a reference to the drug dimethyltryptamine. In "Overdose of Synthesized Prestonia," a
typescript enclosed in a letter to Gysin, Burroughs refers to
**"Souls torn into insect fragments by the Iron Claws
of chess masters—Who Synthesized Dim-N"** (Burroughs to Gysin, April 27, 1961; Berg 85.4). A separate
text, which calls DMT **"the oven drug,"** refers to using
it in experiments on prisoners prior to their being hung:
**"The technician who performed the experiments is
known as Iron Claws—(Actually he has no hands as
result of a birth injury—He exists in a speed up film
and was himself an experiment in film technique)"**
(Berg 16.32). DMT-inspired imagery appears directly in
Nova Express, for example in "Chinese Laundry," where
the sensation of "white hot bees swarming in the body" is
taken from an April 1961 letter describing Prestonia, the
"nightmare hallucinogen" (*ROW*, 70).

56   "casualties and fuck ups": one early draft has an alternative illustration: **"As a result the agent was captured
by The Novia Mob and barely escaped death in their
ovens. However we were able to turn this goof to
our advantage since the enemy is basically a stupid
organism like all criminals and never more stupid
than when they think they are being clever. [. . .] You
can hear the prisoners screaming two galaxies away.
Such noise. Such people"** (Berg 11.6).

57   "the criminal escapes to other coordinates": a very early
typescript continues: **"Now a word about Madame D
herself—We have never been able to touch her—~~In
fact she may not be Madame D~~ Unlike other members
of the mob she is without vices, can occupy ~~immer-
able~~ any coordinate points, and ~~there is no way~~ it is
difficult to follow her colorless trail—"** (Berg 11.47).

58   "Get that writer": Burroughs wrote several different versions
      of this paragraph, including: **"Get that writer—He is too
      close—Bribe him—Scare him with the ovens—Give
      him the orgasm drug—"** (Berg 11.22).

59   "contacted our Tangier agent": one typescript continues:
      **"Shuddering from The Ovens he asked for biologic
      transfer in any direction. He volunteered for any as-
      signment he cared to name. He gave us all the infor-
      mation he had which was considerable. After a short
      training period he was absorbed into the department.
      As it turned out this was not in all respects a fortunate
      decision. Willy had an uncontrollable temper and no
      patience. He immediately aroused the local partisans,
      seized an enemy installation, set up TOWERS and
      opened fire armed only with a transistor radio and
      a few photo collages. The resulting melee narrowly
      skirted total disaster"** (Berg 11.27).

URANIAN WILLY

Under its former title, "THE NOVIA EXPRESS," this was the first
section Burroughs wrote, and he identified the original three-page
typescript as "Chapter I 1st Version" of his March 1962 MS (OSU
2.3). Writing from Tangier, Burroughs quotes from this section when
describing his new novel for the first time to Gysin: "Describes
military action against imaginary invader: 'Area mined—Guards
everywhere—can't quite get through'" (Burroughs to Gysin, August
18, 1961; Berg 85.5).

     Parts would appear in two little magazines: "One Chapter from
The Novia Express" in *The Second Coming* 1.3 (March 1962), a
short-lived avant-garde magazine from New York, and "Novia
Express" in *Rhinozeros* 6 (July 1962), a German magazine that
made striking use of typography and to which Burroughs made
several contributions. Using one passage from near the beginning and another from the end of the section published in *Nova*

Express, nearly a third of "Uranian Willy" appears in *Rhinozeros* with very few differences. The case of *The Second Coming* is more complicated: its "One Chapter" turns out to be Chapter One of Burroughs' manuscript combined with a version of its then Chapter Three ("Towers Open Fire"; see below); a line divides the two parts. Comparing the magazine version with Burroughs' archival typescripts, it is clear how he progressively edited down his material: the earliest source (OSU 2.3) has almost 250 words more than "Uranian Willy" in *Nova Express*; the *Second Coming* version restructured the entire section and cut nearly 150 words of this extra material; the final typescript, on which Burroughs canceled the original title and wrote in "Uranian Willy" (OSU 4.9), cut a further 50 words. Comparing the first manuscript with the published text clarifies the extent of Burroughs' redrafting: sixteen separate cuts, six substitutions of single words, seven small inserts, seven punctuation changes that made one sentence out of two and seven structural relocations. Under the same title Burroughs used much of this section in *The Soft Machine* (1966 and 1968 editions).

59   "Uranian Willy The Heavy Metal Kid": both the March 1962 MS and *Second Coming* begin with a preceding first line: **"His larval flesh shuddering from The Ovens Of Minraud, metal scars on his face cross the wounded galaxies he was wanted for Novia in three solar systems:"** (OSU 2.3).

59   "chance on a crash out": both the March 1962 MS and *Second Coming* continue: **"He would not be falling for any more sweet Venusian con. A heavy narcotic effluvia they spin from green disk mouths. Cruel idiot smiles. Camp followers of The Green Octopus. The colorless vampire creatures from a land of grass without mirrors. From the sewage deltas of Venus. He had been there prisoner for forty years. The memory sickened his flesh"** (OSU 2.3).

59   "One hope left in the universe: Plan D": the March 1962 MS, which refers to Plan D elsewhere, has here: **"ESCAPE"** (OSU 2.3).

60   "THIS IS WAR TO EXTERMINATION": although not part of a draft for *Nova Express*, a two-page typescript overlaps this section precisely and continues with references to a key concept in Scientology that Burroughs would edit out: **"The planet earth has been invaded—This is war to extermination—The entire planet is infected by virus weapons of the enemy—The enemy is in you controlling thought feeling and *apparent* sensory impressions—Fight cell by cell through bodies and mind screens of the earth [...] Who and what is the enemy?—Even told with symbols it sickens—They are known as Thetans—They run on Theta brain waves which are the brain waves of pain and deprivation— They eat pain—Your pain—Organism is precisely anti- human—it is also completely parasitic"** (Berg 15.51).

60   "Life-Time-Fortune": present in the *Second Coming* version, this is one of the few phrases not in the earlier manuscript (OSU 2.3).

60   "Release Silence Virus—": the March 1962 MS continues with two more paragraphs, which did not appear in *Second Coming*: **"He switched off the screen and listened to a brief technical report on Bone Writing. Control gimmick of The Limestone God. Venusian Virus oc- cupying the spinal column.**

Uranian Willy picked up his old grey hat and cursed for the Nth time his body prison. A little present from The Venusians. 'Stupid assed, three dimensional people. A body yet!'" (OSU 2.3).

61   "mirror streets and shadow pools": the March 1962 MS con- tinues: **"Old photo crinkling cracking—'Far shudder of space shaking an iron tree'"** (OSU 2.3). Burroughs

here quotes from Canto VI of St.-John Perse's *Anabasis* in the T.S. Eliot translation.

WILL HOLLYWOOD NEVER LEARN?

The section goes back to 1960 in recycling several phrases from *Minutes to Go*, including the one that gives the section its title, and it was almost certainly part of the March 1962 MS. The earliest draft (Berg 36.3) is much shorter and reveals how extensively Burroughs moved material around within the section. His restructuring is further shown in a heavily annotated three-page typescript (OSU 3.5), which also has numerous variant and unused lines. The final typescript (OSU 4.9) includes a longer title which Burroughs canceled: "WILL HOLLYWOOD NEVER LEARN?—~~UNIMAGINABLE DISASTER~~."

63   "liquidated the Commissar": an early draft has the extra line, canceled: **"But you can't hang me—I'm the Home Secretary"** (OSU 3.5). Variations on this theme in other typescripts include one with a pointed political allusion: **"ZUT ALORS I SAID ELIMINATE LES ALGERIENS PAS LES ALSATIANS"** (Berg 48.22).

64   "blats of Morse Code": corrects *NEX* 63 ("blasts"): the *apparent* error was corrected by the copyeditor on the final typescript, but OSU 3.5 confirms that, as elsewhere (p. 85; *NEX* 82), this is not a typo for "blasts." One instance, "color blats" (p. 100), was not corrected in the galleys and remained in the 1964 edition (*NEX* 95).

64   "speed-up movie": the early typescript continues: **"Enemy advance we retreat—Move back what?—Shadow mirrors and doorways—"** (OSU 3.5). In this unused line, Burroughs cites part of Mao's "sixteen character" formula of guerrilla war tactics ("Enemy advance we retreat"), which he used in other texts, including *The Ticket That Exploded*.

66   "Calling partisans of all nation": corrects *NEX* 65 ("nations"), restoring an *apparent* error that was corrected by the copyeditor on the October 1962 MS; other manuscripts

confirm that the ungrammatical singular was sometimes intentional, and other instances here (pp. 68, 94, 175) have been uncorrected when supported by manuscript witnesses. The phrase is decisively associated with *Nova Express* and in one related page is followed by "**Enfants de la Patrie,**" from "La Marseillaise" (Berg 36.8).

66   "Room— . —": corrects *NEX* 65 ("— — — . —"); the Morse code (which only appears on OSU 4.9) spells out "Word falling photo falling," but Burroughs appears to have first typed the letter "K" ("— . —"), which was misread by the typesetter, who incorporated the double dash he typed after "Room." Burroughs twice refers to learning Morse code in letters to Gysin (May 16, 1960 and February 20, 1962; *ROW*, 28, 99).

TOWERS OPEN FIRE

One of the earliest sections written for *Nova Express*, "Towers Open Fire" was identified by Burroughs as "Chapter III" of the March 1962 MS. He quotes several lines, including one of the most recurrent phrases in early drafts ("Bleep Blop Splat"), in a letter from early September 1961, the night after watching the film *Hiroshima Mon Amour* with Timothy Leary (Burroughs to Gysin, nd; Berg 85.5). The section was partially published in *Evergreen Review* (January 1962) and in *The Second Coming* magazine, although in different forms: *Evergreen* published what Burroughs identified as "Ch III abbreviated version," a one-page redacted typescript (OSU 2.3) that includes a variant final paragraph; in *The Second Coming*, the whole section appeared, almost verbatim, but as the second half of "Chapter One," following what would become the "Uranian Willy" section. Two very similar four-page typescripts (Berg 12.7 and a later draft, OSU 2.3) are substantially longer and include variant passages.

66   "Lens googles": an *apparent* error for "goggles," but confirmed in all manuscript witnesses.

67   "Coordinates 8 2 7 6": these "coordinates" would recur in numerous texts; that they add up to Burroughs' special number, 23, is not coincidental.

67   "Operation Total Disposal": in one quite early draft, K9 has an extra piece of equipment: **"Pilot K9 examined the bottles with his eye torch—"** (ASU 7).

68   *"Return to base immediately"*: a late draft continues with a variant paragraph that again uses Mao's guerrilla formula (see "Will Hollywood Never Learn?"), concluding: **"All pilots—Stay away from that Time Flak—Return to base—Enemy advance we retreat—Return to base"** (OSU 2.3).

68   "The Technician mixed": the one-page "abbreviated version" has an alternative final paragraph discussing military tactics, which appears near verbatim in *Evergreen Review*: **"This operation destroyed enemy installations in the area of Gothenburg. And served a useful purpose in alerting the partisans and organizing partisan activity. However, the risks involved in such total attack was considered disproportionate to the gains realized. Remember that total war is precisely what we have been called in to prevent. Willy was sharply reprimanded in The School of Total Responsibility and transferred to paper work in another area—Fadeout—"** (OSU 2.3).

69   *"Towers, open fire—"*: the four-page draft (OSU 2.3) continues with more text and with an unevenly spaced layout variation: **"A tidal wave of defectors pouring in. And a cry from those trapped behind enemy lines—'For God's sake come and get them'**

  Ground forces moving in—Shift cut tangle word lines—Dismantle Time Machine—Bleep Blop Bleep—Death to the guards—Prisoners of the earth come out—

TOWERS OPEN FIRE
Coordinates Bleep bleep death to the Vampire air hammers
Bleep 8 2 7 6   stutter   FIRE guards Bleeeeeeep
On Board books TOWERS OPEN FIRE Light flak
Tourists— bloop cut bleeeeeepp   Vibrate
FIRE Vibrate   shift   FIRE
FIRE   Death dwarfs—   tangle FIRE Bloop spuut
    Stab cut   Bleeeep Death to The   BLeeeeeep
    Pound shift TOWERS OPEN FIRE Novia Guard FIRE
Flicker   blast tangle   cut word lines
        stab light blasts shift Photo falling
word falling   in Grey Room   Taken
    Break through   Board Books Blue
    Word   Break   Taken Movies
    Falling   through
        Photo   in grey
        Falling   room
            TOWERS OPEN FIRE
    BLEEEEPBLEEEEPBLOOOPSPUTT!"

Crab Nebula

CRAB NEBULA

This section must have been completed shortly before Burroughs submitted his March 1962 manuscript, because it quotes from the February 12, 1962 issue of *Newsweek*. That issue's cover would have caught Burroughs' eye since it featured "GUERRILLA WAR-FARE," a report on the escalating war in Vietnam, which admits that guerrilla war is "a dirty, no-holds-barred kind of business, but it's one the U.S. has to learn how to master." The original title of the section, up to and including the October 1962 MS, was "PLANETS OF THE CRAB NEBULAE." A complete eight-page typescript (OSU 2.2) includes a small number of variant passages.

The quotation from *Newsweek* was also used as a footnote to "They Just Fade Away" in *Evergreen Review* 8.32 (April 1964).

72   "have escaped with the prisoners": one early typescript continues: "**And formed underground movements in the alien planet called earth—**" (Berg 4.42).

73   "smouldering slag heaps": the full eight-page typescript has "**shag heaps**" here and in what follows (OSU 2.2). Both "slag" and "shag" were used in *The Soft Machine* and *The Ticket That Exploded*.

75   "carbon dioxide withdrawal": the eight-page typescript continues with lines that were partially canceled, beginning, "**'Sick picture calling Hospital—Sick Picture calling Hospital,'**" and concluding: "**Patient out of control—Need means of restraint—Need apomorphine—**" (OSU 2.2).

78   "Three thousand years of flesh": the eight-page typescript has a longer variant: "**Two thousand years of flesh—Look at the word and image bank of life time fortune—Enough word and image there to start the whole show rolling some place else—**" (OSU 2.2).

79   "keep the show on the road": the eight-page typescript continues with the canceled line: "**Never was a technician myself—**" (OSU 2.2).

A BAD MOVE

Shortly before submitting the March 1962 MS, Burroughs mailed Gysin a two-page typescript, illustrating his new "fold-in" method, that overlaps this section and includes its specified literary source texts: "Enclose sample of juxtaposed closing page of *The Great Gatsby* and *The Soft Machine* [. . .] I intend to use these preparation[s] in *Novia Express*" (Burroughs to Gysin, March 2, 1962; Berg 85.6). While the typescript enclosure has fragments from the end of Fitzgerald's novel not used in *Nova Express* (e.g., "boats against the current" and "borne back into the past"), it has other phrases that were used (e.g., "word scrawled by some boy"). This cut-up section is especially dense with words from a range of literary sources, from Shakespeare to Wordsworth, as well as from Burroughs' own *Soft Machine* and *Naked Lunch*, and he reworked this material many times. The section's genesis is reflected in its manuscript history, which comprises scattered variant passages and fragments in numerous miscellaneous cut-up pages (OSU 2.2), before he produced the final, near-verbatim three-page typescript (OSU 4.9).

83   "flesh-smeared counter orders": one typescript page continues with a rare self-reflexive fragment: **"Form a cut up of it"** (OSU 2.2).

84   "dont": here (and on p. 187) the lack of punctuation seems to have been intended; Burroughs often typed "dont" and let copyeditors insert the apostrophe, but these two instances were not corrected on the galleys and seem consistent with the use of "dont," three times, in *Nova Express* material published in the January 1962 issue of *Evergreen Review*.

THE DEATH DWARF IN THE STREET

The first draft of this section was "Chapter 16" of the March 1962 MS, so that, as well as lightly revising it, Burroughs moved the section from near the end toward the middle of his October 1962 MS. He also drafted numerous variant pages, parts of which clarify the narrative scenario, extend ideas and make explicit one of his key sources: Rimbaud.

85   "Biologic Agent K9 called for his check": K9 enters (and leaves) a café in "Crab Nebula," so Burroughs seems to have let stand a continuity error, the result perhaps of cutting the longer scenario in an earlier draft: **"K9 walked into the cafe and saw an enemy telepath at the end of the bar—he immediately put on a talk record and left it on while he monitored the mind screen and implanted juxtaposition formulae—"** (Berg 4.35).

85 "L'addition—Ladittion—Laddittion": the incorrect French punctuation and spelling are in all witnesses and long galleys.

85 "Garcon—Garcon—Garcon": corrects *NEX* 82 (missing the last em dash), but again letting stand the incorrect French (lacking the cedilla).

86 "sliding in suggestion insults": several typescripts continue with an illustration: **"(Walked in a fag bar and ordered a dry Martini 'Dry Martini—Dry Martini—Veddy dwy Martini—' The Green Octopus perfect that art along fag lines of the earth)"** (OSU 3.5, Berg 48.17).

86 "in the right—in thee write": the longest of several variant drafts of this passage is probably the earliest: **"RIGHT RIGHT RIGHT RIGHT—Forming nerve patterns to the insult building you into the patterns—Any tape recorder can do the same they are tape recorders machine manipulated by distant fingers—Others can dissolve erogenous holes and leave the sex words tattooed in flesh and bone and spine—Or spit out supersonic light blats of derogatory down grade image of you that burn into the being like acid leaving horrible festering open sores—So the plague of the virus people flashed round the world through the devitalized hosts eaten by The Erogenous sucking dummies and softened for the tearing supersonic buzz saws of the Talk dummies—"** (ASU 7).

86 "Agent K9 was with The Biologic Police": one draft has **"Agent William 'K9' Lee"** (Berg 48.17), a line later canceled (on OSU 3.5), clarifying Burroughs' identification with the agent via his fictional alter ego and former nom de plume.

87 "K9 left the café": the first draft typescript has: **"Biological Lee left the cafe and walked to the corner repeating at supersonic frequencies: 'Billy in a Taxi—Billy ina**

Taxi—Billyinataxi—' A taxi swerved over to his feet and he got in muttering: 'Billy in a taxi'" (OSU 3.5).

88   "The basic law of association": one miscellaneous draft continues: "**From this principal our agents learn to read newspapers and magazines for the juxtaposition statements rather than the contents of individual news items—and we can express these statements in association formulae—There are of course many ways of reinforcing a juxtaposition association—One is the short time hyp—The commonest is sexual images used in all advertisements**" (Berg 48.19).

90   "Or feed in a thousand novels": a miscellaneous draft has a longer variation: "**Or another simple illustration—Put a thousand novels in the machine all of them good if there are a thousand good novels—Now let us look at the last pages of all these thousand novels—That is something of quality no? [. . .] Of course the old machine worked in the other way with bring down and degradation juxtaposition formulae—The machine can be reversed—**" (Berg 48.17)

91   "on the association line": a miscellaneous draft continues with final lines that make explicit the connection Burroughs saw between his "association blocks" and Rimbaud's poetics, citing fragments of several poems, including "Voyelles": "**correlating a certain smile an accent a way of holding a cigarette—The Color Alphabet is useful training—Take a name like IAN—Now assign colors to the letters [. . .] Associate to the poetry of RIMBAUD without words seeing the images in his work—Live ember raining in gust of frost—I embraced the Summer dawn—Corridors of black gauze—banner of raw meat—silk of seas—pensive drowned—a young man has grown up anywhere—perfumes of wine gas—etc.—Images free of word that shift and permutate**

**improbably desertion on the suburban air—candor
of vapors and tents—associate other image poets sad
as the death of monkeys—"** (Berg 48.19).

EXTREMELY SMALL PARTICLES

The date with which this section opens ("Dec. 17, 1961") suggests
both its time of composition and the provenance of the cut-up
material that follows, as is confirmed by Burroughs' identification of first draft material as "Newspaper cut ups — 2 pages with
pages of source material" (OSU 2.2). The source pages in turn help
identify some of the original news items cut up by Burroughs. This
section was almost certainly composed in time to be a part of the
March 1962 MS.

91   "Time: The night before": a variant that names Ahmed Ya-
      coubi confirms that this, and following phrases, are a cut-up
      of Burroughs' text, "Comments on 'The Night Before Think-
      ing'" in *Evergreen Review* 5.20 (September 1961): **"(Re-
      corded 1956 Past Time.) The Night Before Thinking
      came to Yacoubi under the influence of majoun a
      form of hashish jam"** (OSU 2.2).

92   "Might reach 500": references in drafts to **"Niteroi hos-
      pitals"** identify this as the feared death toll of the Niterói
      circus fire in Brazil on December 17, 1961 (a tragedy that
      would have caught Burroughs' eye, bearing in mind a circus
      fire had inspired the title of *And the Hippos Were Boiled in
      Their Tanks*, the novella he co-authored with Jack Kerouac
      in 1945).

93   "two Negro secret service men": the date December 1961
      identifies this phrase as taken from Washington newspaper
      reports that the first non-whites had been appointed to the
      presidential bodyguard.

93   "Another Mineral American formed by meteorite impact":
      references in drafts to **"Stewart L Udall"** identify the
      backstory to this phrase, which derives from a speech

delivered in December 1961 by Udall, Secretary of the Interior in the Kennedy administration, about the discovery of stishovite, a rare form of silica, at Meteor Crater in northern Arizona.

94   "Error in enemy strategy is switchboard": the first draft lacks this final paragraph, but has instead further lines cutting up science news material: **"Forgeries from the next years laying the Photostats—Spells out in chemical code the genetic instructions on rose wall paper—Ribonucleic acid or RNA—Blue Silence for short—The messengers are electrical flesh shifting his crotch—Each link of pleasure through cracked chain consists of an amino acid—Precise crucial question is what is the genitals electro-genetic code?"** (OSU 2.2).

From a Land of Grass Without Mirrors

FROM A LAND OF GRASS WITHOUT MIRRORS

Burroughs identified the first version in the March 1962 MS as "Chapter VIII," so that the section remained in the middle of both his *Nova Express* manuscripts. The first full draft, however, an eleven-page typescript (OSU 2.3), underwent significant restructuring as well as rewriting by the time of the October 1962 MS. A thousand words longer than the published version, this early typescript is revealing formally, both for the lack of em dashes in its first five pages and for featuring a passage where words are spaced on the page (as in the "Uranian Willy" section). This typescript is also revealing in terms of content, featuring Burroughs himself and key friends in his circle as characters within the scenario. Although he redacted the material over several drafts, nearly a hundred words remained in the October 1962 MS that were canceled only at the galley stage in July 1964. The title reworks the phrase "a land of grass without memory" (which appears in *The Soft Machine*), taken from St.-John Perse's poem *Anabasis*, in the T.S. Eliot translation.

99   "Lee was not surprised to see": the first full draft has a much longer version naming various friends of Burroughs ("Jerry G" references Jerry Gorsaline, "Miguel" Michael Portman, "Roger" Roger Knoebber, etc.): **"Lee was not surprised or pleased to see many people he knew. 'I brought them with me,' he decided, 'so there is no doubt at this point who gives the orders.'**

'No doubt about that Bill,' said Jerry G. sycophantically. 'All right where are the women? None of them about you notice. This is ominous under the circumstances. You are all extensions of me so I know what you all can and can not do and there is no question of any one doing anything else except what he can do. You Kiki my aide and body guard. You P.G. chief of staff. Now I need six of you for a patrol. There must be other survivors.'

[. . .] He picked a cop who once arrested him in New Orleans, Jimmy C, Kiki, Tex, and a Spade drummer he knew ~~slightly from Paris~~ **on the junk together. 'All right we will keep in touch with staff by walky talky.'**

'You don't have to tell me how, Burroughs,' said PG sourly.

'You KE are in charge here' . . he indicated Phipps-Stern—Gregory—Miguel. 'Watching them. If they give trouble proceed at once with the only remedy.'

'Roger.' [. . .]

Where was Brion? Lee had not seen him and yet his presence was there but not like the others who were there like bodies. He could feel Brion somewhere over his head and to one side of him but could not contact directly like he could the others. He concluded that

this was because Brion was not part of himself in the
same way as the others were" (OSU 2.3).

100   "In this area the only reason": the first draft (OSU 2.3) has
an extra paragraph here, with six lines of phrases unevenly
spaced on the page:

**"In this area total conditions hideous   Novia Express
of shadow empires   move on   electric
faces of scarred metal   the Venusian front the agents
the Ovens of   back from   orgasm drug on needs
addicts   Minraud   heavy metal   cool blue
of Uranus"**

102   "Heavy scar tissue": first draft continues with longer final
lines: **"Nothing here but scar tissue—will arrange
accident—Suggest overdose of junk or sleeping
pills—Transfer impractical—Damage irreversible—
Workmanship poor—Roger**

**Arrange accident—Suggest overdose of sleeping
pills or junk—Alternatively call 'Mack The Knife'—**

**Original equipment faulty—Hidden miles—Basic
engineering flaws—Damage probably irreversible—"**
(OSU 2.3).

TOO FAR DOWN THE ROAD

The first draft of this very short section was a two-page typescript
nearly 500 words long, and Burroughs canceled over 350 words
using his thick black marker pen at the galley stage in July 1964.
At the same time, he added just over 100 words pasted onto the final
long galleys (OSU 5.12), and this insert, which forms the last lines
of the section, is clearly distinguished in its use of punctuation (its
dozen ellipses contrasting with the em dashes in the first half of
the section). The canceled material is especially important for its
use of the book's original title, *The Novia Express* (which suggests
the section dates from late 1961 or early 1962).

102   "—The Boy": the em dash with which the section begins is
the result and sign of cancellations made on the galleys. The
galley version is identical to the October 1962 MS except
for revisions in spelling (e.g., "nova" for "novia") and one
canceled sentence: **"He projected concepts towards his
aim—The Boy flickering with silent motion, driven
too far down the road in his switch—Stared out
through half face, fear urgent and quivering—With
obscure cemetery hands pointing enemy personnel
and installations to readers of The Daily Express—
Face of novia conditions seared by flash blasts he
shrank in this area of total pain and panic—As if
moved by some hideous electric hand out of any
existence—Back from The Ovens into zero—I don't
know—Venusian Front in the war—Perhaps the boy
never existed—All thought and word from the past—
Twenty-five years flash a frightened face—Danger all
around the familiar station—The music they played
was 1920 Spanish villa—
'What's up with you?—I sed old photo couldn't
reach flesh—'
Looking through Time—The other travel only for
a certain lavatory window—Hate fear and suspicion
quivering emotions washed at his brain in color
blats—He felt through pocket and loaded it—Down
dark streets swept by enemy patrols he moved like
an electric dog sniffing marble installations through
what one called 'The World'—Appalling agony—His
burning metal eyes Uranian born into a school boy—
Past or present whipped away on The Novia Express—
It was in the war—Hideous electric need—I am not
sure—The Boy was still conversing with some reflection of the wisdom game must have given him but saw
only fear urgent and quivering—Huge darkness pressed
the silent fish city—Closed like a store shuttered in a**

riot—Revolver pointing obscure phosphorescent hands
of novia conditions—Brain seared in this area of flames
he shrank in hideous electric pain and panic—Ovens of
Minraud in the war—You can not know the appalling
Venusian Front—The cool blue boy had never existed
at all in this June sunlight—He still circulates in strata
of hustlers—attempts to shift the package game must
have given him—Saw only goof ball bum in 1910 Panama—Lee shuttered like a store in a riot—Both parties
driven too far down the road wanted other identity for
hidden miles—He stared out through faulty equipment
in human contacts—Took the revolver out, intercepted
other people's agent—Obscure hand tapping all messages in and out—To readers of The Daily Express loud
and clear now—Last human contacts—Obscure hand
cross the wounded galaxies removed Mr Bradly Mr—
into zero—Wind hand caught in school boy flesh—Stale
overcoat suddenly withdrawn—The Boy had never existed at all—A wet mouth against the pane—muttering
of marble ape—Appalling agony to neon—" (OSU 4.9).

103   "Never happened is my name": this phrase, which is not
canceled on the long galleys and yet was left out of *NEX*
98, has been restored, and is the only line restored for this
edition.

NO GOOD AT THIS RATE

Burroughs produced numerous drafts of the cut-up material that
would feed into this section (OSU 2.2), but the only surviving
manuscript seems to be the near-verbatim two-page typescript in
the October 1962 MS, written some time before (with its spelling
of "Novia").

104   "walk with the Dib": corrects *NEX* 99 ("with Dib"), an error
in the galleys. As a character, "the Dib" reappears in *The
Wild Boys* and *Exterminator!*

105   "The Controller at the exits": the October 1962 MS continues: **"Don't go to Paris—The typewriter—Shine boy,
collapse it."**

WIND HAND TO THE HILT

Burroughs redacted his first draft of this section, a four-page typescript of uncertain date, and in the course of cutting out a good
deal of repetition he also omitted some of the political and further
literary allusions in the source material. However, together with
fragments of Shakespeare and Joyce, the principal source remains
visible, and Burroughs would identify it in "Intersection Reading":
"1962, *Nova Express*, I made a fold-in with the last pages of Alan
Sillitoe's *Saturday Night and Sunday Morning*" (*The Third Mind*
[New York: Viking, 1978], 138). Fragments of Sillitoe's novel appear
from the phrase "If you or any of your pals" onward, and almost
entirely in the sequence in which they appear in the original novel.

105   "any locks over the Chinese": the first draft has: **"any locks
over Stalin and the Chinese—Accusations of bacte-
riological war of the past igniting the present like a
gambit—instead of bringing you up fair—Changed
places of years in the end is just the same—"** (OSU
2.2).

106   "On the night shift working with blind": the first draft continues, with lines that mix phrases from Sillitoe's novel with
a reference to James Joyce's "The Dead," other phrases of
which would be used in *Nova Express*: **"One more chance
he said touching circumstance—Spanish i come back
to the bait its curtains—Thin air the meet café and
there it'll be fighting every day until Gabriel's eyes
faded—Dreams of us when we are fighting up to hand
they father the last electrician—Slung into khaki at
eighteen wracked and answer Mr Of The Account—
Again in a factory grabbing for us through the hole
in thin air—"** (OSU 2.2).

A DISTANT THANK YOU

Burroughs identified the first version of this long section as "Chapter X" of his March 1962 MS. This nine-page typescript shows a large number of minor differences from the published version, evidence of how carefully Burroughs reworked his manuscript: "Gothic Cathedrals" became "Greek temples," "we are all scheming" became "we are all intriguing," "terrible doom" became "terrible fate," and so on. Burroughs was equally attentive to punctuation and, before the final typescript (OSU 4.9) was tidied up by a typesetter, he used an em dash system made up of two or sometimes three dashes, ellipses using two or three dots and both single and double colons.

117   "Oh yes and whose doing it?": one draft continues (with what is presumably a reference to the Mesoamerican god Quetzacoatl): "Not Garibaldi Qetequatal again? Such a ham—I tell you nobody can scream like Juan Chapultepec—Where is he now?" (OSU 2.3).

117   "he fades out with a train whistle": another line regarding Willy The Rube appears in the draft: "He'll come here and eat all our exquisite food and smoke all the Pakistan Berries lay all our life forms and fade out in word dust of a distant thank you note—" (OSU 2.3).

REMEMBER I WAS CARBON DIOXIDE

It's not clear when Burroughs wrote this section, but it changed significantly at the galley stage in July 1964 through major cuts and insertions. The earliest rough draft, a four-page typescript (OSU 2.2) and the final three-page version (OSU 4.9), have just over 450 words which Burroughs canceled in the galleys, at the same time as he made three separate inserts adding up to 250 words, the new material standing out formally in its use of ellipses.

The section is particularly dense with literary source material, from Conrad's novel *Lord Jim* to Joyce's short story "The Dead" and

Eliot's poem *The Waste Land*. It is revealing that the first draft is headed in autograph "Weilest Du?" which abbreviates the phrase "Wo weilest du?" ("Where do you linger?") from Wagner's *Tristan und Isolde* as cited by Eliot in the first part of his poem. Burroughs' typescripts reveal the extent of his use of *The Waste Land*, and indeed other poems by Eliot: not only "Portrait of a Lady" (whose citation of Marlowe's play *The Jew of Malta* remains in the text as the phrase fragments "in another country" and "committed fornication"), but also "Burbank with a Baedecker: Blestein with a Cigar" (one phrase from the poem, "The boatman smiles," appears twice in the typescripts, and would be used in *The Ticket That Exploded*). Redacting his manuscript from rough to final draft, Burroughs made the largest cuts when revising the galleys and did so in his characteristic way, canceling odd words or entire lines while retaining the original structure and sequence. It is revealing that in 1964 Burroughs made new cut-ups of *The Waste Land* to add onto those made in 1962, and the next year he used a vertical bisection of one such page, entitled "Selections from T.S. Eliot—From The Waste Land and other poems" (Berg 36.8 and 44.41), for a collage (in *The Third Mind*, 102).

120   "in another country—": corrects *NEX* 114 ("country."), restoring the em dash that the copyeditor replaced with a period when Burroughs redacted these opening lines. Appearing twice in the "Trak Trak Trak" section of the revised *Soft Machine*, the phrase from Marlowe's play is also used by Dr Benway and the Professor of Interzone University in *Naked Lunch*. For Burroughs, the unspoken words of Barabas that complete the phrase—"the wench is dead"— referred to his wife, Joan.

120   "Going to give some riot noises": from here to "long time in inquisition . . ." was an insert made in July 1964.

122   "I'd ask alterations": the October 1962 MS begins this paragraph by citing the last line of "Au lecteur," Baudelaire's preface to *Les Fleurs du mal*, via its use as the last line of the first part of *The Waste Land*: **"Mon semblable mon**

frère to neon—Departed have left no address." The
second phrase, which also derives from Eliot's poem (third
part: "Departed have left no addresses"), appears cut up in
this section as "departed file . . . Mrs. Murphy's rooming
house left no address."

122   "Will you let me tell you": from here to "dim jerky far away"
was an insert made in July 1964.

123   "Fading smiles": the October 1962 MS shows that Burroughs
redacted material between these two words, thus obscuring
the citation of Eliot's "Burbank with a Baedecker": "**Fading
in the violet light—Brief moments i could describe—
Damp gusts bringing rain—The boatman smiles.**"

123   "Piece of a toy": from here to "blue kite" was an insert made
in July 1964. Burroughs cites the final line in a June 1964
letter to illustrate the precise intersection points he was
finding between word and image (*ROW*, 163).

Gave Proof Through the Night

GAVE PROOF THROUGH THE NIGHT

The note Burroughs pasted onto the galleys in July 1964 explains
the origins of this material as "first written in 1938" in collaboration with his boyhood friend Kells Elvins. He would recall
this scenario elsewhere (in *The Third Mind* and *The Adding
Machine*), but the most vivid account is in the unpublished draft
of a longer autobiographical sketch: "A hard boiled detective
story bogged down when we read *The Left Handed Passenger*
and got all the references on the *Titanic* and started something
called Twilight's Last Gleamings which I used recently in *Nova
Express* re-written from memory the manuscript is lost long ago.
We acted out the parts giggling in delight over such lines as
'His revolver swung free of his brassiere and he fired twice.' 'I
don't know I feel sorta bad about this old finger.' The innocence
of young writers" (ASU 7).

Burroughs not only produced several versions of this section, he experimented with numerous different layouts. The earliest, an eight-page typescript he identified as first draft for "Chapter VI" of his March 1962 MS (OSU 2.3), has a running banner at the top and foot of every page in block capitals using cut-up lyrics from *The Star-Spangled Banner*. The page format is a direct echo of *The Exterminator*, and indeed this typescript has many lines of material from that text, even though Burroughs' note refers to using the "first cut-ups" from *Minutes to Go*. This typescript is also distinctive for dividing the page into sections by hand-ruled horizontal lines and for using forward slashes throughout and no em dashes. None of these features appear in Burroughs' second version, a four-page typescript that is close to the published text (OSU 2.3). The version in *Evergreen Review* 7.29 (March 1963) is identical except for minor differences.

While most of the first version overlaps the published text, it also includes long passages that seem independent of it, and Burroughs wrote other versions that incorporate anomalous-seeming material. That he produced extensive alternative drafts does not suggest he had any reservations about this section, but apparently Brion Gysin did, and when Burroughs had corrected the galleys he wrote to his editor, Richard Seaver: "Mr Gysin felt that the ship wreck chapter (Gave Proof Through The Night [galley] page 37) was not in keeping with the rest of the book and should be omitted. I am undecided on this point and would be interested to hear your opinion" (Burroughs to Seaver, July 21, 1964; SU). Even though it was precisely interrelated to other parts of the novel—the central image of a man boarding the first lifeboat in drag recurs in three other sections—Burroughs was quite prepared to drop it and offer Seaver "something I think is quite appropriate to substitute"; but, fortunately, "Gave Proof Through the Night" remained in *Nova Express*.

126   "He jerked the handle": a full rough typescript (ASU 7) continues: **"Yage Pintar Yage pintar/"** For the use of this phrase, see *The Yage Letters* (26, 95).

126 "appendectomy in 1910 at Harvard": the earliest typescript (and, near verbatim, ASU 7), continues; **"I Sekuin perfected this art along the Chang Dynasty/ Vegetarian Walkers are *not* subject to appendicitis/ Vestige Organ/ Before White Time/ Dead Hand Stretching The Vegetable People/ Rabbits have Over large appendixes/"** (OSU 2.3).

127 "Mrs. J. L. Bradshinkel": in earlier drafts this is **"Mrs Bryan, Ship Owner"** (Berg 11.24). Lucy Bradshinkel appears in *Naked Lunch* and Billy Bradshinkel in *The Yage Letters*.

127 "Mike B. Dweyer, Politician from Clayton Missouri": in the first version, where the politician is **"Mike Brown"** and he doesn't come from Missouri, this line is preceded by a page of quite distinct material, beginning: **"'Do you think The Captain controls this ship Mr Bane? Unions! Unions! Brown Deal/ Foe Deal/ The West Side Push I told"** (OSU 2.3).

128 "screaming for help like everyone else": in the four-page second draft this is a line of speech: **"—Go on scream like everyone else on the boat—"** (OSU 2.3).

129 "The Captain stiff-armed an old lady": the four-page second draft has **"Captain Norman"** (OSU 2.3).

129 "Perkins brought down his knife": the first version continues: **"Swift Sword/ Switch Blade Preferred/"** (OSU 2.3).

130 "her souvenirs of the disaster": characteristically, the first version interpolates cut-up lines, continuing here: **"Will Hollywood never learn? Unimaginable Disaster Ten Age Future Time / A Life Belt autographed by The Crew and a Severed Human Finger / Remember my medium of distant fingers?/ Talk in flak braille"** (OSU 2.3). The typescript continues with another 150 words before concluding: **"From the First/Raise Out Time Position/ Before Terminal Time/ From The First IN THEE WORD WAS THEE BEGINNING/"**

SOS

Identified by Burroughs as "Chapter 13," the earliest draft of this section appeared in the March 1962 MS under the title "Blue Junction." This seven-page typescript is, in Burroughs' description, mostly "source material" (OSU 2.4) and only about one page (250 words) would remain in the published text. Burroughs produced at least one more version (Berg 48.19) before completing a revised three-page typescript included in the October 1962 MS. This typescript, which has the new title "SOS" (with "SOLID BLUE SILENCE" added in autograph and then canceled), retained a little more from the original draft and included another full page of new cut-up material, but all of this, over 400 words, would be cut at the final galley stage. In July 1964 Burroughs also added almost 100 words of new material to the galleys to give the section a different ending.

130   "The cold heavy fluid settled in a mountain village": Burroughs' redaction at the galley stage started with the opening line, which originally read: **"The cold heavy fluid settled in his spine—He moved slow hydraulic motion to a mountain village of slate houses where time stops in blue twilight—"** (OSU 5.11).

130   "Heavy con men selling issues": one draft has: **"con men who sell whole universes issues of fraudulent universe stock, real estate on Novia Ground and all the money goes back into their Silence habit"** (Berg 48.19).

131   "Martin came to Blue Junction": with minor differences, this is where the first draft (OSU 2.4) begins.

132   "a silent blue twilight": the first draft continues with a canceled line: **"Martin could see the entire ranch and all the workers on his blue view screen of photo collage"** (OSU 2.4).

132   "poker play and flesh trade": the first draft continues with a new paragraph that further clarifies the location ("ranch") and genre (Western) Burroughs had in mind: **"The blues**

clashed with the Yellows who lived in the next ranch a dry hot desert place of crab men with white hot insect eyes" (OSU 2.4).

132 "Empty picture": from here to "flapping gunsmoke" was an insert pasted onto the final long galleys (OSU 5.12).

SHORT COUNT

The manuscript history of this section is itself short: just the final four-page typescript in the October 1962 MS, which shows a small number of minor differences and a few lines of unused text. Burroughs would cancel almost 60 words at the galley stage.

134 "Heavy Metal People of Uranus": the October 1962 MS continues with a longer version that indicates how Burroughs redacted the section on the galleys: **"wrapped in orange flesh robes that grow on them, the little high fi junk note tinkling through cool nerves remote mineral calm entered in a heavy blue mist of vaporized bank notes."**

TWILIGHT'S LAST GLEAMING

This was one of the earliest written sections and Burroughs identified its first version, a three-page typescript, as "Chapter IV" of his March 1962 MS (OSU 2.3), so that it was shifted from near the beginning toward the end for his final manuscript. He reworked this draft at least once more (Berg 11.23) before submitting a revised draft in late 1961 to *Evergreen Review*, where, with very minor differences, it appeared in the January 1962 issue under the title "TWILIGHT'S LAST GLEAMINGS" (Burroughs always used the incorrect plural, which is reproduced in "Gave Proof Through the Night"). The final two-page typescript is verbatim except for punctuation and capitalization changes (OSU 4.9).

136 "The Gods of Time-Money-Junk": the earliest draft has a quintet of evil deities rather than a trinity (here and in the

three later instances in this section): **"The Gods of Time Junk Money Body Death"** (OSU 2.3).

137   "all I said a million silver bullets": the earliest draft has: **"all i sed waiting hole in pain funnel a million silver bullets—"** (OSU 2.3). Significantly, even when this line was edited on both later drafts and for *Evergreen Review*, the spelling "sed" was retained (Berg 11.27 and OSU 4.9); it was changed by the copyeditor on OSU 4.9. Burroughs also used "sed" elsewhere in his manuscripts.

139   "In sun I held the stale overcoat": in a handwritten note beside this line on Burroughs' manuscript, Gysin asked: **"Do you really want the lower case 'I'?"** (Berg 11.27). Burroughs' answer at the time (fall 1961) seems to have been, "Yes," since the change to upper case "I" was almost certainly not made until the galley stage in July 1964. This whole paragraph and the next reproduce verbatim the ending of the revised *Soft Machine* (which used two-thirds of the final three paragraphs of the original 1961 *Soft Machine*).

This Horrible Case

THIS HORRIBLE CASE

According to the book's "Foreword Note," Burroughs wrote this section in collaboration with Ian Sommerville, although there is no obvious difference in the writing. However, by "section," Burroughs meant not the four-part chapter but the specific section "Two Tape Recorder Mutations," and it is logical that Sommerville, with his technical expertise, was responsible for this material. Burroughs' first draft was a five-page typescript identified as "Chapter 14" and entitled "The Biologic Police and Courts" (OSU 2.4). Since its first page appears in the "Coordinate Points" section, Burroughs must have returned to this draft and split it up, as well as cutting over 200 words and adding 300 more by the time of the final near-verbatim version (OSU 4.9).

This four-page typescript, dating from pre-October 1962, has the canceled original title, "THE BIOLOGIC COURTS AND COUN-SELLORS," with "This Horrible Case" added by Burroughs in autograph (and also canceled, as he tried to avoid duplicating *section* and *chapter* titles).

142   "mental and physical cruelty": corrects *NEX* 134 ("metal"); the typo, which is made by Burroughs on OSU 2.4 and corrected by him in autograph, did not appear on OSU 4.9 or on the galleys.

143   "invasion and manipulation": the first draft continues with a canceled paragraph beginning: **"'Better forget those lines altogether' said Uranian U sharply 'Your detestation for the life form you invaded is not regarded as an extenuating circumstance in The Biologic Courts—'"** (OSU 2.4).

144   "Alternative Word Island": *NEX* 136 follows the galleys, but OSU 2.4 and OSU 4.9 both have **"Ward Island,"** a location that also appears in *The Ticket That Exploded*. It is impossible to say whether the "Alternative Word" was a typo, a transcription error or a self-reflexive revision on Burroughs' part.

BRIEF FOR THE FIRST HEARING

The first draft of this material comprises the first two pages of an eight-page typescript entitled "The Biologic Courts and Counsellors" (OSU 2.2), and Burroughs made only relatively light revisions to it for the section's final draft (OSU 4.9). He added the section title in autograph, replacing "THE BIOLOGIC COURTS AND COUNCELLORS (CONTINUED)."

146   "to open biologic potentials for his client": the first draft has a different version: **"to represent a client in a favorable light biologically speaking signalling out aspects of beauty or function tending to survival—"** (OSU 2.2).

BRIEF FOR FIRST HEARING / / CASE OF LIFE FORM A

The published section shows few changes from the last six pages of an eight-page typescript entitled "The Biologic Courts and Counsellors" (OSU 2.2). The verbatim final draft dates from pre-October 1962 (using the spelling "novia"). In first draft there was no subdivision of material to separate it from the previous section, whereas the final typescript includes the title.

150   "Coughing enemy pulled in and replaced": the first draft continues: **"dirty pictures—reverse instructions—Iron claws of pain and pleasure stylishly dressed—"** (OSU 2.2).

152   "suspended pending mutation proceedings": the final phrase is one of the few not to appear on OSU 2.2.

TWO TAPE RECORDER MUTATIONS

The first draft of this section, an untitled three-page sequence, is a continuation of "The Biologic Courts and Counsellors" (OSU 2.2). As with drafts for most cut-up sections, the very rough typescript shows a good deal of unused material from which Burroughs made selections (marked by underlining blocks of text in hand, although this was not always applied). The verbatim three-page final draft (OSU 4.9) has the section title added by Burroughs in autograph. The title phrase appears in his correspondence in early April 1962, referring to "some interesting experiments" carried out with Michael Portman and Ian Sommerville (*ROW*, 103).

152   "message from stairway of slime": the first draft continues with a line referencing either the American military medal or the amphetamine of choice for British Mods (Drinamyl, which came in blue triangular tablets): **"Voice fading into advocate—Not that a client ever gets The Purple Heart—"** (OSU 2.2).

152   "civilization and personal habits": the first draft continues with lines that include a reference to Burroughs' publisher

at Olympia Press, Maurice Girodias, and the philosopher and writer Gerald Heard, whose work Burroughs had long known and whom he met with Timothy Leary in September 1961: **"With the Leica first pressure—Instructions to stay away from my supply—Flesh froze to supply Girodias—Amino acid directs all movement to """ that is—A book by Heard leapt into my hand to be read telepathic misdirection—"** (OSU 2.2).

153   "c-Sequential choice": from here to "That is a 'book'" is one of the few lines not present in OSU 2.2.

Pay Color

PAY COLOR

Under its original title, "Photo Falling—Word Falling," the section appeared as "Chapter V" in the March 1962 MS (OSU 2.3), so that Burroughs moved it from near one end to near the other of his manuscript. He produced two three-page typescripts which he redacted, and the text was printed under the same title, almost verbatim, in the January 1962 issue of *Evergreen Review*. Only on the final draft (OSU 4.9) is this title canceled and "Pay Color" added in autograph. The new title emphasized this section's return to the "Pay it all back" call in the opening section, and Burroughs wrote numerous variants on this theme, including at least one directly related to *Nova Express* that he typed in blue ink to materialize on his page the color he associated with apomorphine (Berg 6.9). The origins of the section go back to summer 1961 in Tangier, when Burroughs gave himself a "brief rest from writing" to make color photo-collages (including one entitled "Word Falling—Photo Falling"), and came up with the "Pay Color" refrain that would conclude the section (*ROW*, 76, 82). In 1965, Charles Plymell literalized the color calls in the second issue of his *Now* magazine by printing the section's last paragraphs in red, blue and green ink.

Only mentioned in previous sections, The Subliminal Kid is here fully introduced, joining the ranks of Burroughs' other Western-style characters (The Intolerable Kid, The Carbonic Kid, The Heavy Metal Kid, etc.). The Kid uses the latest technological weaponry, and Burroughs saw the section as not just a fictionalization but a lesson, "suggesting some extended use of tape recorders" (*ROW*, 97). The Kid also appears in the revised *Soft Machine* as "Technical Tilly," and in *The Ticket That Exploded* he's identified as a "technical sergeant" and "charter defector from the Nova Mob." The character was based on Ian Sommerville, and Burroughs paid tribute to the name by signing one 1965 text (in *My Own Mag* 15) "for the subliminal kid."

157   "the river of all language": the first draft has a longer paragraph here and continues: **"So that people could not control their words or accents and no one knew what he was going to say"** (OSU 2.3, first version).

158   "watching a gangster movie": early drafts continue: **"whether he was man woman beast or monster from outer space"** (OSU 2.3, both versions).

159   "*Pay Red*": typed in blue and including four lines of text spaced out on the page, one typescript page overlaps and extends the color theme: **"Marx Freud colors you stole PAY RED pay back the red you stole for your Einstein decade—apomorphine in the beginning was the word Coca Cola signs and your lying flags pay back that red to penis and apomorphine pay blue pay back the only begetter the blue you stole for your police—"** (Berg 6.9).

PAY OFF THE MARKS?

The manuscript history of this section comprises only a few variant cut-up passages (OSU 2.2) and Burroughs' pre-October 1962 draft (with its spelling "novia"). He cut almost a third of this draft at the final galley stage in July 1964. At the same time, he made two short inserts, so that the section lost over 400 words and gained just over 100 (distinguished by their telltale use of ellipses).

163   "Comte Wladmir Sollohub": from here to "exploded star). . . ." is an insert made on the galleys in July 1964.

163   "I watched the torn sky bend": the phrase recurs in several texts, including "St. Louis Return" (1965), where Burroughs identifies it with a massive tornado that hit his hometown in 1927 (although he misdates it as 1929).

163   *white white white as far as the eye can see ahead*": in his essay "Hemingway," Burroughs cites this as "the last line" of "The Snows of Kilimanjaro" (*Adding Machine*, 68). Neither the last line nor an accurate quotation from the short story, Burroughs' words rewrote the original: "and there, ahead, all he could see, as wide as all the world, great, high, and unbelievably white in the sun, was the square top of Kilimanjaro. And then he knew that there was where he was going" (Hemingway, *The Snows of Kilimanjaro and Other Stories* [New York: Scribner's, 1961], 27). The phrase "where he was going" in turn gave Burroughs the title for a short text in *Tornado Alley* (1989) beautifully read by Burroughs on the 1990 album *Dead City Radio*.

164   "Bicycle races here at noon": the October 1962 MS continues: "**Sombre anger steaming to a room is far away—Faded this violence is a calm by some boy thighs—Sad look caught in throat—Whiffs of my Spain—Lost dog space of lontanza.**" Burroughs' redaction of these last lines (to "boy thighs—Sad—Lost dog") is characteristic of how he canceled phrases in his cut-up texts to produce a new, more elliptical text. Like numerous other word combinations, the phrase "**space of lontanza**" occurred repeatedly in drafts for *Nova Express*, but all were edited out.

164   "He had come a long way": from here to "died during the night. . . ." is an insert made on the galleys in July 1964.

SMORBROT

The section's title seems to have been a late revision, added in autograph onto the October 1962 MS, and Burroughs first refers to this section under its previous title in a letter to Rosset at the end of February 1962: "Do you feel that the section called *Outskirts Of The City* can be published as it stands?— If not I will provide you with an expurgated version" (*ROW*, 100). In fact, an erasure on the archival typescript of the letter shows a still earlier title, one that more clearly relates to the section's content, which Burroughs canceled halfway through, typing: "~~Operation Se~~"—for "Operation Sense Withdrawal" (SU). Burroughs' concern about expurgating the material reflects the fact that "Smorbrot" contains the only sexually explicit passages in *Nova Express* (and, unusually for Burroughs, describes both heterosexual and homosexual acts), which in turn reflected the hopes of writer and publisher that this book would make it easier for Grove to publish *Naked Lunch* without a censorship trial. This strategy also explains the appearance of "Outskirts of the City" in *Evergreen Review* 6.25 (July 1962), albeit in a redacted version (identical to the October 1962 MS, but with over 400 words cut—mainly of sexually explicit material, although much remained).

Aside from some early partial typescripts (ASU 7, Berg 9.11), the first draft proper shows a very large number of minor differences and about an extra page of material. This draft, identified as "Chapter 17" of the March 1962 MS (OSU 3.5), had the section's original title: "Operation Sense Withdrawal." Burroughs canceled 50 words at the final galley stage.

165   "Doctor Lilly in Florida": the draft of this footnote has: **"Doctor Lilly in Miami and by Doctor** [blank] **in Oklahoma"** (OSU 3.5). Lilly had worked on isolation tanks and sensory deprivation at the National Institutes of Health near Washington since the late 1950s. After the phrase "Science—Pure science," which evokes Dr Benway from *Naked Lunch*, this draft has a canceled line: **"And what sex is this body**

floating half in and half out?" The footnote is repeated verbatim in the "substitute flesh" section of *The Ticket That Exploded*, as is the following footnote regarding Reich's orgone accumulators, although in reverse order.

170   "one of them flicked my jacket": the first draft alternates first- and third-person narration and, using a name recurrent in *Naked Lunch* and *The Soft Machine*, here has not "my" but **"Carl's jacket"** (OSU 3.5).

171   "white—red—white—": Burroughs rewrote this passage across several drafts, and the earliest integrates color association with his special "coordinate" number: **"Jack off red—8 red . . . two green 7 blue 6 black—Flash red 8 . . . green two . . . blue seven 6 black . . . In the underwater medium converse in flashes of color a system like Morse code—with two coordinates intensity and repetition—setting off immediately the appropriate response in the other nervous system color circuits . . ."** (Berg 9.11).

171   "Color-music-smell-feel": the first draft has: **"Color-music-smell-taste-kinaesthetic—You got it??—Now associate without words"** (OSU 3.5).

171   "from ferris wheels": corrects NEX 161 ("wheel"), as per the first draft. Burroughs used the incorrect lower case for "Ferris" throughout the trilogy.

173   "open shorts flapping": "shorts" seems to be a typo, since in the first draft and elsewhere this is "open shirts"; however, the proximity of "genitals" to "shorts" warrants leaving the "error" alone.

ITS ACCOUNTS

A section made from cutting up other parts of *Nova Express*, literary sources and news items from daily papers, "Its Accounts" has a short archival prehistory in scattered pages of cut-up variants (OSU 2.2) and a final, two-page typescript (OSU 4.9). Since it recycles material from numerous sections including "There's a Lot Ended" and "Are These Experiments Necessary?" and since these sections contain news items dating from March 1962, it is very likely that "Its Accounts" was written at the same time. In his "Section Heading And Layout of Nova Express" (Berg 36.7), Burroughs typed the title as "It's Accounts," but dropped the apostrophe in autograph on the final typescript.

173   "Ewyork, Onolulu, Aris, Ome, Oston": like several other phrases in the section, this derives verbatim from Brion Gysin's "First Cut-ups" in *Minutes to Go*. Burroughs also experimented with variations on the phrasing, adding **"Lgiers, Ran"** (Algiers, Oran) and **"Adrid"** (Madrid) to the list in one draft (OSU 2.2).

174   "Venus Vigar choked to passionate weakness": on Vigar, see under "There's a Lot Ended."

SIMPLE AS A HICCUP

Like "Its Accounts," the history of this short section consists of scattered pages of cut-up variants (OSU 2.2) and a final, two-page typescript (OSU 4.9), where the spelling "novia" dates its composition as pre-October 1962. On the final typescript, Burroughs wrote in the title after canceling its original heading: "Notes on Distinction between Sedative and Hallucigen [sic] Drugs." In 1961, he had delivered a controversial paper entitled "Points of Distinction between Sedative and Consciousness-Expanding Drugs" to the American Psychological Association, later published in *Evergreen Review* 8.34 (December 1964). When Burroughs sent Rosset the March 1962 MS of *Nova Express* he had suggested that a transcript of his talk "might serve as appendix" (*ROW*, 102), but he seems to have changed his mind. For three days later he mailed Rosset what sounds like "Simple as a Hiccup": "a cut up from the talk given to The American Psychological Symposium Sept 6, 1961 Points of Distinction Between Sedative And Hallucigen [sic] Drugs—" (Burroughs to Rosset, April 2,

1962; SU). A few fragments from the talk ("classified as narcotic drugs," "Morphine is actually," "Dimethyltryptamine," "cortex") are recognizable.

176   "blue sky writing of Hassan i Sabbah": draft cut-up pages for this section include alternatives such as **"Glyphs of Hassan i Sabbah"** (OSU 2.2).

THERE'S A LOT ENDED

Burroughs opens this section with a dateline ("New York, Saturday March 17, Present Time") that announces the provenance of its material in daily newspaper items, while the date is clarified by the complementary opening to the later section "Are These Experiments Necessary?": "Saturday March 17, 1962, Present Time Of Knowledge." The final two-page typescript (OSU 4.9) drew from a large number of variant cut-up pages, which include many other references to items in the news that spring, some clarifying the sources of enigmatic details in the published text, others suggesting the range of Burroughs' interests and the precision with which he made selections.

177   "Great Gold Cup—Revived peat victory hopes of Fortria": Fortria achieved fame in 1962 by winning the Mackeson Gold Cup for the second time. The other horse named here, Sheila's Cottage, won the Grand National in 1948. "Maharani" refers to the Indian Princess, celebrity, politician and horsewoman, Gayatri Devi, **"one of the world's most glamorous wealthy,"** as a source draft page describes her (OSU 2.2).

178   "already watched Identikit": in a source draft this line follows a reference to the Duke of Edinburgh's visit to Peru in February 1962: **"Lima Wednesday Prince Philip—Wore a Peruvian sombrero of a man seen—'Why, we all take satisfaction—Rode a dancing horse on Sugar Avenue—Well publicized visit to Peru's capital—'"** (OSU 2.2).

178   "The capsule was warm": in a source draft the "capsule"
        is clearly identified even as its referent is scrambled with
        other elements in news items that competed for headlines
        in February and March 1962: **"On the heels of Colo-
        nel John Glenn Rickard's body—Triple orbit of the
        earth failed with another—There are many similari-
        ties—between the two killings and Colonel Glen's
        wife—Think it possible that children and parent of
        the same man may be Colonel and Mrs Glen—"** (OSU
        2.2). John Glenn had become the first American to orbit
        the earth on February 20, 1962, his flight watched by a live
        television audience of up to 100 million. Burroughs mixes
        the historical milestone in space exploration and the cold
        war with a crime story in London: the "two killings" refer to
        the case of the "wardrobe killer" (the same draft page has
        the phrase **"wardrobe victim"**), whose victims were both
        homosexual men, Norman Rickard and then, in a "carbon
        copy" killing, Alan John Vigar, murdered in west London
        not far from where Burroughs was living that spring. These
        cases were linked at the time to the recent killing of two
        other homosexual men in Derbyshire, known as "the Car-
        bon Copy Murders." This last phrase appears several times
        in one draft page that includes verbatim the references to
        Vigar used in *Nova Express*. While newspapers brought to
        lurid light the generally hidden world of gay men in early
        1960s England—in contrast to "well publicized" royal vis-
        its and ticker tape parades—Burroughs also drew on mur-
        der cases where the key issue was not sexual identity but
        capital punishment. Hence, the reference in this section to
        "[James] Hanratty," who was hanged amid much controversy
        on April 4, 1962: "Portman Clinic" was where Hanratty had
        received psychiatric treatment. Other draft source pages cite
        the British press coverage itself, one naming the *Daily Mail*,
        another suggesting disagreements between papers (**"But
        one newspaper—*The Observer*** [which is named in this

section and in "Are These Experiments Necessary?"] **Another newspaper *The Express***") (OSU 2.2).

179   "He plays Mark even Anthony with Liz": one of the few news stories that could compete with Glenn's orbiting of the Earth in spring 1962 was the scandal caused by the Taylor-Burton affair, which started during the filming of *Anthony and Cleopatra*. The affair made the April 13, 1962 cover of *Life*, and the film nearly bankrupted the studio, which Burroughs names in one of the section's source pages: "**Twentieth Century Fox trying to eat my breakfast**" (OSU 2.2).

179   "Sir, I am delighted to see": clearly taken from a Letters to the Editor column, in the source typescript this line is preceded by references that mix up anticolonial uprisings, cold war conflict, and the celebrity marriage of film stars: "**Today's killing as curtain raiser for Linda Christian and Romina and Taryn—See daughter by her marriage let loose the seven year old Algerian war to the late Tyrone Power—Both murdered men is Edmund Purdom 33—he and Linda terrorists of the European secret 37 have said they will marry next month—Opening national rumors about Castro—**" (OSU 2.2). In March and February 1962, the U.S. Secretary of Defense received CIA plans for "false flag" covert ops designed to justify invading Cuba; although no "rumors" leaked out, the plans included proposals to blame Fidel Castro should Glenn's space flight end in disaster.

ONE MORE CHANCE?

The manuscript history comprises a one-page untitled rough typescript (OSU 2.2), which has numerous minor differences compared with the published opening of the section, and a verbatim one-page neat typescript with the title in Burroughs' hand in the October 1962 MS. The last three-quarters of the section, over 1,200 words, were added only at the final galley stage in July 1964, a distinction made visible on the page through the difference in punctuation (ellipses replacing em dashes).

180   "Told me to sit by Hubbard guide": L. Ron Hubbard had previously been named in *Minutes to Go*, already establishing the connection between cut-up methods and Scientology.

181   "hotel room in London—": from here until the end of the section was inserted onto the long galleys in July 1964 (OSU 5.12).

184   "It has a 3D effect sir": corrects *NEX* 173 ("third effect"), an error introduced by the copyeditor, who misinterpreted "3d" in Burroughs' typed insert. Needless to say, the error is peculiarly serendipitous, since the copyeditor's "collaboration" had the effect of creating the very *third* defined by Burroughs and Gysin's "third mind."

ARE THESE EXPERIMENTS NECESSARY?

Composed by cutting up a good deal of the previous two sections, this section exists as an untitled two-page typescript with a number of small differences and about 175 extra words compared with the published version (OSU 2.2), and the final verbatim typescript (OSU 4.9). Most of the unused material comprises phrases used in the previous two sections.

185   "Saturday March 17, 1962": the early draft begins: **"New York Saturday March 17 present time of knowledge—"** (OSU 2.2).

186   "creating and aggravating conflict": the early draft continues with a phrase not used elsewhere: **"The game of life demands total war of the past—"** (OSU 2.2).

MELTED INTO AIR

On March 15, 1962 Burroughs mailed Kerouac a four-page typescript to illustrate the new fold-in technique he had used in his current novel: "Page I was made by folding your letter and placing it on a section i had just written entitled The Carbonic Caper—Page 2 i copied out of the ending section of *The Subterraneans*—Then I folded page two and laid it on the end of *Naked Lunch* and some other texts including the end of *The Soft Machine*—Result was page 3 which i consider not only contains some beautiful prose but is most meaningful to me" (Burroughs to Kerouac, March 15, 1962; CU, Kerouac Collection). Page 3 is, absolutely verbatim, the "Melted Into Air" section as published in *Nova Express*. The result was exactly "half Kerouac half Burroughs" in terms of word length, while almost every word not deriving from *The Subterraneans* appears in the earlier section "A Bad Move." Burroughs' choices were highly calculated: by using a phrase that names the title of Kerouac's novel, for example, he invited the reader to recognize the source text, while he chose the openly self-reflexive last words of *The Subterraneans* ("this book") for the last words of his section (the penultimate section of his own book).

187   "Mr. Beiles Mr. Corso Mr. Burroughs": Gregory Corso appears in Kerouac's *The Subterraneans* (as Yuri), while he and Sinclair Beiles were, together with Brion Gysin, Burroughs' collaborators on *Minutes to Go* (1960).

188   "Yas, he heard your"; corrects *NEX* 177 ("Yes"), confirmed by the recurrence of this apparent typo in other drafts; also later used in *The Ticket That Exploded*.

188   "And I go home having lost—": what is lost at the end of Kerouac's novel is itself lost in Burroughs' cut-up of his last lines: "And I go home having lost her love. And write this book" (*The Subterraneans* [London: Penguin, 2001], 93).

CLOM FLIDAY

Taken from the last words of *Naked Lunch*, the section title certainly seems like a gesture of finality, but "Clom Fliday" was not the final section of either the March or October 1962 manuscripts. The first rough draft of this section (OSU 2.2), which was a fifth longer, and the final draft lack the last half-dozen lines, including the date and signature after "You are yourself Mr Bradly Mr Martin—" (OSU 4.9). The existence of a different ending to *Nova Express* is confirmed in a letter Burroughs wrote to Rosset just after mailing the first draft, which he admitted was "not in as good order as I would like": "The last section I forgot to put in the chapter head which is: Punishment And Reward, What?—Never Existed At All—" (Burroughs to Rosset, April 2, 1962; SU). In fact, as the October manuscript and the galleys reveal, "Clom Fliday" was followed not only by the ninth chapter to which Burroughs refers here (which consisted of a single section entitled "Never Existed At All") but also by another short section at the end of Chapter Eight, entitled "Wind Hand Thy Father."

Some 250 words long, the text of "Wind Hand Thy Father" in Burroughs' manuscript is almost identical to that published in 1962 in the German magazine *Rhinozeros* 7 as "Be Cheerful, Sir, Our Revels Touching Circumstance," a title taken from the opening words of the piece. The text recycles familiar elements, including valedictory phrases from Shakespeare's "final" texts (both *The Tempest* and the playwright's epitaph, which had already been used in *Minutes to Go*) and from Joyce's "The Dead," including a direct reference to the character Michael Furey. In July 1964, Burroughs canceled all but the very last line of this section on the galleys (leaving only: "all the living and the dead— You are yourself—There be—"), and then pasted in the ending as published.

As for the ninth chapter, it was probably composed just before Burroughs submitted his March 1962 MS, based on the occurrence of the date "Saturday March 17, 1962 Past Time" in the five-page typescript titled "PUNISHMENT AND REWARD, WHAT?—NEVER EXISTED AT ALL" (Berg 9.21). The title on this typescript was a typed addition, suggesting it is the manuscript to which Burroughs referred in his April 2 letter to Rosset. After recycling material from "Melted Into Air," the typescript ends: "Good bye to 'William'—You are yourself 'Mr Bradly Mr Martin' who never existed at all—'" Burroughs later redacted this highly repetitive material, and the October 1962 MS has a much shorter (590-word) version that also includes such new phrases as "Rings of Saturn in the morning sky" which would appear in *The Ticket That Exploded*. Under the handwritten title "Never Existed At All," this two-page typescript ends with Burroughs' autograph signature and the dateline: "Paris, Oct 24, 1962."

However, Burroughs continued to revise the ending, and a year later he sent Grove a one-page text on legal-sized paper which he recommended "as a much more powerful end to *Nova Express* than the one we now have following right on from the present end" (Burroughs to Seaver, October 10, 1963; SU). Starting, "telling me/ dead birds falling/lacer guns 'washing'/'''''''" 'Annie Laurie' had no luck," this 350-word typescript concludes: "A distant s̶o̶l̶d̶i̶e̶r̶ officer from uh special police never returns. He made an arrest. . . . 'September 17, 1899 over New York' (a silent Sunday to the post.)," after which the copyeditor added the signature and 1962 dateline. Whether this had, as he put it to Seaver, "much more impact and surprise than the present ending" is debatable; it was certainly different. But Burroughs was still not done revising the ending. In July 1964, he sent a 180-word insert to add onto the beginning of "Never Existed At All"; the insert was sent but may not actually have been made, since it does not appear on the galleys. Burroughs' indecision is reflected in the copyeditor's instruction on the galleys: "*delete to end / But do not kill. Hold until we tell you to kill*" (OSU 5.11). In the end, he changed his mind and indeed killed the entire ninth chapter along with the "Wind Hand" section of the previous one. At the last minute, Burroughs recognized that the solution to a highly repetitive ending was neither to redact it nor to add anomalous new material, but to just cut it.

190   "Melted into air—": in one of a small number of variants, the first rough draft continues: **"And beings all went away—No good no universe in setting forth—Clom Fliday—Dead—"** (OSU 2.2).

190   "Well that's about the closest way": from here to the end was
a typed insert that Burroughs pasted onto the long galleys
(OSU 5.12).

190   "July 21, 1964": this was indeed the date on which Burroughs mailed Richard Seaver the corrected proofs of *Nova
Express*.